Running Away F

A Detective

Running won't solve your problems

Mary M. Cushnie-Mansour

Mary M. Cushnie-Mansour

Books by Mary M. Cushnie-Mansour

<u>Adult Novels</u>
Night's Vampire Series
Night's Gift
Night's Children
Night's Return
Night's Temptress
Night's Betrayals
Night's Revelations

Detective Toby Series
Are You Listening to Me
Running Away From Loneliness

<u>Short Stories</u>
From the Heart
Mysteries From the Keys

<u>Poetry</u>
picking up the pieces
Life's Roller Coaster
Devastations of Mankind
Shattered
Memories

<u>Biographies</u>
A 20th Century Portia

<u>Children/Youth Titles</u>

<u>Novels</u>
A Story of Day & Night
The Silver Tree

<u>Bilingual Picture Books</u>
The Day Bo Found His Bark/Le jour où Bo trouva sa voix
Charlie Seal Meets a Fairy Seal/Charlie le phoque rencontre une fée
Charlie and the Elves/Charlie et les lutins
Jesse's Secret/Le Secret de Jesse
Teensy Weensy Spider/L'araignée Riquiqui
The Temper Tantrum/La crise de colère
Alexandra's Christmas Surprise/La surprise de Noël d'Alexandra
Curtis The Crock/Curtis le crocodile
Freddy Frog's Frolic/La gambade de Freddy la grenouille

<u>Picture Books</u>
The Official Tickler
The Seahorse and the Little Girl With Big Blue Eyes
Curtis the Crock
The Old Woman of the Mountain

Published in Canada by
CAVERN OF DREAMS PUBLISHING
www.cavernofdreamspublishing.com

CAVERN
OF DREAMS
PUBLISHING

ISBN 978-1-927899-87-8
Ebook ISBN 978-1-927899-88-5

Cover Art by
Jennifer Bettio

Cover Design by
Terry Davis
https://ballmedia.com/

Dedicated to everyone

who has a dream

and

has the courage

to follow it!

Chapter One

Some things in life are worse than loneliness. Everyone around you thinking that all is good in your life—that you are a rock they can come to, to pour out their troubles to, that you will fix everything with a smile and an assurance all will be well in their lives and in the world—*that* is worse than loneliness.

Such a person was Violet Saunders, but she had finally come to a breaking point. She was tired of being there for everyone else. She was tired of trying to fix everything for the people around her. She was tired of not having the moments to herself she longed for, for so many years—for too many years. She was just plain tired of her lonely life.

Violet sat curled up on the couch, her knees hugged close to her chest. There was nothing on television; it was one of those off nights when not one of her favourite shows was playing. A tear slid out of her right eye, followed by another on the other side. Suddenly, the dam burst. It was a flood that had been hiding for a long time, just waiting until she was ready to release the gates. She grabbed a pillow from the couch and buried her face in it, letting the material absorb her pain.

~

The cuckoo clock on the wall chimed nine times. Violet jerked awake, startled. She must have fallen asleep. She sat up straight and looked around the room, at the darkness she sat in, and reflected on her life.

It had been difficult growing up in the country, especially with not a neighbour around that had children her age. School, for Violet, had been torture from the first day. Her grade one teacher had decided, for whatever reason, Violet was the child she was going to make a daily example of. It had started as a weekly example before escalating to a daily one. Violet had dreaded getting on the bus every morning, dreaded getting off the bus at school, dreaded going into the classroom that promised nothing more than humiliation for her.

As the years went by, nothing improved. Violet had been made an outcast in her first school year and the label stuck to her like a tongue on a frozen pipe. She prayed her parents would move away and she could start over again in a new school where no one knew her, but it never happened, at least not soon enough. One day, her father came home and said they were going to move. His father had left him a piece of land, and he'd decided it was getting too expensive to keep up two properties. He wanted to build a house on the acreage, and by September they would move in and Violet could start her school year in a new school.

Violet had been ecstatic. Her dream of moving away and starting fresh was going to come to fruition. She would be thirteen in the fall and starting grade eight, which would give her time to make new friends before heading off to high school. Her walk took on a refreshed rhythm, and more times than not, her mother caught her humming— even singing—as she helped around the house. Violet couldn't remember when she'd been so happy.

But, as fate decreed, the new school was no different. Violet hadn't realized how difficult it might be to fit in when everyone already had their little cliques. And, to make matters worse, she stayed in that school for two years. Devastation at the loss of her dream had worked its way so deeply into Violet's demeanour that her marks failed miserably and even though she passed—on the borderline—the principal and her parents felt another year in elementary school would help her to mature, making her readier for high school. Little did the adults know Violet's suffering.

Through all these years, only one thing held Violet together—her pen. She entered her fantasy world and created a life she thought would be beautiful to live in. She wrote her stories and her poems and stored them away in a secret place no one knew about. No one knew the real Violet, and she was content to keep it that way. Why give anyone the opportunity to mock her more than they already did?

Time passed quickly through the high school years. Violet stayed as nondescript as possible, drawing as little attention to herself as possible. It worked, for the most part. She managed to make a few friends, mostly misfits like herself, and she began to share some of her writing with a select few. They were impressed. Violet even joined the drama club and landed a couple leading roles in the school plays. Acting was another outlet for her, where she didn't have to face the reality of her everyday loneliness. She could be someone else—anyone else.

High school finished and Violet went straight to work in a factory. She'd had enough of school, and things weren't so great at home. She'd been a good girl but her parents thought otherwise. They constantly harped at her and accused her of not being one. Finally, she determined to strike out on her own and moved out.

Eventually, Violet decided she'd had enough of working in a factory, so she applied to a college and was accepted as an adult student. She was able to collect unemployment insurance as long as she finished her course. She'd never dreamed of becoming a secretary, which was a far cry from being the writer she had always imagined being, but the writing wasn't going to put bread and butter on her table.

Violet had a certain calmness that drew her fellow female students to her at the college. Many of them were there for the same reason she was, trying to expand their job opportunities. Some were trying to escape dangerous living situations. One young woman was in an abusive relationship and hoped that by improving her employment prospects, she could move away, somewhere the boyfriend would never find her. Violet heard from her friend a few years later and was happy she had made a new life in another province, well out of reach of the fist that had blackened her eyes on far too many occasions.

Drawing near to the end of Violet's course, she had landed a job with an oil company. The only drawback being she had to start immediately, and she wasn't quite finished one of her courses. The guidance counselor told her to take the job; jobs like that didn't come along too often.

Violet excelled at her job. She was a hard worker, and she also had a good head on her shoulders when it came to dealing with people. She was elevated quickly to a management role in the office, and her self-esteem began to develop. Plus, as had happened in college, the other women in the office always turned to Violet with their troubles—work-related and family.

After a couple years of keeping her nose to the grindstone and not doing much other than working, Violet finally met a fellow she thought might be The One. She'd been on a few dates, mostly set up by her friends, but none had gone any further than a couple outings before she would end them. Frank was different. He was a bit older than the others she'd dated, seven years her senior. She liked his maturity and his commitment to family. She liked his family, which was enormous and boisterous, unlike the quiet one she'd grown up in.

Violet and Frank dated for a year and then, one night, he popped the big question. She'd been elated, of course, and had said yes. They talked about the type of wedding they both wanted, something small and frugal, and one that could be arranged in a short time period. She approached her parents with the news, and even though her relationship with them had improved over the years after she'd left home, they weren't sure about Frank. First, he was much older than her, and the fact he hadn't been married yet and had lived quite a single life had them thinking he wasn't really the marrying kind. Second, he was from a different ethnic background—French—and they feared that might cause problems for Violet. Third, and most likely the most serious apprehension—Frank was a Catholic.

Regardless of their concerns, Violet's parents had mellowed enough that after voicing their apprehensions they gave their daughter their blessing and helped out with the wedding. They felt it their Christian duty to try and understand their daughter, and in doing so, had hoped she would one day see the light and return to the church she had grown up in. As time passed, they gave up on that desire.

Violet settled into married life. She and Frank had a good grasp on what they wanted out of marriage, and she felt right at home with his large family of three brothers and three sisters—all who were married already, some with children, some expecting their first. Frank was the baby of his family and they were all happy to welcome the woman into the family that had finally tamed their little brother. Especially was his mother pleased because that meant more grandchildren for her.

Frank worked hard. He took on extra jobs outside his day job so he and Violet could get ahead quicker. Violet kept her employment at the oil company until it decided to close that office and amalgamate with a more extensive operation located too far away from where she and Frank had made their home. Besides, it was time to start thinking about making a family. Violet wasn't getting any younger, and she told Frank, neither was he. If they didn't have their first child soon, before she turned thirty, she wasn't going to start after that age.

Their first child came along when Violet was twenty-eight, a boy. He was followed by a set of twins—a boy and a girl—eighteen months later. Three years after the twins were born, another boy, and two years after him, another girl. At that point, Violet knew she'd had enough children; the last two hadn't been planned. She was content with the five she had and didn't want any more. Frank did the honours of ending their baby boom.

During the years that followed, Violet lost a lot of who she was—who she had started to become during her college and working years—as she became absorbed in her children's lives. At the same time, she developed a small circle of acquaintances, mostly parents whose children went to school or played sports with her kids.

Frank continued working two jobs so Violet could stay home with the children. He also joined an old-timer's hockey team and began to hang out with the boys more and more.

When all the children were in school, Frank mentioned to Violet that it might be a good idea if she returned to school and continued her studies. He thought she would make an excellent teacher; she had a way with children. She enrolled in correspondence classes, with the intention of becoming a teacher. However, during the first few courses, a flame that had almost been extinguished began to flicker. Many of Violet's essays were story-like. She started writing on the side, mostly poetry at first, and then children's stories for her kids and their friends. Eventually, she told Frank she didn't want to be a teacher, she wanted to write. He finally agreed to let her quit her university courses, and he said that when the kids were grown up and on their own, she could pursue her writing. In the meantime, she could write her stories, and maybe even join a writing group—something for her to do. After all, Frank had his outside interests; he felt she needed something as well...

~

The cuckoo clock struck ten. Violet got up from the couch and made her way down the hallway to the bathroom. She splashed water on her face, then patted it dry. She leaned over the sink and stared into the mirror, noting the loneliness in her eyes. Frank was out again tonight. They had very few mutual friends; in fact, there were no couples they did anything with, and this bothered Violet more than anything. Frank had his friends; she had hers. But Frank spent a lot of time with his buddies, and Violet found less and less of her time being spent with hers.

Violet wandered into the room she'd set up as an office and ran her fingers over the keyboard of her laptop. The laptop held all her poetry and stories. It kept her secrets, secrets she didn't want anyone to find out, which is why she'd password protected her computer. Even Frank didn't know the password. She sat down in her office chair and turned it to face the window. It was raining outside. She picked up a pen and tapped it on her desk. She was lonely. Lonelier than ever she had been. Her life was busy, but it was a life spent looking after others, listening to others' problems, and trying to pursue her dream amid everything else. Violet stood, a grimly-defined firmness to her jaw. She knew what was required—to save herself.

Chapter Two

Jack Nelson, a retired cop who lived with his oversized orange tabby, Toby, was tired. He needed a break from the everyday routine. The Camden Gale case had drained him mentally, especially when Toby was recovering from the injuries he'd sustained saving the final victim of Camden's scourge, Jack's friend, Andrew.

Camden Gale murdered five people because he thought they'd insulted him in some way or another. Camden's sister, Emma, had needed Jack's emotional support when her brother, the only family she had, was sent off to prison.

But Toby was wholly recovered now and Emma seemed to be managing on her own quite well. Jack decided he and Toby should take a short, but well-earned, vacation. He knew of a quiet little lake up in the Kingston, Ontario area, and had a friend who owned several cottages there. The cottages were spread far apart so Jack could be assured of peace and quiet.

"Maybe we should ask Tessa to join us, eh, Toby?" Jack looked down at the overweight orange tabby. "And Andrew … but not until we've had a few days to ourselves. How's that sound, old man?"

Tessa was the police profiler who worked on the Camden Gale case with Jack and they'd become more than friends. Andrew, a paramedic and long-time friend of Jack's, was Camden Gale's intended sixth casualty, but

Toby, having solved the crime, saved Andrew from the same fate as the other victims by jumping off a gym roof and knocking a poisoned drink from his hand.

Toby flattened his ears and switched his tail sharply. *Even after everything I've done … solving all those crimes … saving your friend's life … you still "old man" me!* Toby turned away and looked out the living room window. *Maybe I'll take a walk and go see how Emma is later. Still feeling a bit stiff from all the surgery after jumping off the roof to save Andrew!* Toby closed his eyes and purred as he thought about his friend and the last case he helped solve.

Emma recovered quicker from her brother's murder trial than Toby thought she would. Camden was admitted to the inpatient unit of the medium-security facility in St. Thomas. They had a forensic program there that focused on providing consultation and assessments of individuals who were in conflict with the law. In Camden's case, it was apparent he suffered from paranoid delusions, thinking everyone was out to get him. Thus, his reason for killing before his victims could destroy him.

As of yet, Emma had not made the trip to see Camden, despite the close proximity of St. Thomas to Brantford. Camden's lawyer fought hard to have him in St. Thomas as opposed to the higher security facility in Penetanguishene, which is where the prosecution had wanted to send him. At the trial, Emma pleaded she would not be able to visit her brother if he were so far away and his healing might highly depend on those reassuring visits that she had not abandoned her twin. Toby thought it strange that, despite her pleas, Emma still hadn't taken any opportunity to visit her brother. Jack had offered to take her several times, so had Tessa.

Toby could hear Jack rustling up his breakfast in the kitchen. Jack was a good man, and Toby knew how lucky he was to be sharing a house with him. The fact that Jack was a retired cop and still had ties to the local police department helped with Toby's own detective work, allowing him the inside scoop on cases Jack got called into the precinct to work on. The smell of bacon wafting through the rooms almost encouraged Toby to leave his perch and join Jack at the table. Almost.

As the morning progressed, the house was filled with the sounds of Jack getting ready for their trip. Annoying as it was—the noise disturbed Toby's sleep—he was excited to be getting away. Toby loved the camping trips he and Jack occasionally ventured out on, the walks along the beach, making sure the waves didn't lap up and wet his paws; adventures on uncharted trails in the woods, chasing birds and chipmunks; nightly campfires, feeling the warmth of the fire and smelling the wood smoke. Yes, a couple weeks away would be good.

Jack walked into the living room and plunked down in his chair. "Hey there, old man, you going to sleep your entire morning away?"

Toby heard the chuckle in Jack's words and cracked his eyes open. *Well, I guess I could get up and investigate how much you've actually got accomplished for our big trip.* Toby stood, balanced himself on the back of the couch, and stretched. He yawned, then made his way over to Jack and jumped up on the arm of his chair.

Jack's fingers curled around Toby's neck, rubbing behind his ears. Toby purred and pushed into the massaging fingers. *Oh, Jack, you certainly do know how to please a man!*

"If I get everything packed up today, we can set off first thing in the morning," Jack stated. "I already called my friend and he said there was one cabin left, but told me it hadn't been used in a while and might need some tender loving care before we could settle in. A bit of hard work never bothered me, though." A pause. "I'll let Tessa and Andrew know where we're going to be and give them directions to join us if they want, but not until the second week. Sound good, Toby?"

Sure, anything you say, Jack. Toby purred and then jumped down and headed to the kitchen, straight to his dish.

As Jack followed, he continued on with his plans. "I'm not taking a radio or television or computer with us, old man; I've no desire to know what is going on in the world. Just two old boys having a few days relaxing on the beach … maybe doing a bit of fishing…"

Hmmm … fish… Make my day, Jack! As long as you're the one in the boat doing the fishing. Toby rubbed around Jack's legs. *For now, I'll settle on some kibble.* He looked at his dish and gave a hungry meow, then purred.

Jack poured the kibble into Toby's bowl, then went to the fridge and pulled out some lunch meat and fixed himself a sandwich. Sitting at the table, Jack continued his plans out loud, as though Toby understood everything he said.

"I've got to go to the grocery store after lunch and grab the rest of our food supplies, Toby. No sense you coming along, though, 'cause I can't take you into the store with me. Then the hardware store—need some bottles of propane for the camp stove, in case I want to cook outside—and some charcoal for the little barbeque … can't waste a good fish in a frying pan when one is roughing it in the boonies!"

~

Shortly after Jack left for his shopping expedition, Toby headed over to visit Emma. It had been a few days and he missed her. As he crept up to the fence, keeping a watchful eye out for Duke, her oversized—in Toby's mind— Doberman/Shepard cross, Toby noticed Emma in the three-season room tending to her plants. Duke was following her around.

Toby pushed himself under the fence and headed toward the house, stopping at the back screen door. He sat down and meowed loudly, twice, to get Emma's attention. She looked up, and Toby was rewarded with a big smile.

"Just a sec, Toby," Emma called out as she grabbed hold of Duke's collar and directed him to the sliding door that opened into the kitchen. With Duke safely inside the house, Emma opened the screen door for Toby.

As Toby rubbed around Emma's legs, he threw mocking glances at Duke, who was whining at the glass doors. *Serves you right, you overgrown dog! If you were nicer to me … no, wait … that would mean I'd have to share my time with Emma with you … no, keep up your nasty disposition toward me.* An outsider, if they were observing carefully, they would swear the old cat was grinning!

"Where've you been, Toby?" Emma's question cut into his daydreaming. "You haven't been around for a few days. Oh well. You're here now." Emma scooped Toby up into her arms and gave him a squeeze, then set him down on one of the tall stools.

Toby looked around the room, searching to see if the castor bean plant had been removed, the plant that grew the beans Camden had used to poison his victims. *I don't see that plant anywhere ... good ... Emma got rid of it.* Toby arched up, hinting he needed a backrub.

Emma reached over to a shelf and took down some garden gloves. "Want to join me outside, Toby? I need to tend to a few weeds in the flowerbeds." She headed out the door, pausing to hold it open for Toby.

Over the next hour, Toby followed Emma from spot to spot as she pulled weeds and talked about her life without Camden. He listened as she told him how lonely it had been for the first few weeks: Camden and she had been each other's rocks throughout the years, especially after being abandoned by their parents, and even more so after the rape.

"But, you know, Toby, I'm adjusting. It's getting easier. I've been opening up the rooms in the house, one's Camden kept closed off, and spreading my belongings out, so the place won't look cluttered." She paused a moment and sadness crept into her eyes. "I haven't been able to bring myself to touch my brother's room yet; still can't wrap my head around what he did to all those people."

You're better off without that scumbag! I don't blame you one little cat's paw for not going to see him. Next thing you need to do is get rid of that big mutt you have in the house and then life around here will be just perfect! Toby sauntered over to lie under the big maple tree; it was getting too hot in the sun.

Emma stood and wiped her brow. "I think maybe I've had enough for today," she noted as she went around the flowerbeds gathering up her tools. She approached Toby

14

under the tree. "Want to come in the house for a nice cold drink of water?" she asked.

Only if you let the big mutt out!

As though Emma read Toby's mind, "Don't worry, I'll let Duke out in the yard; it's time he stretched his legs."

For the next half hour, Emma showed Toby what she was doing in the house and snuck him some cat treats she purchased just for him.

How I love you, let me count the ways! Toby crunched the treat and absorbed the back rub Emma was bestowing on him. Life was good. He was going to miss Emma when he and Jack went away. *Maybe, I should try and get Jack to bring Emma along… On second thought, that would mean the mutt, too. No, I'll just have to go without her.*

Realizing it was time to be getting back home, Toby made his way to the front door. He had no means of telling Emma he was leaving for a couple of weeks; he hoped Jack informed her so she wouldn't worry.

Emma glanced at her watch. "Wow! Time has flown by, hasn't it, Toby? I guess you need to get going, eh?" She opened the door, reached down and gave him a goodbye pat, and watched as Toby headed down the sidewalk.

~

Toby found Jack busy putting the last of the supplies into the camper. "Hey there, old man, have a nice visit with Emma?"

You bet. Toby sat in the driveway and began grooming his fur as he watched Jack finish loading the camper.

"I'll be back in a sec," Jack began. "I think it's wise to let Emma know we'll be away for a couple weeks, maybe ask her to keep an eye on our place … pick up my mail and paper, too."

Good man, Jack. I was hoping you'd do that. Toby headed to the house, and his dish.

~

Early the next morning, Jack and Toby left for their quiet vacation on a remote lake in the Kingston area. Jack notified Tessa and Andrew of his intentions and invited them to join him and Toby during the second week. They both said they would think about it, so Jack provided them with directions.

Chapter Three

A week after Violet made the decision to do something about her life, she was driving along a country road toward a cabin she'd rented just outside Kingston, Ontario. Her mind wandered over the events of the past few days, to the working out of her plan. Violet felt guilty for leaving the way she had, but hopefully, in the long run, she would be able to repair any damage she might have inflicted on her relationship with her husband. She'd left Frank a letter explaining why. She had faith he would understand and give her the time she needed. She hoped, anyway.

The song on the radio finished and the newscast started with the breaking story of an escaped killer from the Kingston penitentiary.

Great, just what I need, an escaped killer to add some excitement to my life!

The newscaster droned on about what everyone in the cottage district should do to protect themselves: lock doors and windows, keep cell phones charged, never go out alone, etc. The man was thought to be armed and wouldn't hesitate to kill anyone who got in his way.

Violet turned the radio off. She didn't need to hear anymore. She wasn't going to be put off her course of action by letting something like an escaped killer worry her. What were the chances he would end up at her cabin on the lake?

After driving for another half hour, Violet finally reached her destination. She turned onto a narrow, tree-lined driveway and made her way slowly to the cabin she knew was waiting for her at the end. The owner had warned her the road was full of potholes and he hadn't been exaggerating. Finally, she pulled into a clearing and there it was—a log cabin—looking much different than what had been pictured on the internet. The structure in that picture had been pristine; this one was anything but.

Violet sat in the van for a few minutes before turning off the ignition. She sighed as she opened the door and stepped out. She would just have to make the best of it. She reached into the backseat and gathered her suitcase and computer. She didn't need the internet; she'd come here to write a novel and didn't intend to leave until she'd done so.

Stepping up onto the porch, Violet set her cases down and walked over to a flowerpot sitting at the end of the porch. She lifted the pot and found the key the landlord said would be there. Opening the cabin door, Violet was hit with a musty smell. The door carved an arc in the dust as it swung inward. She picked up her cases and stepped inside, observing the mess. The man hadn't been kidding when he'd said it hadn't been rented for a few weeks— more like a few months, maybe years, from the look of the neglected room.

Once again, Violet heaved a sigh. She'd paid for two months and wasn't about to lose her money. There was supposed to be hydro, according to the landlord; she hoped he hadn't been lying—exaggerating—about that as she made her way back to the van to bring in her food supplies. She was thankful she had thrown in a few cleaning supplies, as well; she was going to need them.

Violet left the boxes in the corner of the cabin and began cleaning. She found an old broom and dustpan and embarked on a sweep through the main room and the bedroom. Unfortunately, there was no toilet in the cabin, just a dingy sink and a rusty shower stall. Violet gazed out the window over the kitchen sink and noticed an outhouse several yards out. Her heart sank but she pulled herself together. She was here to write, not bask in luxury. Her grandparents had coped with an outhouse all their lives; surely she could for a couple months.

Violet hoped the lake would be suitable for swimming and bathing. She decided to check it out before dark. Besides, she had to go pee, and now was as good a time as any to check out the outdoor facility. She grabbed a box of Kleenex and the broom and dustpan, knowing she would probably have to get rid of some dust and cobwebs in the outhouse.

Surprisingly, even though it was cobweb and dust infested, the outhouse didn't smell, an indication it had been cleaned and not recently used. Quickly, Violet swept it out before relieving herself. *Everything will be okay ... I just need to focus on my goal.*

A few minutes later, following the path down to the lake, Violet began to relax as she took in Nature's beauty. She breathed in the freshness of the air and felt the tingling in her lungs. Stepping onto the beach area, she gasped. The sun was just beginning to set in the west, and its reflection on the water was the most glorious sight she'd seen for a long time. She walked to the water's edge and gazed down into the clearness, noticing the rippling sand. Content that the water was a satisfactory place to bathe in lei of a proper shower, Violet headed back to the cabin.

She spent the next hour scrubbing the kitchen area. A stove, obviously propane, and a small fridge plugged into the wall were her prime challenges. Apparently, the cabin owner hadn't thought to clean them after the last tenant— whenever that might have been. Finally finished her cleaning, she began unpacking her boxes and the cooler and set about making something to eat. She had been so busy, she hadn't realized how famished she was.

After supper, Violet made another quick trip to the outhouse. When she returned, she flicked on the light switch located just inside the door and gazed around, searching for something she could use as a desk. She noticed a small table in the corner of the bedroom that she wouldn't need there, so Violet grabbed it and dragged it out into the main room. She set the table in front of the second window in the room, retrieved one of the kitchen chairs, then took her computer from its case and placed it on the table—her new, crude desk, a far cry from the elaborate one she had at home. *Oh, Frank … I'm so sorry… Please understand why I had to do this.* She pulled a stack of lined paper from her case and set it beside her computer. A backup in case the hydro went out.

Violet got down on her hands and knees and searched for an electrical plug. Finally, she located one, but it meant she would have to move the table a few feet from the window. *Oh well, this will have to do.* She plugged her computer in and checked that the light came on to confirm it was charging. She stood and dusted her hands off, satisfied.

Standing on the porch after changing into her nightgown, Violet took in the vast beauty of the northern sky. The air smelled crisp—like pine—despite it being the middle of summer. Crickets chirped endlessly, and the scuttling noises told her the woods were alive with small wildlife. At least, she hoped they were all small.

Violet turned and headed back into the cabin. It was time for bed. It had been a long day—a long week. Tomorrow, she would begin her novel, one she'd never had the courage to write but always wanted to. She crawled into bed. As she lay under the covers, she remembered she'd forgotten to lock the door.

"Oh well," she muttered to herself, forgetting all about the news report about a killer on the loose.

Chapter Four

When Frank arrived home from work, he called out for Violet. Not getting an answer, he went back out to the garage to see if she took her bike out. It was still there. So was her vehicle. He didn't notice the big cooler was missing because he didn't think to look on the shelf where the coolers were stored. Why would he? Assuming she probably left a note that she'd gone to a movie with a friend and the friend had picked her up, Frank returned to the house, poured a beer, and turned the television on. It had been a long day and he needed to put his feet up. Violet would likely be home before he found the note.

As usual, Frank fell asleep and when he woke he looked at the clock on the VCR. Ten o'clock. The house was still quiet, no signs Violet had returned yet. He called out: "Violet!"

Silence.

Frank got up from his chair and headed to the bedroom. First, though, he checked the kitchen table for a note, the usual place his wife would leave one if she went out.

Nothing.

Upon entering the bedroom, Frank noticed an envelope with his name on it sitting on his night table. He approached nervously, a sudden feeling of uneasiness welling inside him. Thinking about it, Frank had noticed a subtle change in Violet lately but had dismissed it, figuring she just had a lot on her mind.

He sat on the edge of the bed and turned the envelope over and over in his hands, afraid to open it. Decisively, with a shuddering breath, he ran his thumb under the seal and ripped it open. Inside was a folded paper. He took it out and noted Violet's firm handwriting.

> *Dear Frank: I know this may come as a shock to you, but I have decided I needed to get away for a while. I didn't want to have to explain my reasons to you because they are complicated even for me to understand. I want you to know I love you more than life itself and hope you will still be there for me when I return. I will explain everything then. You won't be able to reach me; I've left my cell phone behind. I took money from the bank account, enough to sustain me for a couple months, the amount of time I figure will be sufficient for me to find—figure out—what I'm looking for. Please don't call the police or send out search parties for me. I'm okay. I'll be okay. Have faith in me, as you always have in the past, and just allow me this time. I'll be back before you know it.*
> *Love, Violet*

The letter dropped to the floor as Frank buried his face in his hands. He didn't usually cry—couldn't remember the last time there'd even been a reason to—but this was one of those occasions when the tears flowed without inhibition. He didn't know how long he sat there, but finally he stood and walked into the bathroom. He turned on the shower, stripped his clothes, stepped in and let the water wash over him, an attempt to wash away his pain.

Half an hour later, as Frank prepared himself a plate of fruit, he thought about why Violet would leave so abruptly. It wasn't like her to just take off. She was his rock, the foundation he'd built his life on. She was the breath in his lungs, his reason for living. Nothing mattered if he didn't have her. From the moment he'd first laid eyes on her, thirty-two years ago, he'd known she was The One—his other half. And she'd stood steadfastly by his side over the years. What had he missed? Why hadn't he paid attention when he noticed an unusual sadness about her lately?

He picked at the fruit, not really hungry but knowing he had to eat. He would have to tell the kids something, eventually. They would want to know where their mom was. The girls depended on their mom to help them out occasionally with their children. Violet loved babysitting and spending time with the grandchildren—he had always thought so, anyway. Not so much the boys, though—they had their wives but no children yet.

"I'll just tell them their mother took a trip and I'm not sure exactly when she'll be back … but she'll be in touch soon," Frank mumbled a possible reason he could give. "Maybe I'll tell them she had the opportunity to get away with a friend for a few weeks … maybe she won't stay away two months like she said in her letter. But if she doesn't return sooner, what will I say?" Frank closed his eyes. Fatigue took over.

The next morning, Frank woke, showered again, and headed off to work. He needed to get out of the house, out of the emptiness, before it devoured him.

Chapter Five

Violet opened her eyes and stretched her arms above her head. It took a few moments to realize where she was. She'd been dreaming of running through the woods, but there had been no sense of fear in her. She glanced up at the small, un-curtained window and noticed the day was just beginning. Violet sat up and, slipping her feet into her slippers, headed out to the outhouse.

"Thank God it's not winter," she laughed as she stepped through the grass, heavily laden with early morning dew.

Back in the cabin, Violet put a pan of water on the stove to make tea; there was no kettle. In fact, there were very few dishes, but she'd make due; it wasn't as if she'd be doing any gourmet cooking over the next few weeks. Opening the fridge, Violet took out the quart of almond milk and set it on the table, then retrieved a bowl, spoon, and box of cereal. After finishing her breakfast, she made a cup of tea and headed out to the porch; Violet remembered seeing a rocking chair there.

Watching the day begin in such a peaceful setting washed over Violet like a veil of tranquility. She sighed and a tear escaped the corner of her eye. She wondered what Frank was doing. How had he taken her letter? Would he wait for her? Would he respect her request and not call the police to try and find her? Violet sipped her tea and set her cup down on a rickety side table beside the rocker. She stood, walked to the railing, leaned over it, and wept.

Violet was startled out of her distress by a rustling in the woods. She looked up and searched the perimeters, holding her breath, hoping it wasn't anything bigger than a deer. A few moments later, a mother deer and her fawn stepped into the clearing and looked nervously around. Violet remained still, not wanting to disturb them, wishing she'd brought her camera outside with her. She'd remember tomorrow.

The mother deer caught sight of the stranger on the porch and shooed her baby back into the woods. Violet headed back into the cabin. What she needed was a dip in the lake to wash yesterday's sweat from her. She grabbed a towel and a bar of soap. She'd dress when she got back—after all, who would be around but the wildlife to see her swimming in the buff?—something she would never have thought of doing when she was younger.

Refreshed and ready to start her novel, Violet fired up her computer and opened her Word program. Her fingers lightly touched the keyboard. "Where to begin..." she muttered. Finally, she started to type, the words pouring onto her screen with a fury of their own...

Karen McCray left her house early in the morning, heading out to get her supplies. She'd be gone a few weeks and needed to make sure there was nothing she would need during that time. Throughout the morning, Karen made several stops at different stores, picking up the non-food items she would need for where she was going. Then she headed home and packed a couple of suitcases.

Karen checked her watch, noting the time—she had an appointment to look at a van. It would be an easy deal and she already secured a location to hide her car until she returned … if she did. If Karen decided to stay where she was going, it wouldn't matter.

When she arrived at the house where the van was, she noticed junk everywhere and smiled to herself. *Perfect.* She offered cash for the vehicle and told the owner it might take her a few days to get it registered and not to worry. He looked like the type of person who wouldn't care either way. He just lit a cigarette, popped open a can of beer, and shoved her money into his pocket.

When Karen arrived home, she loaded all her supplies and suitcases into the van. Before leaving, she looked around the house she was temporarily vacating, pausing at the picture of her and her husband on the fireplace mantel. A tear escaped the corner of her eye, knowing how much hurt she was inflicting on her husband, Darryl, leaving like this. Finally, she turned away from the picture and went to retrieve her purse and computer. Before leaving the house, she pulled an envelope from her purse and placed it on the kitchen table.

Arriving at the cabin in the woods, Karen surveyed her surroundings. *Perfect—isolated—not a person in sight.* She had listened to music tapes while on her way to the cabin, so decided to turn the radio on and listen to the news and weather. It was 10:00 p.m.

Violet leaned back from the computer and smiled. *Why not use the escaped prisoner angle?*

Karen's blood raced as she listened to the newscast. An inmate had escaped from the maximum-security prison not far from where she was staying. He was armed and dangerous. Karen's fingers tapped nervously on the steering wheel.

It had taken longer than she'd expected to arrive at her destination. Cautiously, Karen exited the van and made her way to the cabin. It appeared shabbier than the picture she'd seen online. She located the key in the flowerpot by the door where the rental agent had said it would be and opened the door. Karen groped for a light switch, finally locating it about a foot away from the door. She flicked it on and was rewarded with a dim light. She looked up and noticed the lamp in the middle of the ceiling only had one bulb working: three others were burned out. The air was stale but everything looked neat, other than a thin layer of dust.

As she walked back to her vehicle, Karen thought it might be better if she slept in the van for the night. She preferred to dust the cabin before moving in, mainly because of her asthma. Karen piled some of the boxes of food, clearing a space for her to lie down, pulled out her sleeping bag and spread it on the van floor. She would just lie down on it; the night was hot, and she didn't think she needed a cover. She reached over and pushed the buttons on the doors down, locking herself in for the night.

Violet stopped typing and glanced at her watch— almost noon. She pushed away from her make-shift desk and headed outside to the porch. A chipmunk skittered away, running across the path and into the woods. She smiled. "I'll leave you some nuts tomorrow," Violet called after the disappearing tail. She turned and went back into the cabin.

After lunch, Violet decided to take a walk and further explore her surroundings. The cottage still smelled musty, so she opened the windows before leaving. She followed the trail down to the water's edge, took her sandals off, and walked along the shore, allowing the gentle waves to tickle her feet. A light breeze blew in off the lake. Violet swung her arms like a little girl. She kicked her legs in a formal march-style and laughed.

"If only Frank and my friends could see me now—how funny I look, am behaving. 'Why look at that silly woman,' they would say. 'Does she know how ridiculous she looks … why doesn't she grow up?'" Violet grinned mischievously. She hadn't felt this sort of freedom for a long time—actually, never, when she thought about it.

Violet came to a part of the lake that buffered right up to the land, the expansive beach she'd been walking coming to an end. She turned and began her trek back, sure the cabin would be cooled down by now. As she walked, Violet remembered the newscast about the escaped prisoner and thought to check if there was any more news about him. Since she'd failed to pack a radio, she'd have to make do with the one in her vehicle.

After listening to the newscast, Violet couldn't stop shaking. The prisoner was still at large. The penitentiary was a bit too close for comfort. Inside the cottage, she checked to see what kind of lock was on the door—not much of one. The windows had no locks at all.

"Guess what will be, will be," she muttered. "Let's see what Karen is up to. That'll take my mind off escaped prisoners." Violet laughed. "Except I wrote the same incident into my story." She giggled nervously and brought the story back up on the screen.

Chapter Six

Jack was almost having second thoughts as he drove down the rutted lane to the cottage and saw the condition his lodging for two weeks was in. He cursed his friend under his breath. Fred said it hadn't been used for a while, but from the looks of it, it had been a long while, and Fred hadn't bothered to check on its condition.

"Well, old man," Jack tapped his fingers on the steering wheel, "good thing I brought my trusty toolbox."

Toby placed his paws up on the dashboard and stared out the van window at the cottage. *There are moments when I'm delighted I'm a cat—gets me out of a lot of menial tasks in life, like work!* Toby threw a dramatic look in Jack's direction.

Jack opened the truck door and stepped out. He stretched before heading to the back of the camper to retrieve his tool chest. First order of things would be to see if any wild creatures had taken up residence inside the cottage and then fix the door, which looked, even from the driveway, to be hanging by a couple of screws.

Toby decided to do a little investigating of his own. He jumped out of the van and began exploring around the cottage. Not seeing anything that really interested him, he headed down to the shoreline. He sat on the sand, staring out at the calm waters. A light mist hung over the islands that spotted the lake.

I could get used to this quiet but I'd miss the comforts of home. I'd miss Emma, and the trips to the police station, the attention bestowed on me for solving yet another case. Toby closed his eyes and dreamed of the comforts of home.

The sun began to dip behind a distant island and the odd star twinkled in the sky. A dark moon rose, attempting to replace the sun. Toby stood and headed back to the cottage to check on Jack's progress.

When he arrived, he was greeted by Jack, sitting in a deck chair, his feet resting on the wooden railing and a beer in his hand.

You are obviously finished for the night, Jack; I hope my dish is filled and waiting for me! Toby took a spot directly in front of Jack and meowed hungrily.

"Well, old man, about time you got back. Nice how you always seem to manage to shirk the work," Jack grinned. "I set out your dishes in the kitchen area, by the fridge," he added, leaning back in the chair and opening the now-working door for Toby to slip through.

Good man, Jack … you must have read my mind.

"There's an old canoe behind the cottage; only one oar, though. I guess it doesn't matter because you can't row, now, can you, old man?" Jack chuckled.

Who says I'd even go with you, in a boat, in the water? No, you go fishing yourself … I'll just help you eat whatever you catch! Toby disappeared through the opening, heading straight to his dish. Watching the water and the sunset had built up his appetite.

~

Syd Lance couldn't believe his luck, having escaped the two lazy—in his opinion—guards who had been transporting him to the hospital in Kingston for a procedure that couldn't be done at the prison hospital. He had told them he needed to use the restroom to take a piss and a shit, his condition worsening, he'd said. They'd pulled into a gas station, seen him to the bathroom, removed his chains, and waited outside the door.

The idiots hadn't thought to check for a window, which Syd thought was a bit off, especially for George. George had a bad reputation around the facility for being a hard-ass; Larry, on the other hand, was new to the prison and Syd hadn't seen him before. Syd could hear them laughing and joking outside the door and was thankful for their noise—it made it a lot easier for him in case there was any unforeseen sounds involved with what he was about to do.

Having worked out every day in his cell, Syd was as fit as he could be and small in stature—small enough to slip through the undersized window in the washroom. As he fiddled with the window, trying to get it open, one of the guards—sounded like George—knocked on the door and asked how he was doing.

"Doing okay ... ahhh ... shouldn't be long ... stomachs just ... ahhh!" Syd replied, as the window finally opened for him.

Standing on the back of the toilet, Syd squeezed his body through the opening. Fortunately, the drop to the ground was not far and he quickly found his footing and took off to the wooded area behind the station. He was deep in the woods before he heard the siren and knew he was going to have to pick up his pace and get somewhere that he wouldn't be found. Taking a deep breath of freedom, Syd quickened his pace. He wasn't a praying man—God had never done him any good that he knew of—however, in this case, he sent up a quick prayer to the Almighty asking Him to provide him with a heavily secluded hideaway, sooner rather than later.

Syd pushed on for what seemed like hours, sweat pouring from his brow, dripping into his eyes. His muscles were weakening and his stomach growled with hunger, his last meal had been breakfast. He glanced up through the trees, trying to see where the sun was, and noticed it well on its way to leaving the sky for the night. Syd took a moment to sit on a fallen log to catch his breath before pushing on.

Listening carefully to the forest sounds, Syd listened for sounds that didn't belong, like someone chasing him. Nothing. He'd been smart, taking several twists and turns on the trails and sometimes breaking through virgin territory to throw off whoever might be in pursuit. He'd even traversed down and across a few small streams, hoping to throw off his scent in case they brought in dogs to track him.

There seemed to be nothing out of the ordinary in the woods. Syd relaxed. He looked around, hoping to see a bush with berries, anything to quell the hunger he was feeling, to give him the strength to push on. He sniffed the air.

"Water," he mumbled. "Must be close by. Should be some fruit bushes near that, hopefully."

Syd stood and followed his nose until he came to a small clearing in the woods and was rewarded with a lily-laden pond. On the far side he noticed some red berries; he made his way over to them.

"Raspberries. Small but good enough," he said, starting to shove them into his mouth.

Having eaten his fill of berries, Syd stretched out on his stomach and drank from the pond. He'd tasted better water, even in prison, but a beggar couldn't be choosy. Standing, he looked around, hoping to see a place where he could curl up and grab a bit of shuteye before heading out again. Finally, his eyes lit upon a huge fallen tree trunk with vegetation growing out of it. Syd made his way over to it and climbed to the other side.

"This should do if I crawl under it and camouflage myself with a few branches."

Finally feeling secure enough to close his eyes, Syd drifted off to sleep. He had no idea what the next day would bring—probably being captured and returned to his ten-by-ten cell, or worse yet, to isolation. Whatever happened, it would be worth it for the few hours of freedom he'd had.

Chapter Seven

Violet had a violent dream during the night. A man was chasing her through the woods, and she, trying to escape him, was heading to the lake, running into the water. But he kept coming, closer and closer. She plunged into the water, but he was still there, right behind her. He grabbed hold of her foot and dragged her under. As she was about to lose consciousness, she beheld his malicious grin.

Violet woke in a sweat, her stomach knotted with nerves. Hugging her knees to her chest, she shivered. "What's the chance he'll find this place?" she questioned the empty room. "Maybe I shouldn't have written him into my novel, makes the situation seem more real," she continued, the sound of her voice comforting to her. She laughed nervously.

Getting up and heading to the fridge for a glass of milk, Violet stubbed her foot on a chair. "Damn!" she cursed, hopping on one foot to the ratted couch. She pursed her lips and held her throbbing toe until the pain eased off. "Probably'll be bruised by morning."

Even though the pain subsided, Violet's mind kept spinning. "What the hell was I thinking coming up here by myself?" she muttered. "How could I do this to Frank after all these years … he's always been there for me … supporting me … I wonder if it's all going to be worth it…" Violet drew in a shuddering breath.

A rustling sounded through the screen window, sending a shiver up Violet's spine. She froze and cocked her head to the side, listening for more. A few seconds later, there was another rustling, closer this time. Cautiously, Violet got off the couch and tiptoed to the window. Looking into the dark night, she folded her arms around herself, wishing again she hadn't left Frank behind. She'd give anything to have him with her right now.

Squinting into the night, Violet tried to see what was making the noise outside. It was a cloudy night and the moon was having difficulty doing his job, but suddenly it managed to get clear of the clouds and shine down on the yard around the cabin. Violet breathed a sigh of relief as she saw the reason for the scuttles: a family of raccoons scavenging in the yard, looking for something to eat.

Wide awake now, Violet went to her computer and turned it on. She might as well write a bit more in her novel.

~

Toby was restless, unable to sleep. He was thinking to blame it on Jack giving him nothing more than dry kibble for supper, not the fresh fish he'd been expecting. He jumped off the end of the bed where he'd been trying to catch some sleep and wandered into the main room of the cottage.

Noticing an open window minus a screen, Toby jumped up onto the sill and stared out into the darkness. The night sounds were soft in the distance—crickets and frogs. A rustling in the nearby trees drew Toby's attention. He narrowed his eyes in that direction. *Shouldn't be leaving windows open, Jack. Don't like thinking someone could just come in while we're sleeping and knock us off!* Toby jumped down onto the porch.

He moved silently across the yard to where the sounds had come from. *While you're sleeping away, Jack, I'll keep an eye on things for you—one of us needs to be on the job.*

As Toby approached the edge of the woods, he paused as another rustling hit his ears. *Maybe this wasn't such a good idea, coming out here in the pitch dark. Might have been safer at the foot of the bed. At least that way, if someone was going to attack us, they'd get Jack first—he's a larger target, and despite my slight over-weightiness, I can still get under the bed!*

Toby waited a few more seconds, listening intently for more rustling, however, all was quiet except for the crickets and frogs. *Must have been a false alarm. No sense freezing the fur off my toes out here.* He turned and made his way back to the cabin, jumped through the open window, and headed to the bed. As he nestled back into the covers, Jack groaned and changed positions. The night air must have made Toby sleepy because he was snoring within minutes.

~

In the woods near Jack and Toby's cabin, Syd, hunkered down behind a half-decayed log; he thought maybe the old cabin was uninhabited. However, as he'd been about to leave the woods, he noticed an orange tabby cat in the window. As he'd stepped back into the safety of the trees, the cat jumped down from the window and headed in his direction. He wasn't afraid of a cat catching him and turning him into the police, but there was probably someone inside the cabin whom the cat belonged to. Syd couldn't take any chances until he was long-gone from the area. He was sure his name and picture was all over the television.

Syd closed his eyes and tried to sleep. The crime he'd committed and his early years in life flitted through his mind. He'd not had the best childhood, in fact, it had been terrible.

Syd's father had come and gone as he pleased, but Syd, as much as he longed to see his father, hated the minute the man walked through the door. It meant his mother would get a beating—usually for no reason—and if he dared to shed a tear over her, his father would turn the belt on him.

The day Syd's little sister was born had been another dark day. He'd only been ten, and it was a big responsibility his mother had to give him. Money had always been another big problem for his family, Syd's father never bringing home enough to sustain a decent living for those he was supposed to be responsible for, so they didn't even have a phone.

Syd's mother was horribly sick and he had no idea she was getting ready to have a baby. After hours of listening to her painful cries, she had instructed him to run down the street to Mrs. Nelson's house and ask her to call an ambulance. Syd was to tell her the baby was on its way.

He had rushed out into the dark night, into the rainstorm that had started in the early evening and hadn't let up one bit. The rain pellets didn't take long to soak his threadbare clothes, and by the time Syd reached Mrs. Nelson's, he was shivering uncontrollably.

Approaching the house, Syd noticed there were no lights on. What was he going to do if Mrs. Nelson wasn't home? Syd pounded on the door and waited. He pounded again and waited some more. Just as he was about to turn and leave, wondering what he was going to do to get his mother help, the porch light flickered on, and the door opened.

"Who the hell is bothering me at this time of night?" Mrs. Nelson yelled. "Oh, it's you," she added when she saw Syd. "What do you want, boy? Is your mother okay?"

It seemed, at the time, to Syd, Mrs. Nelson might know more about his mother's condition than he did. "Mama said to come and ask you to call an ambulance … she said the baby's on its way."

Mrs. Nelson put her arm around Syd's shoulders and drew him into the house. "You poor dear," she said as she directed him to a chair in her kitchen, before going to her living room to make the phone call to 911.

Syd sat still as a cat stalking a mouse. He'd learned early in life to be seen and not heard, and sometimes it wasn't even good to be seen. He could hear Mrs. Nelson in the living room talking to someone on the phone, he heard her say his mother's name and the address where they lived.

A few minutes later, Mrs. Nelson returned to the kitchen and walked over to Syd. She put a delicate finger under his chin and looked into his eyes, then moved his head from side to side. The welts his father had left across his face and on his neck a few nights ago before he'd left the house for a few days were still visible.

"You poor child," Mrs. Nelson mumbled. "When is that girl going to leave that no-good son of a bitch! And bringing another innocent into the world … better off if the child weren't born," she went on as though Syd wasn't there.

Mrs. Nelson went to her fridge and returned to the table with a piece of cake and a glass of milk. "Get this down you, boy, and then I'll wrap you up in a blanket and get you back to your mother's house."

Syd shook his head. "C -c-can't g-go back … h-he'll th-think I d-d-done somethin' to her." Tears welled up in his eyes at the very thought of having to face his father if something awful happened to his mother.

"Is my mama g-going to d-die?" he asked.

Mrs. Nelson heaved a big sigh and pulled up a chair beside the distraught boy. She reached over and gathered him into her arms and hugged him close. Syd remembered how sweet she had smelled, not like his mother, who hardly ever changed her clothes or took a shower. Syd didn't think she had many clothes because the closet in her room was pretty bare. He didn't have many either.

"Your mama's just going to have a baby, she's not going to die," Mrs. Nelson explained patiently. She brushed the tears from Syd's cheeks. "Now you finish up this piece of cake and your milk, and we'll go along to your house, so you can see for yourself that your mother is okay."

Syd wolfed down the treat, not wanting to waste any time getting back to his mother. When he finished, Mrs. Nelson put on a pair of rain boots and a raincoat and lay a small crocheted blanket around Syd's shoulders. She picked up an umbrella and together they headed out the door.

The ambulance siren was drawing closer to his house as he and Mrs. Nelson reached the front step. Syd heard his mother's screams beyond the door. He wondered where his father was. He wondered if the man was inside beating his mother again, and that was the real reason she was crying.

Mrs. Nelson rushed into the house and raced up the stairs to the living room where Syd's mother was lying on the couch. Syd stood in the doorway of the room, watching, his eyes filled with terror at the scene before him. His mother was covered in blood, and he was sure his father had come around. It—the blood—was a familiar scene. But where was his father now?

"Excuse us, son," a firm, gentle voice said as a hand touched Syd's shoulder. The person behind the voice guided him out of the doorway. Two paramedics rushed over to Syd's mother, and Mrs. Nelson stepped out of the way to let them get to work.

Everything that happened over the next half-hour went over Syd's head. He had no idea what was going on, only that he thought his mother was going to die and his father was going to blame him and maybe kill him this time. Syd remembered considering how he might be better off dead. He recalled a couple stories he had heard on the few occasions his mother had taken him to Sunday school, about how when you died you went to a place called Heaven and everything was beautiful, and you got a new body and maybe even a set of angel wings. That would be a beautiful thing to have; he'd be able to fly then.

"It's okay, Sheila, I'll take your boy back to my place for the night, or for as long as needed. You just concentrate on having this baby, and when you get out of the hospital, I think you should come and stay with me until you are strong enough to handle things on your own." Mrs. Nelson was talking to Syd's mother, who was laid out on a stretcher.

Syd had been scared more than ever when he'd seen all the wires hooked up to his mother. It was inevitable now—he was going to get in trouble from his father. Syd knew it was about time for him to show up. As though on cue, the front door banged open, and like a gust of harsh wind, Syd's father burst into the room.

"What the hell is going on here?" he demanded, his voice slurring with alcohol. "Where are you takin' my wife? Get her off that thing!" He tried to push his way past the paramedic standing at the front of the gurney.

The other paramedic, noting there might be real trouble, took out her phone and dialled 911. "We have a situation here at 410 Glenwood Road, a woman in distress, bleeding badly, almost ready to deliver a baby, and the husband is trying to stop us from getting her out of the house and to the hospital! He's violent." The paramedic was sputtering because Syd's father was advancing on her, rage written all over his face.

Mrs. Nelson, foreseeing what might happen, quickly ushered Syd toward the back door but she was too late. His father saw her make her move and advanced on her and Syd.

"Where do you think you're takin' my son, bitch?" he bellowed as he reached the neighbour and Syd. Grabbing hold of Syd's arm, he yanked the boy from Mrs. Nelson's grasp. "Come here, boy! You responsible for all this?" he leered, shoving his face up close to Syd's.

Syd shook his head. Tears flowed unchecked.

"Speak up, boy! I can't hear you!" The fumes of stale cigarettes and whiskey were overwhelming.

Syd still couldn't find his tongue. He cowered, waiting for the first of the blows to hit him. His body shook. He peed his pants, feeling the warmth of his urine soaking down his leg and into his shoe. He could see the shadow of a fist in the air above his head, ready to strike like a viper.

"Put your fist down, sir!" a new voice bellowed authoritatively through the room, freezing Syd's father's fist in the course of its intentions.

A second officer entered the room and approached Syd's father, forcing his arms behind his back and clipping on a pair of handcuffs. After realizing that he couldn't get out of the cuffs, Syd's father settled down but the scowl he threw his son guaranteed this was not the end of it.

While the police had taken control of her husband, Sheila had been loaded into the ambulance and it was on its way to the hospital, sirens roaring through the still night. Mrs. Nelson looked around the house then turned to Syd and asked him where his room was so they could pack some clothes for him to bring to her place.

Syd had hung his head, ashamed there weren't many clothes in his room to be packed. His father only left enough money to buy essential food items and most of his clothes were what his mother had been able to scavenge from bins outside the Goodwill stores. He'd been with her several times when she'd gone late at night to search for necessities. She'd told him what they were doing wasn't really right but they had to have clothes, and there just wasn't enough money to buy any. She'd assured him God wouldn't punish them for such an act.

Mrs. Nelson saw the look of horror on the boy's face as she put the meagre belongings into a bag. It had been a rough night. She turned and led Syd out of the house and back down the street to her place.

Syd had never slept in such a comfortable bed. The sheets smelled of flowers and the pillow cradled around his head. He fell instantly asleep, despite the drama of the night.

But morning brought dreadful news to the young boy. The hospital called Mrs. Nelson and told her Sheila had passed away giving birth to a baby girl. The child was in intensive care but not likely to make it. If she knew how to reach the father of the child, the hospital would appreciate it very much.

Mrs. Nelson hung up the phone and turned and looked at Syd. Noticing the tears in her eyes, he began to cry. It was as though he knew his mother had died. He didn't even think about the baby. The elderly woman pulled herself together and began to rustle up a good breakfast for Syd. She had nothing more than a cup of coffee.

After breakfast, Mrs. Nelson called the police department and asked to speak to someone in charge. She sent Syd to the living room to watch television while she filled the officer in on what had happened to the wife of the man they'd arrested last night. Mrs. Nelson didn't want to, but she had to tell them about Syd. She couldn't keep him long-term; he wasn't hers, and she was getting on in years and didn't want to start raising another child. Wouldn't be fair to either one of them.

Syd's life took a turn for the worse. His father had been charged with domestic abuse. A few days after the birth, the baby followed its mother to Heaven. The police charged Syd's father with manslaughter after the autopsy on the baby showed fetal damage and the autopsy on his wife indicated she'd been severely beaten numerous times in recent months.

The Children's Aid came to Mrs. Nelson's house and took Syd away. He'd clung to her apron, not wanting to leave her, tears running freely down his cheeks. She tried to explain to him she had no rights to him and that the kind people were going to find him a good home. He'd be okay.

But he hadn't been. He'd been shuffled from home to home until he was sixteen when his father got out of jail and demanded his son be returned to him. The system seemed tired of trying to find a suitable home for Syd, who'd become quite the troublemaker, so they gladly handed the boy over to his father.

His father picked up where he'd left off, only this time Syd was bigger and stronger and he fought back.

One night, after a horrific brawl in which both parties were well bloodied, Syd staggered out of the house, leaving his father in a pool of blood on the kitchen floor.

"You fucking bastard!" Syd screamed as he gave his father another kick in the gut before leaving. "You fucking bastard—you'll never lay another hand on me again!"

Syd hit the streets, scavenging for food in garbage cans, living in cardboard boxes in back alleys. He kept to himself. One night, when he was looking through a dumpster behind a restaurant, he felt he was being watched. When Syd turned around, he saw a well-dressed gentleman looking at him, a smile on the man's face.

"What's a good-looking boy like you doing rummaging through the garbage?" he'd asked.

Syd scowled at him.

The man moved closer and extended his hand. "Name is Arthur." He paused. "I'd like to offer you a job." He smiled again.

Syd had learned over the past six years in foster care not to trust anyone. He turned his back on the stranger. But Arthur wasn't about to give up.

"Seriously, I'd like to offer you a job and a place to live."

Syd turned back to the man. "You fucking with me, man? Why would you want to do that for me?" he asked warily. The thought of a roof over his head and a paycheque was enough to at least make him curious.

"I just had a couple openings come up in my club, and I noticed you hanging around here a few times, thought I might be able to help you out, get you off the streets. But, if you don't wa—"

"Okay, man … Arthur … what's the job?" Syd figured if he didn't like it, he could just leave.

Arthur smiled widely. "Follow me. My place isn't far from here."

For the first couple months, Syd did odd jobs and errands for Arthur and slept in one of the rooms off the kitchen. It wasn't much, but it was better than the streets, and winter was just around the corner. He had money in his pocket to spend, and during his time off he spent his time in pool halls, drinking and hustling.

One night, Arthur came to his room with a tuxedo. "I have a little something different for you tonight," he said, the usual wide smile on his face. "Shower, put this on, and meet me upstairs in half an hour."

When Syd came upstairs, he noticed Arthur was sitting with a middle-aged man. They were laughing. When Arthur saw Syd, he motioned him over to the table.

"I'd like you to meet my friend, Jarvis. He's just got into town and would like someone to show him around. I'm busy, so thought maybe you might like to do the honours in my stead."

Syd nodded, happy to be doing something more than errands. Little did he know exactly what he would be expected to do. He'd thought the beatings his father had given him were depraved but what he suffered at the hands of Jarvis made those whippings seem trivial.

After spending a few hours sightseeing around town, Jarvis suggested they go back to his hotel and have a bite to eat, said he didn't want to eat in a crowded restaurant, so if Syd didn't mind, they would go up to his room and order a meal by room service, after which they would kick back and watch some television. Syd didn't see any harm in that. He was just short of seventeen, still innocent to certain things.

When Jarvis was finished with Syd, he whispered in his ear that if he breathed a word to anyone about what had happened, he'd be a dead man. Arthur wouldn't like it if an employee didn't please one of his friends.

Syd had been too distraught at the time to argue—shock was a better word to describe his feelings. Jarvis came to the club every night for a week and Syd was expected to *service* his boss's friend. At the end of the week, Arthur found another friend that wanted—needed—entertainment. And it went on and on. The only good thing was Syd's bank account was growing exponentially. He began to plan how he was going to get away—far away. He learned to shut his mind off when the men were doing their deeds, think of a beautiful place, the Heaven he'd heard about when he was a boy.

Arthur, however, was more difficult to escape from than Syd had thought, not willing to let one of his "boys" go. After two years of turning tricks for Arthur's friends, Syd had had enough. He figured there was only one way to get out of the life he'd found himself trapped in, but in doing so, Syd found himself in a different prison, one with bars. The only satisfaction he had was that Arthur would never be able to turn another innocent boy into a prostitute.

His mind racing, Syd still couldn't sleep, and the sun was creeping over the horizon, sending beams of light through the trees. He knew he'd have to search further down the lake if he hoped to find an empty cabin to hole up for a while and get some rest before pushing on. He stood and slipped out of the woods, walking down to the lake, hoping a walk along the shoreline might render something. He decided it best to walk in the water, just in case.

Chapter Eight

Toby awoke with a start. A loud bang resounded through the cottage, followed by an even louder "Damn it!" The old cat jumped off the bed and ran to the main room to see Jack hopping around on one foot, a frying pan on the floor nearby. Jack's face was riddled with pain.

"Hey, old man," Jack greeted through clenched teeth as he made his way to a kitchen chair. "I'll get your breakfast in a minute," he added, sitting down.

Toby walked over and sat by Jack's chair. He noticed Jack's foot was an angry red colour. *Guess I can wait for my meal, probably just dry kibbles again anyway.*

Rubbing his foot, Jack looked at Toby. "Are you sure you don't want to go fishing with me, old man?" The grinning grimace on Jack's face was enough for Toby to know Jack was joking.

Toby stood and walked to his dish. *You'd think Jack would know by now that I have no interest in going out on the lake in a boat to catch fish, my only desire in the process is the finished product, nicely filleted, in my dish!* Toby sat down by his empty bowl and swished his tail. A cat could only exist so long without food, even if the person who put the kibble in his dish was wounded.

As he waited, Toby's thoughts turned to his night venture, wondering if he'd heard something worth further investigation. *After you leave for your fishing, I think I'll take a little walk and investigate if there was someone there in the woods.*

An hour later, Jack limped off to the boat to spend a few hours fishing on the lake. Toby sat on the veranda watching him go, and once Jack was well out in the water, Toby headed to the woods where he'd heard the noises in the night.

Stepping gingerly through the damp leaves, Toby came upon the fallen log where Syd had taken refuge. Toby jumped onto the trunk and gazed down at the flat terrain. *Something more substantial than a racoon was here … and recently. Not a bear or a deer … the compacted area isn't big enough… Could it have been a human? Hmm...*

Toby jumped down to the flattened ground cover. He sniffed around. *Definitely human—and one who hasn't showered for a while.* He looked around and saw tracks leading away from the spot. *Well, why not? No harm in following the prints. Someone hiding like this may be up to no good. It's best to make sure they are well away from our cottage.*

Toby followed the pathway out of the woods and down to the beach, where the tracks confirmed whatever had been in the woods was human. *Interesting … I wonder what someone was doing sleeping in our woods?* Some of the footsteps were faint, the waves having washed traces of them back into the lake. Periodically, they disappeared, only to reappear a little further on.

Toby kept a watchful eye as he went along because he knew there could be any number of animals around. He climbed over a fallen tree and noted where the human had done the same—the imprints in the sand were more pronounced on the other side where they'd jumped off the tree trunk.

This is thirsty work. Toby stepped to the edge of the water and lapped up a few drops to quench his palate. Moving away from the splashing waves, Toby sat down on the sand and observed his surroundings. Lots of trees just off the beach edge, tufts of grass and weeds spotting the area, and then, in the near distance, the roof of another cabin. *Interesting … we aren't as alone up here as Jack thought we would be. I wonder if anyone is there … if whoever was in our woods last night rents the place. But if so, why would they be sleeping out in the wild? Why not safely in their cabin?*

Toby's thoughts spun as he made his way toward the building. He kicked into detective mode as he got closer. The windows were all closed, curtains drawn. The door was shut tight. There was no smell of morning coffee or breakfast cooking. *Something's not right.* Toby slunk down in the grass and shimmied his way to the cottage. His feline sense that all was not well was strong.

~

Syd had come upon the cottage as he made his way along the shore. At first, he'd thought it a godsend—until he noticed the vehicle parked at the side of the building.

"Damn!" he cursed. "Well, whoever is here probably doesn't know about my escape and I'm hungry … I could use a good breakfast." Syd made his way to the door, paused and listened for any movement from within. Nothing.

He jiggled the door to see if it was locked. The knob turned effortlessly and the door creaked open. Syd stepped inside and observed the area carefully. An open concept with kitchen, living room, and two doors on the far side—one ajar, presumably a bathroom because a small sink was visible—the other door closed, probably a bedroom.

Shutting the door behind him, Syd made the decision to hole up for a time, whether the current occupant liked it or not. After all, the element of surprise was on his side and he had a lot more to lose than whoever was here.

~

Jack's foot was still throbbing, but nothing was going to take away the enjoyment of a good morning of fishing on an open lake. The conditions were perfect. Not a wave to be seen, not a breeze to rustle a noise and scare the fish away by rocking the boat. He wondered what Toby might be up to.

"Probably sleeping," Jack mumbled as he hooked a worm on his line. "Oh well, he deserves it with all he's been through." He cast the line into the water, leaned back, and waited. The boat floated lazily on the water, lulling Jack to sleep.

Suddenly, the fishing pole jerked: Jack sat up quickly and began the joyful job of bringing the fish in. "Well, old man, it'll be a fish dinner for us tonight."

Chapter Nine

Toby approached the cottage. He heard voices coming from inside. One of the voices—a woman—didn't sound too happy. The other voice—a man—sounded angry.

"What do you think you're doing?!" the woman hollered.

"I was out walking on the beach and thought to make a friendly call. I'm staying at a cabin just down the lake," the man replied.

Toby knew the guy was lying; he wasn't staying at any cabin. *You slept in the woods last night, liar! Why are you fibbing to this woman? I'm going to have to get Jack; she might be in danger. Not much I can do on my own, limited as I am. Still a bit achy from my last big case.*

"But what makes you think you can just walk into my cabin and start helping yourself to my food?" The woman demanded.

"Well, if you think bein' neighbourly is not nice, lady, I'm sorry 'bout that." A pause. Then, "I've been comin' up to this lake for years, and it's just the way cottage life is in these parts."

"You should have knocked; that would've been the proper thing to do."

Toby heard the strain in the woman's voice. He thought about turning around and trying to bring Jack back here somehow, but thought maybe it might be best to get a full cat's-eye view of what was going on inside. *Who could resist a handsome devil like me?* Toby walked up to the door and let out a loud meow.

The talking inside the cabin ceased. Toby meowed again and was rewarded with approaching footsteps. Within seconds the door swung open—the woman. The man was fast on her heels and shoved her aside. Toby hissed.

The man stepped out onto the porch and scanned the area. Toby, seizing the opportunity, raced into the room and hid behind the woman—safe zone. Backing into the room and closing the door, Syd turned and faced the woman and Toby. He ran a hand through his hair.

The woman, looking shaken, spoke up. Toby could tell she was scared. "Look, mister, I don't know what the protocol up here is with cottagers, but I would prefer if you left. I came up here for some peace and quiet…"

"Did you now?" Syd cut her off. "Mighty unsociable of you."

Toby slunk around to the front of the woman, protectively leaning on her legs. *Really something off with this guy, good thing I happened along. Why don't you just beat it out of here, mister … leave the lady alone.* Toby hissed at Syd.

All Violet could think of was the news about the escaped prisoner. She couldn't help thinking this might be the guy. Years of watching police programs had taught her that the worst thing she could do was let him know what she knew, if that were the case.

Syd raised a foot to kick at Toby. He hated cats. Violet, not feeling overly brave but also not wanting an innocent cat hurt, scooped Toby up in her arms.

There, buddy. She's got your number. Hands off! Toby nestled into Violet's chest and began to purr.

Syd hesitated, then put his foot back down on the floor. He rubbed his chin thoughtfully and pointed to the table. "Why don't you sit down, lady, and let me make you a coffee and some breakfast; show you how to be hospitable." Syd laughed, a scratchy sound from his throat.

Violet hesitated.

"Go on." Syd's words took on a dark tone as he reached out and put his hand on Violet's arm and propelled her to the table. "Be better all around, I'd say, if you just obliged me."

Violet stumbled on the way across the room, but managed to keep hold of Toby. Her mind was working overtime, realizing the man likely was the escaped prisoner. *And here I am, stuck in the middle of nowhere, no one knowing where I am, with only an old cat to cling to.* Violet clutched Toby tighter and buried her nose in the fur around his neck. "Where did you come from, old fellow?" she whispered in his ear.

Toby struggled to get off Violet's lap. *I need to get out of here and get this lady some help. Jack will know what to do.*

"You want down, old fellow? Here you go." Violet released her hold on Toby and he headed right for the door.

How he was going to open the door and get out was a problem. Syd noticed the sudden movement and stopped what he was doing. He couldn't let the cat get out and take a chance on the feline bringing someone back to the cottage until he was long gone. He needed a good meal and a few hours of decent sleep.

Violet made a move to get up, with the intention of opening the door for Toby.

"What do you think you're doin'?" Syd snapped.

"I think the cat wants out," Violet replied nervously.

Syd rubbed his fingers on his temples. "Cat's not goin' anywhere. Sit back down!" he ordered. "Don't make this hard on yourself."

Violet, despite her fear, shouted, "Who the hell do you think you are, coming into my cabin and ordering me around like this? I'll have you know my husband will be up here any time…"

Syd's face clouded with anger. "Don't lie to me, bitch. You just told me a few minutes ago you came up here to get away from everyone. I'd bet you don't even have a husband! Ain't no one comin' to help you out, sweetheart." Syd's laugh bordered on diabolical and Violet knew she was in real trouble.

Toby was sure the guy was up to no-good. He made his way to the door and began to paw at the wood, attempting to open it. Syd was on him in a flash.

"You ain't goin' anywhere, pussycat," Syd snarled as he shoved Toby away from the door with his foot.

Toby hissed, despite knowing he was no physical match for the man. He walked back to the woman. *I'll have to bide my time and make my escape when he's off-guard.* He planted himself under her chair.

Syd began pacing in front of the door. He hadn't planned on involving anyone else in what he had to do. It wasn't enough he'd killed Arthur—he needed to find Jarvis, and then go down the list he kept in his head. He'd be a lot more careful this time and not get caught. Arthur had been a crime of passion, one he'd committed in front of witnesses when his temper got the better of him. He definitely wouldn't make the same mistake again.

But this woman was going to complicate things for him. Why did he have to enter the cabin? Having seen the vehicle there, he knew the place was inhabited. Syd was almost positive the woman knew who he was, despite not seeing a radio or a television in the room. She would have one in her vehicle, and if she'd gone anywhere, or had just arrived, she probably heard about his escape on her way in.

Finally, his decision made, he turned to Violet. "You know who I am?" he asked, ambling over to the table.

Violet looked away, deciding not to answer him immediately. The scrape of a chair being pulled back from the table caused her to turn back to the man in her cabin. Syd sat down and leaned toward her. She tried to back away, from fear, and from his overwhelming odour.

"Answer me!" Syd shouted.

Finally gathering a morsel of courage, Violet swallowed hard and whispered, "I think you might be the guy who escaped from prison recently." She looked away again.

Toby, catching the words "escaped from prison," came out from under the chair and jumped up on Violet's lap. *I definitely have to escape and figure out a way to get Jack over here to save this poor woman!*

Syd stood, still leaning over the table. He slapped his hand on it. "Bingo! You got it right, lady. So I have a problem now—what to do with you!"

Violet swallowed hard. Her mouth opened, closed, and then opened again. Finally, "Please, mister, just go. I won't tell anyone you were here … I don't even have a cell phone that I could call to tell anyone…"

"You think I'm a fool, lady?" Syd chortled. "You have a vehicle." He paused. "Actually, that might be a good idea—me leaving. I can take your van. But I still have to do something with you, I can't leave loose ends. I need to finish what I started—what they started—I have to..." Syd was rambling.

Toby decided to make a move. After all, an old cat couldn't be expected to hold it in for too long, and from the looks of things in the cottage, there was no litter box for him to use. He jumped down from Violet's lap and headed back to the door, meowing as he went. When Toby reached the door, he stretched up and began scratching it, looking back at Syd and then Violet. When neither one made a move to open the door, Toby started to scratch on the small doormat and then pretended he was squatting to go pee.

If this manoeuvre doesn't get this guy to open the door and let me out, I don't know what will!

"I think the cat has to go to the bathroom," Violet spoke up. "You best let him out. Not much chance of the cat telling anyone about you, is there?" she added matter-of-factly.

Syd ran his hand through his hair again. The woman was speaking the truth about the cat not being able to tell anyone. *Think, man! Think!* But, it was a well-fed and well-groomed cat, inferring the owner was probably not far off.

Violet, apparently thinking along the same lines, continued. "It might be best that you let the cat out and he'll make his way home … might save the owner from looking for him, something you probably don't want to happen."

Good for you lady! Why hadn't I thought of that? If I don't show up at Jack's cottage, he'll come looking for me. I wonder if my paw prints are still visible down by the shore...
Toby started meowing again, louder, and scratched more

furiously on the mat. *Come on, you sick bastard, open the door and let me out; I really don't want to make a mess on this lady's rug!*

Syd finally made his decision. Moving quickly to the door, he opened it and booted Toby out onto the veranda. Toby was slightly unsettled from the rough treatment. While he was shaking off the assault, he heard the door slam and the lock click into place.

Toby made his way back to a grove of trees near the cottage. *I can't leave her. She's right; Jack will come looking for me, which means I can't go back to our cottage… What to do, though… Jack's out fishing and God knows when he'll return… He might not even notice I'm missing … hmmm … I wonder if I have time to slip back and finish up that breakfast I only half ate then get back here and keep an eye on the lady until Jack comes looking for me… Maybe even go back into the cottage, pretend I'm lost or something… Yeah, that's what I'll do; it's the only way to get Jack here. Boy, detectiving never stops!*

Toby wandered back the way he'd come, hoping the plan he'd derived in his head would work.

Chapter Ten

Jack was exceptionally pleased with his morning catch. He wondered how Toby was making out back at the cottage but knowing the old cat for as long as he had, figured he'd still be curled up on the end of the bed, sound asleep.

"May as well take a little cruise around the lake and check the area out," Jack said to the fish in the pail. "You guys aren't going anywhere."

Jack started the motor and put it in the lowest gear: he wasn't in a hurry. The boat made small ripples in the water as it chugged along, following the shoreline. There weren't many cottages up this way, and Jack wondered why because the area was beautiful.

Passing by another heavily wooded area, Jack noticed a cabin with a van parked beside it. "Maybe I'll take a walk in a day or two and meet my neighbour," he said as he continued on his way around the lake.

~

Toby was just about ready to leave the wooded area when he heard the boat motor. *Maybe I won't have to try and get Jack here!* But, his hopes were dashed as the boat continued on its way. *Oh well, at least this will give me time to get to my cottage, grab a bite to eat, and get back here!*

~

Syd wanted nothing more than to finish making the breakfast he'd started, eat it, and then have a good nap. Being tormented by his past during the night had prevented him from getting any sleep. He looked around the cabin, searching for something to tie the woman up with. He couldn't take a chance on falling asleep and having her escape. He'd figure out what to do with her before he left. Taking her van, of course, was a first logical step. Maybe he could even change into some of her clothes and pose as a woman. He was small enough, and his hair was long.

"What do you plan to do with me?" Violet asked again. "Like I told you, I won't tell anyone. I do have a family … a husband … children … grandchildren … please."

Syd ran his hand through his hair, a nervous habit Violet realized. "Right now, lady—"

"Call me Violet," Violet suggested. She'd seen it on one of her detective programs that it was good to personalize yourself to the criminal. They might be less likely to do away with you if you put a name to the face. "What's your name?" she added.

"Don't try and get into my head, lady!" Syd said.

"Not trying to. I just thought it would be nicer if we knew each other's names since we're going to be spending some time together."

"I won't be here long enough," Syd lisped, his lips curling sarcastically. "I've got places to go, things to do. Right now, I just want to get some food and have a nap."

Violet decided to try another tactic even though her insides were churning. *Maybe if I'm genuinely kind to him, he won't kill me, because I think that's what he believes he'll have to do, kill me.* "How say you let me make you something to eat? I don't mind, really. I'm hungry, too."

Hand through the hair again. Pacing. Thinking. *What to do ... I don't want to kill the lady ... Violet ... what a pretty name ... like a flower... What to do?* Syd's eyes lit on the computer on the table by the window. *The computer will have a cord; I can use that to tie her up while I get some sleep. No harm in letting her cook for me either ... probably taste better than anything I can rustle up.*

Syd finally turned to Violet: "Okay ... Violet ... you can make me something to eat but no funny stuff—you make a move toward that door, and it'll be lights out for you. Understand?"

"Perfectly."

Half an hour later, Violet set a breakfast of eggs, bacon, and toast in front of Syd, then fixed herself a plate of the same. Not that she felt like eating, but she needed to keep up the façade she'd begun. Syd dug into his meal with a savage hunger.

"It's been a while since you ate?" Violet asked.

"Ate some berries in the woods," Syd mumbled through a mouthful of eggs.

"Oh, I'm sorry, I didn't get you a drink," Violet tried to keep the conversation on food. "Can I get you a coffee?"

"Yeah, a coffee would be great."

"Let me put some water on to boil." Violet left the table and went to the sink.

"Syd. That's my name."

Violet, her back to Syd, smiled. *Maybe there's hope after all!* "Syd. That's a nice name. I had a great uncle with that name," she lied.

Syd grunted as he shoved another mouthful of eggs in his mouth.

~

Toby slunk up to the cottage cautiously, just in case Jack had turned around and headed back. All seemed quiet. The screen door was still slightly ajar and it was easy for Toby to push into the living area and go to his dish. The thought of the fish dinner he should be feasting on tonight was foremost in his mind, but dry kibble would have to do for now. At least it was better than having to catch a mouse. Toby couldn't stand the thought of eating raw meat!

Finishing his meal off with a drink of water, Toby headed back out the door. He felt he had no time to waste; the lady could be in real trouble. He needed to return to that cottage and do whatever he could to save her. In the meantime, while on his way back, he'd leave as much signage as possible for Jack to follow once he realized his beloved cat was missing.

As Toby approached Violet's cabin, he caught a whiff of eggs and bacon. *Am I too late? Has he already killed her?*

Toby manoeuvred quietly up onto the veranda. He could hear talking inside, a good sign that the lady was still alive. Had he been mistaken that she was in real trouble? He made his way over to the window and jumped up on the sill and looked in. The lady and the guy were sitting at the table eating but she still looked nervous.

Well, here goes nothing! Toby let out a couple of loud meows, getting the attention of the cottage inhabitants.

Syd looked over at the window, angrily gesticulating with his knife. Toby heard him yell: "It's that damn cat you told me to let out, what the fuck does it want?"

"Maybe he's lost, or maybe his owner left him behind accidentally," Violet said. "I think we should let him in."

Hand through the hair again. "Damn!" Syd finally bellowed, getting up and going to the door. "Get in here, cat. At least you can keep the lady company while I get some sleep."

Toby raced into the room and settled himself by Violet's chair.

After Violet and Syd finished eating, Syd walked to the computer and pulled the cord from the wall and the unit. Approaching Violet: "Sorry, Violet, but I gotta tie you up while I get some sleep."

As afraid as she was, Violet nodded. She hadn't expected anything less. Syd tied her wrists together behind her back, then looked for something to bind her feet and to muzzle her. He couldn't take a chance on having her scream out in case someone happened by.

Rummaging around in her room where she'd put her clothes, Syd ripped one of her T-shirts into strips and then tied her feet together. He took another piece and tied it around her mouth. Satisfied she was going nowhere, Syd went into the bedroom and stretched out on the bed. He was asleep within seconds.

Toby curled up beside Violet. There was nothing more he could do now but wait for Jack.

Chapter Eleven

J ack arrived at the cottage shortly after the noon hour. He was hot and tired and wanted nothing more than to have a nap. He looked around for Toby. "Where are you, you old bugger?" he questioned as he looked in the bedroom and noticed there was no furball nestled in the covers.

Deciding to make himself a quick sandwich before lying down, Jack noticed Toby's dish was empty. "Well, wherever you are, you aren't hungry," he mumbled. He proceeded to fix his lunch, washing the sandwich down with a can of beer.

Thinking no further about the old cat, Jack stretched out and closed his eyes. The fish he'd caught was on ice and would be waiting for him when he woke up. Toby was going to be pleasantly surprised with the fish dinner he would have whenever he arrived home, which Jack was confident would be in time for supper. One thing Toby didn't like to miss was a meal.

~

Violet struggled against the cord that tied her hands together behind her back. Whoever this Syd was, he certainly knew how to tie a proper knot. She strained against the cloth wrapped around her ankles, hoping the material would rip apart, rendering her legs free to possibly make a run for it.

Nothing was working.

She looked down at the big orange cat that had decided to come back. "What's your game, old fellow?" Violet whispered. "Why'd you return? You were free."

Toby glanced up at Violet's voice and purred. He wanted to let her know that, in the end, all would be well. He couldn't tell her Jack would save them, but in his heart of hearts, he knew his friend would. Toby rested his head back on his paws and closed his eyes. *Need to get some shut-eye to preserve my strength for what might come if Jack doesn't show up.*

~

Despite having fallen asleep quickly, Syd's rest was short-lived. Dreams of the past once again invaded his mind. He saw Jarvis's face leering at him, beckoning him to come and get him—if he dared. He could feel the man's hands around his neck and the soft clicking sound he made as he shoved his penis into Syd's anus. He could hear his own sobs as the man thrust deeper and deeper, only releasing the pain when his satisfaction was complete.

Time after time, Syd had endured the man's torture, which was what Syd considered it to be. Despite not having a positive male role model in his life, Syd knew that a man's cock was supposed to go in a woman, and only those who chose to be man-on-man should behave as Jarvis did. Syd hadn't chosen.

Syd had often wondered why Jarvis just didn't go after another gay guy, why did he have to go through Arthur to find him young men to get off on? It had finally occurred to him many of Arthur's clients were well-known within the community, and such a lifestyle might not be tolerated within the walls of their stations in life. They were married men, as well, which made it even worse—even more secret. Syd had found out about Jarvis—what he did—and what all the others who came after Jarvis did. And Syd was going to make them all pay.

His dream thoughts turned to the most brutal of them all—Leno Cartelli, the Italian. Leno liked to torture Syd before he finished his business. Syd still had scars on his body from what the crazy man had done to him: whips, bites, ropes, pokers made of steel and wood, fists... The list went on of instruments of torture Leno had used. But Leno had never touched Syd's face, saying the boy was too pretty. Syd knew it was because his face couldn't be covered and Leno didn't want anyone asking questions. He was an important man.

Leno would be his last victim, and Syd would draw his death out as long as he could. While in prison, he studied medieval tortures, many that would be perfect for the job.

Syd startled awake in a cold sweat. The nightmares always hindered his sleep, and he'd learned a long time ago to adjust to having little rest, however, lately, the dreams came more often, even tormenting his subconscious when he was awake. He sat up and ran his hand through his hair, feeling the dampness.

"Shit," he cursed. "Gotta get this over with." He leaned over his knees, resting his elbows and cradling his head. "What to do with the woman, though, Violet. Don't really want to kill her but..."

Syd stood and walked to the doorway of the bedroom, looking out at the chair where he'd left Violet tied. She was sleeping, her chin resting on her chest. The orange cat slept by her feet.

"Maybe I should just find her keys and sneak out while she's sleeping," he muttered. "I'd be long gone before she reached someone to tell them what happened here." He paused. "But, what if someone is close by … the cat indicates there might be a neighbour within walking distance."

Tiptoeing into the main room, Syd scanned the area, searching for a purse, the most likely spot Violet would keep her van keys. He noticed something black sitting underneath the computer table and tiptoed over to it.

Bingo!

Gingerly, he pulled the purse out from under the table and was relieved to see a side pocket from which hung a key ring. He gently lifted it out, stood, looked around the room, and made his decision. Violet hadn't woken, and the old cat was snoring.

The door creaked faintly as he opened it. He hesitated, glancing back at his prisoners. They hadn't moved. He slunk the rest of the way out, leaving the door open, taking off in the direction of the van. Figuring it would be locked, he quickly located the right key and pushed the unlock button.

Climbing into the driver's seat, his hands were shaking as he put the key in the ignition. Syd heard the groan of the engine as it sputtered before starting. He glanced at the needles on the dashboard and then hit the steering wheel hard with the palm of his left hand. The gas needle showed the vehicle was almost empty. Syd knew he would not get far, and he didn't have any money. Why hadn't he thought to see if Violet had a credit card?

Syd turned the engine off and walked back to the cottage. With any luck, Violet would still be asleep; maybe he could get a credit card or some money out of her wallet—money would be best because it couldn't be traced.

Luck wasn't with Syd, though. As he approached the still-open door, he noticed a small shadow. As he entered the room, Toby's back arched, and he hissed loud enough to awaken Violet. Furiously, Syd kicked out at Toby but the old cat saw it coming and scurried back to Violet.

"She can't protect you, you beast!" Syd cursed, running his hand through his hair nervously.

Violet took in the scene before her. She noticed the keyring in Syd's hand, and the open door. He seemed to be returning. She couldn't help the half-smile that curled on her lips despite the cloth across her mouth. *Thank goodness I didn't fill up with gas at that last station before my turnoff; I just wanted to get here, and it was going to be dark soon. Idiot probably didn't think to grab my wallet, which has only a bit of cash and a couple credit cards.*

Syd returned to the purse and rifled through it for Violet's wallet. Pulling it out, he opened it, a look of disappointment at what he'd found on his face. Toby walked over and jumped up on the table beside him, hissing. Syd whirled around and confronted Violet.

"Do you have any other money hidden around here?" he demanded.

Violet shrugged her shoulders and moaned, indicating she couldn't answer him because he'd gagged her. Frustrated, Syd made his way to her chair and roughly released the cloth across her mouth.

"Where's the rest of your money?"

"That's it, Syd; there isn't anymore. I spent most of my cash on supplies. You'll have to use one of the credit cards, although I don't think there's much credit left on them, they're almost maxed," Violet explained. "And I missed last month's payment," she lied, "so they may not even be usable. You know how credit card companies are pretty strict about clients paying their bills on time." She tried hard not to smile, not wanting to give away her deceit.

Syd wasn't having any of it. "Don't tell me, lady, someone as organized as what you seem to be, wouldn't pay her bills on time! I ain't stupid, you know!"

Violet had to think quickly of something believable. "Well, I hate to disappoint you, Syd, but I was so absorbed in planning my getaway I forgot to pay those credit card bills. Simple fact, simple truth."

Syd studied her. Ran his hand through his hair. Pressed his fingers to his temples. "I think you're lying, but why would you? If I were to take off, you'd be free to get out of here; why warn me? Doesn't make sense. And there's this cat … maybe he's really yours and you're both playing a game with me, maybe you really are all alone up here and there isn't another cottager anywhere close by…" Syd rambled, trying to think what was the correct scenario.

By this time, Toby was chuckling inside. *Is this guy for real? How the heck did he escape from a maximum-security prison? What a go, lady; keep him guessing and confused.* Toby glared at Syd.

Syd walked to the door and slammed it shut. He slipped the keys into his pocket then headed for the refrigerator. "Don't you drink beer, lady? Of course not," he answered his own question. "You probably drink white wine or are a teetotaller."

Even with the predicament Violet found herself in, she couldn't help smiling. She wouldn't tell him about the bottle of wine tucked in her suitcase under the bed, one she'd hoped to save for a night by an outdoor fire. The last thing she needed was a drunk psychopath.

"I guess you've got that right, Syd," she confirmed. "Nothing but tea, the odd coffee, and water for me." She halted briefly before continuing. "Do you think you could untie me long enough to let me go to the bathroom? I don't know how much longer I can hold it." Violet squeezed her legs together to emphasize her immediate need.

Syd procrastinated, as though he had a choice in letting Violet use the facilities. Toby meandered over to Violet and, looking from her to Syd, let out a loud meow, as though saying: *What are you waiting for; the woman has to go!*

"Okay ... okay," Syd said, walking over to the chair and undoing the cord around Violet's wrists. He wasn't dumb enough to undo her feet himself and take the chance of her kicking him in the face and escaping. "What do you want, cat?" Syd grumbled at Toby, who was watching every move he made.

Toby hissed. *Your demise.*

"Undo your feet, and then go to the bathroom. The cat stays out here with me," Syd said as Toby tried to follow Violet. "Since you seem to like the kitty so much, if you try anything stupid, I'll ring its neck."

Toby hissed again. The one thing he'd failed to do was walk around the cottage and check for windows. *Oh well, if this place is designed anything like the one Jack rented, the window in the bathroom is barely big enough for me to squeeze through!* Toby glared at Syd, knowing it wasn't the time to play the hero—yet.

"I'm afraid there's no toilet in the bathroom; I'll have to go to the outhouse at the side of the house. The fellow that rented me this place didn't inform me of the facilities, or lack of," Violet said.

Syd hadn't checked out the bathroom yet, so did so now, not believing Violet. Seeing she wasn't lying, he took her arm and propelled her to the door. "Make it quick and don't try anything funny or kitty-cat will meet an untimely death. You got that? I'm watching you."

"Got it," Violet returned as she made her way out the door and over to the outhouse.

~

Jack slept longer than he thought he was going to and when he finally woke, it was past mid-afternoon. He swung his legs over to the floor and felt the coolness of the boards. He shivered. "Getting old," he mumbled.

Standing, he looked around for Toby. No sign of the old cat. "Well, wherever you are, old man, I hope you're having fun." Jack headed to the bathroom and splashed water on his face. He kept talking to himself, "May as well get those fish cleaned and on the fire. Toby hasn't missed a meal on purpose yet; I doubt he'll do so tonight."

~

Frank read Violet's note over so many times the edges were warped from wear. He'd seen the signs his wife wasn't happy but chose to ignore them. Violet never complained much during all the years they were married. He hadn't told the kids yet that their mother had gone off, hopefully not for good because that would be like ripping out his heart. The past couple days had been torture enough.

Knowing Violet had a couple of their personal credit cards in her wallet, Frank made the decision to call the credit card company and put a trace on any current purchases and where they came from. That might give him a starting point to track her down and plead with her to return home, despite her requesting time.

Frank called both card companies, then went into the kitchen to prepare a bite to eat and wait for a phone call that might tell him where his wife was. As he ate, he turned on the small television Violet had asked him to install in the kitchen. The first thing he saw was the all-points bulletin about an escaped prisoner in the Kingston area. He prayed his wife hadn't gone up there but he also knew how much she loved that region, and there were plenty of secluded areas around Kingston where a person could hide out.

Chapter Twelve

The two guards, Larry and George, were dressed down by the prison warden.

"How could you two have been so careless? Syd Lance is a dangerous criminal, and there are a few people out there in danger if he was to get to them." The warden, John Harley, had heard rumours from some of his inmate snitches that Syd had unfinished business on the outside. It was surprising what a warden could find out by offering special privileges.

"I don't think Syd will get far on foot. The first thing we need to do is put roadblocks up all around the area, and then start checking out the remote cottage areas," the warden continued. "There's a lot of places he could hole up in until the heat dies down." John Harley's eyebrows furrowed downward.

"I know Syd's crime was one of passion, and in my opinion, for what his victim did to him, even the sanest person might have done the same," he resumed. "But take a young street kid who'd already seen more than enough heartache—kid was bound to turn up bad! From what I understand, his mother died in childbirth but probably would have eventually been beaten to death by her no-good husband had she survived. Syd was regularly beaten by his old man, too. When his father was incarcerated for manslaughter when all the evidence, even on the newborn, showed signs of constant beatings, the boy ended up in foster care, and he has quite the record there.

"Went from home to home for numerous years, never settling … a lot of anger and complete withdrawal from the world. No one was able to reach him. Eventually, he ran away and lived on the streets, which is where his victim found him.

"I investigated this Arthur fellow—I like to know my inmates and what they might be capable of—and discovered, up-front, he ran a legitimate nightclub. However, behind the scenes, he pimped out a few of the young men he hired to some very exclusive customers, ones that didn't want society to know what they were up to.

"I guess our boy, Syd, finally had enough of being used as a pincushion for every sicko Arthur made him go out with and he snapped. Who better to start with than the man at the top? My greatest fear—not that any of these sadists wouldn't deserve a bit of reckoning for what they do—is that Syd isn't finished yet. I'll bet he has a whole list of people he wants to rid the world of."

Larry and George stood quietly, listening to their boss as he filled them in on what the escapee had gone through in life. They'd had no idea. Larry was too new to know much about Syd but George knew him as an inmate who didn't cause trouble. Syd stuck to himself, staying out of gangs. He had worked in the library and occasionally in the kitchen. He kept himself in good shape, and if appearances were to be believed, they would suggest he had been a model prisoner. George knew more about Syd but those were his secrets to tell, or not to tell. He was shocked Syd had managed to escape at the gas station and cursed inside. Syd knew too much about other things–

–goings on—that George couldn't afford to have made public knowledge.

John Harley stood and walked around to the front of his desk and leaned back on it. He folded his arms and stared at the two guards. "I hate it when a prisoner escapes, despite any sympathies I might have for the reasons they committed their crime. But you know what I hate even more?"

Not waiting for either of his employees to reply, the warden continued: "I hate carelessness. This was a simple job, boys—transport a prisoner to the hospital and back. I would like to know why one of you wouldn't have gone around to the back of the building just in case there was a window in the washroom, which, by the way, boys, there usually is." The warden's statements had more than a hint of sarcasm in them.

"So, can you tell me, why didn't that happen? What were you guys doing while your prisoner was crawling out a small window and running into the woods and disappearing?" John Harley stood. "Especially you, George. You're a seasoned guard; transported prisoners several times over the years!"

Both guards shuffled their feet nervously. Larry, the younger of the two, blushed and looked at the floor. George, having had the most experience—ten years, in fact—shrugged his shoulders, temporarily tongue-tied.

Eventually, George spoke up. "Syd appeared to be so sick, we didn't think he'd do anything like that," he started. "The guy was doubled over with pain—at least that's the way it looked to us. We decided to have a smoke while we waited for him to finish in the washroom; I guess we just got to talking about stuff and didn't realize how much time had gone by. It wasn't much, though; Syd must have gone through the window immediately." George looked at Larry as though he wanted him to confirm what happened.

Larry nodded but kept his mouth shut. He didn't want to rat out his fellow officer and tell the warden that, in fact, he had suggested they check around back to ensure there was no escape route and George had laughed and said Syd wasn't going anywhere but to have a big shit; they had time to have a smoke and relax a bit before continuing to the hospital. Larry hadn't worked with George for long but rumour around the Pen was George had his own rules, his own way of doing things, and they didn't always fall in line with the prison protocol.

George had a reputation amongst the guards, and Larry had learned quickly when he first started working at the prison there was not only a hierarchy amongst the prisoners, but one amongst the guards, as well. George was a ringleader, not to be messed with. A couple guys who'd started after Larry had found that out pretty quickly—the hard way.

John Harley studied the two men in front of him. He was by no means a fool to what went on in his prison, and he knew George was a bully amongst the guards and the prisoners. But he was useful, especially with the ornerier inmates, and there had been more than a few times John turned a blind eye to how an inmate ended up in the infirmary.

Walking around back to his chair, the warden shuffled a few papers on his desk. He knew there was no better man to track down a prisoner than George. George knew this area like the back of his hand, having grown up on the lakes, his father still owning several cottages in some of the more remote areas.

"I'm putting you in charge, George," the warden stated. "Maybe you can catch Syd before he accomplishes what I think he's set out to do." He drew a deep breath, then carried on: "I think you should call in Joe Simmons and his dogs. Take them to the point of escape; they've helped us several times before. In the meantime, make sure the roadblocks are set up. Syd is a smoking cannon about to explode."

Turning to Larry, "I have another job for you. There is a list of men who abused Syd and might be on his radar. I want you to contact each one of them—discretely—and let them know Syd might be coming after them. They need to take precautions if they want to live. What that young man did to his boss is probably minor compared to what he'll do to the guys that actually abused him."

John handed Larry a file. "Don't waste any time, men; we need to put this situation to bed and get Syd back behind bars where he belongs. I don't want us to be the reason another woman becomes a widow or more children become fatherless." John turned his back on George and Larry and walked to the window. "Dismissed," he added, folding his hands behind his back.

Chapter Thirteen

Syd was hungry again. When Violet came in from the outhouse, he shoved her toward the refrigerator. "May as well make us something to eat," he said, "before I tie you up again."

Even though she didn't feel like eating, Violet was only too willing to oblige. Her wrists were sore from the computer cord, having strained to get out of it. She opened the fridge and took out some cheese and ham.

"How about a grilled ham and cheese?" she asked, holding up the packages.

Syd nodded.

"Tea?"

Syd shook his head no.

"Okay then." Violet went about preparing the lunch, taking as much time as she dared. She didn't want to anger Syd.

"Hey there, kitty … you want something to eat? I can maybe give you a bit of cheese … sorry, I wasn't expecting you to drop in."

Toby made his way to Violet and rubbed around her legs, purring.

"Cat's fat enough, don't you think?" Syd pointed out. "I wouldn't be wasting good cheese on him if I were you."

"Well, you aren't me, are you?" The sarcastic retort was out of Violet's mouth before she could stop it.

Guess she told you, didn't she? Toby glared at Syd.

Thankfully, Syd decided to ignore Violet's off-colour comment. He sat down at the table and waited for the lunch to be served, thinking how he was going to kill the next person on his list.

Violet, not able to waste anymore time, walked to the table with two plates. She set one in front of Syd and then sat down across from him. After a few seconds of silence, she decided to try and have a conversation with her captor.

"So, tell me, Syd … What is it you did to land yourself in prison?" Violet took a bite of her sandwich.

"Why should you care?" came the terse reply.

"Just making conversation."

"Killed a man."

Violet swallowed her mouthful of sandwich. "I see," was all she could manage to say.

Great! A killer. Another killer to try and apprehend. Toby sat protectively by Violet's chair.

"Who'd you kill?" Violet continued, hoping to get a handle on what might be making this young man tick. He didn't look like a cold-blooded killer. He was young, of slight build, bright blue eyes, and sandy-coloured hair. Could have passed for a girl, his features were so delicate.

"You don't know him; why should it matter to you?"

Violet thought to try another tactic. "Did he deserve to die?"

Syd leaned back in his chair and observed the woman he'd still not determined what he was going to do with. *What's your game, lady?* Talking to Violet about what had happened to him, Syd figured wouldn't hurt. She might not be around long enough to tell anyone what his plans were anyway—once he decided what he must do.

"Yeah, he deserved to die."

"Why?"

"He wasn't what he portrayed to the outside world. He preyed on young people who had nothing more to lose in life, giving them hope for a better life. He made them feel comfortable and secure, and then … well, then…" Syd hesitated, unsure how to say what had happened to him, embarrassed by the enormity of it.

"Then what?" Violet encouraged.

Breathing in a shuddering breath. "He pimped us out … and not to women."

Violet let out a low whistle. She hadn't expected that. Even Toby was taken aback by what Syd revealed.

"That's awful," Violet breathed. "Did it come up in court what was done to you?"

"Not really. My lawyer tried, but he was young and inexperienced—court-appointed, of course. I couldn't afford a professional criminal lawyer."

Violet had an idea. "You know, Syd, I'm a writer; I could tell your story. If the courts knew what really happened to you, they might lessen your sentence."

Toby looked at Violet. *I think I know where you're going with this and I like it. Buy as much time as you can; I'm sure Jack will show up eventually; he has to be missing me by now.*

Syd thought hard about what Violet had suggested, but it didn't solve his current problem. "I don't think you can help me, lady."

"Violet … please," she interrupted. Trying to personalize things as much as possible was her primary goal at the moment. Anything not to end up being tied up again.

It was working. "Okay … Violet. If you recollect, I'm here 'cause I escaped from those guards; I'm supposed to be serving a life sentence for killing someone."

"Someone who harmed you terribly; the court needs to hear your story." Violet paused. "I can't do anything about your escaping, but this I will promise you: I'll write your story for you, and I'll try and get your case reopened with representation from a proper criminal lawyer."

Syd looked at Violet, suspicion written all over his face. "Why would you do that for me?"

Violet took a moment to reply, trying to be careful of what she was going say, how she could convince him she wanted to help and, at the same time, not set him off. She knew her life could be in jeopardy if she didn't get through to him.

"I've always had a problem with injustice, not that I agree with you killing a man, but I think you should have had the opportunity to tell your side of the story. What that person did to you was wrong, and he should have been the one thrown behind bars."

"How you gonna tell my story?" Syd asked.

Violet pointed to her computer. "You talk and I'll type."

Syd ran his hand through his hair.

Toby looked admiringly at Violet. *That's right, keep him here.* He made his way to the table with the computer and jumped up on it, situating himself by the window. *Come on, Jack, where are you?*

Syd stood and began pacing. Violet waited patiently, not wanting to rock the boat, praying he agreed to do as she suggested, and that somehow she'd be able to get through to him—or better yet, the authorities, who were undoubtedly searching for him by now, would find the cabin and end her nightmare.

"Okay … I'll tell you my story; but, if I do, I need something more from you. I need you to give me your credit card and your vehicle so I can get out of here when we're done. I need you to fix me up with an outfit so I can pass myself off as a woman, and I need you to promise me you won't tell anyone I've been here for at least two or three days."

Violet knew she had no choice but to agree. What she did with the information once he was gone, out of her life, would be her choice. She walked to the computer and turned it on. "Shall we begin?"

Chapter Fourteen

Jack finished cleaning the fish and wrapped it with foil, readying it for the barbeque. He decided not have a potato; he'd just make a big salad. Heading out onto the porch, he scanned the area, looking for Toby.

"Where are you, old man? This isn't like you to wander off for so long." Jack resorted to calling out, "Kitty, Kitty!" hoping if Toby was nearby, he'd get his tail home.

After calling out a few more times, Jack gave up and returned to the cottage. He looked around, not believing the peace and quiet he'd wanted to have for a few days was *too* peaceful and *too* quiet. He missed Tessa and wished he'd just invited her from the beginning. Hopefully, she'd decide to surprise him and show up before the designated time they'd agreed on. There was only so much an old cat, who seemed to have disappeared, could do to entertain a lonely old man.

Jack headed to the couch and picked up a crossword puzzle book. After finishing two of the easiest ones, Jack found himself falling asleep again and, deciding there was nothing better to do, he put down his pencil and stretched out on the couch.

~

Frank was on his way out the door when the phone rang. He raced back into the house and picked up the receiver. It was one of the credit card companies, letting him know when the last time the card had been used—well before Violet left.

"Would you like us to track your card use?" the girl on the other end of the line asked. "We can notify you if anyone tries to use it."

Frank thought about it for a few seconds, realizing it might not be a bad idea, "Yes ... yes ... that would be perfect."

As luck would have it, as Frank was ready to head out again, the other credit card company called and they repeated the process. Feeling good that if Violet, or anyone else for that matter, tried to use the card, he would get a call and be able to get a location of where she was, Frank finally went out to do some errands. He had called his kids and asked them to come over for a barbecue, deciding he should tell them their mother had gone off for a holiday by herself.

~

George got hold of Joe Simmons, but Joe said he couldn't bring his dogs out until the next day. They had been loaned out to another police department and wouldn't be back until late that night. They'd need to rest before another job.

"Is that a for sure, Joe?" George asked.

"Pretty much. I actually just came from the job ... got a real pain in my one leg, arthritis, I think ... and they were closing in on the suspects they were after," Joe affirmed.

"Okay, I guess we'll have to live with that. What time should I come by in the morning?" George didn't like that another day would be lost before they could get on Syd's trail; he could really be making tracks. George had already arranged for roadblocks, but he was anxious to get a search party out to the remote lake districts to check out the cabins, especially the isolated ones.

"Seven o'clock should be good."

The line went dead.

~

Larry was astounded at the number of names on the list who might become victims if Syd got to them before they were warned. He wondered how safe they would be even with a pre-warning.

His first call was to a man named Jarvis.

"Hello, is this Jarvis Cameron?"

"Yeah ... who's this?" Jarvis asked rudely.

Larry swallowed hard. He hated rude people. He should just let the guy get what he deserved, but that wasn't his choice to make.

"I'm calling you, Mr. Cameron, from Kingston Penitentiary, to inform you Syd Lance has escaped from jail and we have reason to believe he might be coming after you. The prison warden wants you to be aware so you can take extra precautions, and if he should show up on your doorstep, please call the police immediately. He is considered very dangerous; we're not sure if he's managed to find a firearm yet, but he may not need one with what we think he might have in mind for you."

There was silence on the other end of the line and, for a moment, Larry thought Jarvis hung up on him. As he was about to hang up and make his next call, Jarvis spoke, his voice tempered, "Thanks for the warning."

Larry finished his list. A couple of the names didn't answer, so Larry left them a message to return his call; it was urgent. The last name on his list was Leno Cartelli. He made Jarvis sound like a saint. He told Larry the little wimp could try whatever he wanted; he'd be sorry. He said Syd had been a wimp when he knew him and figured there wasn't much the kid could do that he couldn't handle.

"You have no idea, mister," Larry muttered after hanging up the phone. "No idea at all."

Larry looked around the office where he'd been making the calls from and decided to call it a day. On the way out of the prison, Larry bumped into the warden.

"Make the phone calls, Larry?" he asked.

"Yes, sir."

"Talked to everyone on the list?"

"All but two; I left messages for them to call me back."

"Then why are you leaving?" The warden looked annoyed. "Get back to the office and wait for their calls. I don't care if you have to sleep in there tonight. I want everyone on that list to know they could be in danger. Have I made myself clear?"

Larry blushed. "Yes, sir. Quite clear." It was time to start looking for another job. He was beginning to hate this one.

The warden, as though realizing the time and what he was asking of his employee, conceded, "I'll make sure you get some supper sent up to you." A slight pause. "And, if I were you, I'd just keep trying to get hold of whoever you didn't talk to yet; don't wait for them to call you. It might be too late for them if you do." With that final statement, the warden continued on his way out of the building.

At six o'clock, a pizza was delivered to the office where Larry was holed up. He had made several attempts to reach the two names on his list, to no avail. He didn't bother to leave another message, no sense. He'd just keep trying. Finally, by eleven o'clock, Larry had talked to both and was able to head home.

Larry couldn't help thinking about the young man, Syd Lance, who had escaped his custody. He'd glanced at Syd's file, which the warden had left on his desk, and was surprised at the detail in it. Some of the information was from the trial, but some notes were in the warden's handwriting. Larry wondered why the warden left such pertinent material on his desk, knowing that Larry might be curious and take a look, particularly since it was the only file in view.

"I think I might have offed those guys myself," Larry uttered as he closed the office door and headed out of the prison and into the darkness of a chilly northern night.

~

George decided there was nothing more he could do until the next day when the dogs were ready to go. All the roadblocks were in place and he had a team prepared to go in the morning, to follow the dogs when they picked up Syd's scent.

Grabbing a beer, George went into his living room and sat down in his easy chair. He flicked on the television and turned to the national news. Nothing new popped up, so he flicked to the comedy station.

George knew all about Syd's past. The warden had shared more than enough information with him to give him an understanding of how important it was to capture the man and get him back behind bars. Unlike Larry, George had no sympathy for the young man who had been so severely abused by his employer and by the string of men his employer forced him to go with. In George's opinion, the kid could have said no and walked anytime he wanted to.

George figured the kid stayed for the money and that he enjoyed what he was doing—he hadn't been forced at all. His boss was probably going to cut him off or something and the kid snapped, not wanting to lose his cash cow.

There would be no sympathy from George once they caught Syd Lance, and maybe, if he came upon him alone, George might have to do something desperate—especially if Syd tried to make a run for it. And there were always ways to make a prisoner more than uncomfortable once he was put back behind bars.

Syd knew a lot about George, and that was something the guard wasn't happy about.

~

Frank fired the barbeque up at five o'clock, having told his kids, minus spouses and children, to be at the house by five-thirty. He'd thrown potatoes in the oven and made a large Greek salad. The steaks had been lightly spiced with a mixture Violet always had made up and ready for such an occasion.

How he missed her.

Everyone arrived in good time, except Frank Jr., who was consistently late. Frank waited until he got there to throw the steaks on, and by six-fifteen, the family, minus their mother, sat down to a hot meal.

"So, Dad, where's Mom?" Heather asked. She usually talked to her mom every other day and had been wondering why she hadn't been able to reach her over the past couple days.

"Well," Frank began, "your mom decided to get away for a bit; I'm not sure for how long, maybe a couple weeks, maybe three." He hesitated, wanting to be careful of how he worded what he was going to say. "You all know your mom has always wanted to write a novel ... well, she thought she might be able to do it better if she got away from the busy life she leads here, so she could focus on her work."

"So where is she?" Heather pushed. Being the oldest daughter, she usually took the lead on most family meetings.

Frank looked down at his plate. He picked up his glass of water and took a sip.

"Dad ... where is Mom?" Heather's brow furrowed in frustration at the lack of specifics from her dad.

"I don't know." Frank looked around the table at his five children, ashamed he had to tell them he had no clue where their mother—his wife—was.

There was a clang of forks falling on plates as the information processed. Ten eyes turned on their father, but once again, it was Heather who spoke up.

"Excuse me? You don't know where our mother is? You're kidding, right? Mom just wouldn't go off like that and not tell any of us where she was going. She isn't that stupid, to begin with, and she knows it would worry all of us."

"Maybe that's why she didn't tell anyone," Mark, the youngest boy, mentioned. "Maybe, like Dad said, she just wanted to be alone to pursue her dream. We all know we lean on her way too much, and she's sacrificed so much for us over the years. I think it's great she got away, and I, for one, look forward to reading whatever she comes up with when she gets home." Mark picked up his fork and resumed eating.

Frank Jr. nodded his head in agreement. "Mark has a point. I don't think we have anything to worry about. Mom's a big girl; she can take care of herself."

Frank thought that might not be the case, especially if she had gone to the Kingston area, where there was a dangerous escaped prisoner. He decided not to mention that to his children; he didn't want them to worry unnecessarily if Violet was okay, which she probably was—he hoped.

Heather noticed the gloomy look on her father's face. "Is there something you aren't telling us, Dad? You seem preoccupied; are you holding something back?"

Frank shook his head. "All's good, kids; I just thought you should all know, and to be truthful, I was in need of a bit of company … kind of lonely without your mom here."

Heather opened her mouth to say something, then closed it, knowing she wasn't going to get anything more out of her father.

The rest of the meal was conducted pretty much in silence. When finished, the kids cleared the table and did the dishes while Frank went out to the deck to clean and cover the barbecue. A half-hour later, he bid his kids goodnight and turned back into his empty house.

Chapter Fifteen

"**W**ould you like to take a break?" Violet asked after an hour of listening to and typing Syd's story.

"Why?" Syd looked at her suspiciously. "Too much for you? Change your mind about telling my story?"

Violet looked at Syd, tears in her eyes. "No, I don't want to quit. I think your story needs to be told."

Silence hung heavy in the room as Violet and Syd stared into space. Toby studied them both, happy with what he was seeing but also wondering where the heck Jack was; he should have noticed the signs by now.

Finally, Syd stood and walked to the kitchen area. "I guess we can take a little break," he conceded. He hesitated a moment before moving toward the door to go outside to the outhouse. "I need to take a piss—don't try anything—you won't get far."

"Where would I go?" Violet returned. "I told you, I want to tell your story and it's only partially finished. Why would I leave now?"

Syd shrugged. "I haven't had a lot of reason to trust anyone in my life; not sure if you're really trustworthy or just playin' a game with me, waitin' for a chance to slip out and make a run for it."

Violet used her motherly voice: "Go to the bathroom, Syd; I'll be here when you return."

Toby stood and stretched, gazing out the window. He purred as Violet scratched his back. *Where are you,*

Jack? Violet—should have taken this opportunity to make a run for it. Of course, he has the van keys in his pocket but you could reach the main highway and flag down help—I could have held him off long enough to let you get away… Toby leaned into Violet's fingers, pondering what her real game was. *Feeling sorry for the guy, aren't you, Violet? Don't forget: he's a cold-blooded killer! One little slip on your part and it could send him in a less friendly direction.*

Toby jumped up on the window sill and glanced at the outhouse. Syd had left the door cracked open. *What's your game, buddy? Your story sounds pretty spectacular … I wonder if any of it's true or you're just making this up to gain sympathy? You still have killing on your mind, don't you?*

Syd smiled when he returned and saw Violet fixing them each a cup of tea and putting out some cheese and crackers. After they finished their snack, they got back to work. Syd's voice became more animated and aggressive at points, and occasionally, Violet had to ask him to slow down.

The sun started to fade, and a mist began crawling to the shore from the lake. Toby was genuinely worried now. *Jack will never find all my clues now! Maybe I better head back myself and figure out another way to get him here in time to save Violet.*

Toby stood up on the table and meowed, then jumped down and walked to the door and scratched at it to be let out.

Violet paused and pointed to Toby. "I think the cat wants out again," she mentioned.

Syd scowled but obliged by opening the door for Toby. "Out you go, cat—and don't come back!" He slammed the door.

~

Jack woke from his nap and sat on the edge of the couch. He put his head in his hands, then stood up and looked around to see if Toby had returned yet. No sign of the old cat.

"Where the heck are you, Toby?" Jack murmured. He walked to the door and opened it, stepping out onto the porch. A heavy mist gathered over the lake, making its way inland. Jack went down the steps and checked the landscape around the cottage. He noticed a faint set of overemphasized paw prints, and periodically some scratched lines joining them together.

"What the heck are you up to, old man?" Jack scratched his head. He glanced at his watch. "Well, if I don't get that fish on the barbecue, we won't be eating tonight." He returned to the cottage, mumbling, "I'm sure as soon as the smell of cooking fish hits the air, Toby'll be here in no time."

~

Toby was having a difficult time finding his way back to Jack's cottage. The mist thickened with each passing minute, and the waves had begun to sweep up onto the shore, eliminating the tracks Toby had left for Jack.

I definitely need to get to Jack; I don't know if Violet is going to be safe once Syd finishes telling her his story. He said he was going to take her vehicle and credit card and leave, but what if he has second thoughts and decides she's a liability ... maybe even takes her with him...

Toby sat for a moment and looked around. This country living wasn't up his alley, he was a city cat, out of practice in the ways of tracking and all the other stuff outdoor cats never have to give a second thought about. Finally, making a decision, he set off again.

About a half an hour later, Toby found himself back where he'd started. *Damn! I'm a cat—I should be better at this! Now, it's way too dark, and I have no idea where I am … no sidewalks to guide me…no streetlights to light my way … damn!* He looked around, utterly disgusted with himself.

Well, I guess I have no other alternative but to find a bit of shelter and hope Syd doesn't do anything foolish tonight. I should be able to get to Jack once the sun comes up. I hope he doesn't worry too much about me.

Toby noticed a fallen tree not far from where he was sitting and meandered over to it. He curled up on a bed of leaves in the crook of the log and closed his eyes, knowing there was nothing more he could do tonight. The fog covered the area like a thick blanket, blocking out the moon and the stars. Nothing stirred in woods.

~

Syd finally stopped talking around five o'clock. He ended with what the Italian, Leno Cartelli, had done to him. By the time he was finished, Violet was crying uncontrollably. What Syd had endured, time and time again, no person should have to go through.

Violet saved the document and shut the computer off. "So now what?" she asked.

"Now, we have something to eat." Syd looked out the window and noticed how thick the fog was, realizing he probably wasn't going to get very far in this weather. *Might be best I wait 'til morning.* Turning back to Violet, "I think I'm going to have to hole up here for the night and leave in the morning."

Violet swallowed hard. She'd been hoping he would leave and the weather changed his plans. She missed the old cat; at least he'd brought some comfort with his presence. She hoped, wherever he was, he was safe. She rose from her chair and went into the kitchen, opened the refrigerator and looked for something to prepare for supper—not that she felt like eating much after hearing such a story as what Syd had just told her.

After supper was over, Violet asked Syd about sleeping arrangements, telling him she was exhausted and needed to lie down.

"I'm not as young as I used to be, Syd, and your story has … well, let's just say, I need to sleep, and not in a chair." Violet was pleading for some sort of consideration, figuring she'd earned it by being so kind to her captor.

Syd ran his hand through his hair. He looked around the room. There was a small couch by the far wall; that's where he would sleep, but he felt, despite Violet having been willing—so she said—to tell his story, he still didn't entirely trust her.

"I'm afraid I'm going to have to tie you to the bed. No offense, I just can't take any chances on you escaping before I get on my way."

Violet nodded, not wanting him to get upset and do something worse. "I can give you my word that I won't go anywhere, where would I go in this weather, but, if you must tie me, you must."

Syd felt a twinge of guilt as he tied Violet's hands to the bedposts, but not enough to not do it. "Goodnight," he said as he started to leave the room. "I'm sorry."

Violet closed her eyes. He was sorry? But, under the current circumstances, there was nothing she wanted to say to Syd at the moment. She tried to turn and get as comfortable as possible and prayed for salvation.

~

Night closed around everyone—a restless night for many. Frank missed the love of his life. Larry was bothered by the files he'd read about what Syd endured. The warden didn't like that one of his prisoners escaped and that it was taking so long to recapture him. Jack was worried about where Toby was. Toby was afraid of the night and what might be happening to poor Violet. Violet couldn't get comfortable and couldn't stop dreaming about what had happened to Syd. Syd was confused about what he should do with Violet, wondering if he could trust her to keep her word to tell his story. The only one who slept like a baby was George—a man without a conscience.

Chapter Sixteen

The morning sun could not penetrate the blanket of fog that hung over the area. Syd rose early and was disappointed, but felt he had no choice but to get on the move. He knew the place would be crawling with cops and roadblocks would be set up, so when he woke Violet, he reminded her about putting together some clothing for him that would enable him to pass as a woman. He leaned over and untied the cloths he'd secured her wrists with.

Violet rummaged through the drawers in the dresser where her clothes were, pulling out a pink turtleneck sweater and a pair of pink track pants.

"Would you like a bra?" she asked, holding up one of her brassieres. "We can stuff it with Kleenex and it will make you look more like a woman."

A crooked grin swept across Syd's face. "You think of everything, don't you?"

Violet smiled and handed Syd a razor. "Might be advisable if you shaved, as well. I don't think your beard will pass inspection if you should get stopped; no one will believe you are a woman."

Syd studied the woman he had happened upon and couldn't help but think maybe he'd come across someone whom he could actually trust. *Perhaps I should take her with me as extra security … but I won't say anything until the last minute.* Syd took the razor and went into the bathroom, totally forgetting about keeping an eye on his captive.

~

Jack rose early and staggered into the bathroom. He'd had a restless night worrying about Toby and hoped the old cat had finally made his way home. Coming out of the bathroom, Jack looked out the door to see if Toby was back. He stepped out to the porch and looked around the yard, still heavy with fog. No sign of his furry friend.

Returning to the cottage, Jack first filled Toby's dish, then downed a glass of orange juice and set a banana on the table for after he got dressed. He could eat it while searching for Toby.

Making his way down to the shoreline where he'd seen the strange tracks the day before, Jack began to wonder if Toby had actually left him a clue. After all, he was a smart old cat, no doubt about that, and, if that were the case, what kind of trouble had Toby gotten into—or found?

"His tracks went toward the shoreline. I bet he was following that somewhere. Hopefully, he left me more clues. Poor Toby, he'll have a hard time surviving out here in the wilds, being so citified."

Jack noticed the last remnants of paw prints just before the wave line on the shore. He knelt and detected the long scratch between prints, just like the tracks by the cottage. "You really are trying to tell me something, aren't you, old man?" Jack decided to skirt along the shoreline and see if there were any more tracks he could pick up as to where Toby had gone.

~

Toby woke and stretched. He felt damp and cold and shuddered as he left the woods to investigate which direction he should take. *Darn creaky bones! Sucks getting old! With any luck, there's enough sun for me to get my bearings and get to Jack. Hopefully, I'm not too late to save Violet. I feel it in my bones that Syd might make an unexpected move—maybe change his mind and take her with him, or worse, kill her.*

Standing on the grass at the edge of the woods, Toby looked up at the sky and caught a glimpse of the sun rising in the east. Knowing the sun had been in the west when he'd found Violet's cabin, Toby headed east, setting as fast a pace as possible for an overweight, elderly cat, who was also feeling the pangs of morning hunger.

He moved along for a good ten minutes, making his way closer to the shore, when he heard a familiar voice calling his name. Toby quickened his pace in the direction of the sound, letting out a couple loud meows, which he hoped would carry through the lifting mist.

~

Frank rose early from his restless sleep. He intended on staying close to his phone in case the credit card company called with news.

Wandering through the house, Frank tried to fathom why Violet had thought it necessary to just up and leave without talking out her feelings with him.

"You always talked to me, Violet," he voiced to the empty rooms. "At least I think you did." Frank sighed entering the living room and heading for the shelves where Violet stored all the photo albums.

Starting with their wedding album, Frank sat down on the couch and opened it to the first page. There she was, so beautiful in a wedding gown adorned with daisies and a long silk veil edged with sequins. Her hair, at his request, was swept off her face and cascaded down her back in ringlets. The veil was held in place by a comb garlanded with off-white flowers. Violet's face beamed with happiness.

Frank turned the page, running his finger over picture after picture—the ones in her family home with her parents and grandparents. Her father looked stern in the photographs. Frank knew he'd not approved of the marriage but had sucked it up for his only child. Violet's mother didn't appear too happy either, but then she always found it difficult to find joy in life. Violet continually justified her mother's distance because of the mental problems she suffered from.

Violet's grandparents were a different story, standing for their photos with big smiles on their faces as they gazed upon their granddaughter.

The pictures moved to the church, where Violet was greeted at the door by his sister and her children—a girl and a boy who they'd chosen to be the flower girl and ring bearer. Frank's sister was the matron of honour; his brother, the best man.

Violet continued to beam throughout the pictures in the church, at one time even laughing when they exchanged rings when he had held his finger up in the air to receive his ring.

"God, you were beautiful … still are." Frank closed the album, and went to the shelf and picked out the next one. Violet was meticulous about keeping things in order.

Pictures of their honeymoon … the births of their children … the children growing up—all five of them. As the pages of images turned, though, Frank started to notice something different about Violet—she was not smiling much. Why hadn't he detected that before? Had she ever mentioned to him she wasn't happy? He couldn't remember.

He'd been busy trying to provide for such a large family. And he'd had his hockey. Frank thought Violet was happy raising the kids and looking after the household. She'd often mentioned writing but he'd always fluffed it off and told her once the kids were grown and out of the house, she would have time to do whatever she wanted.

Frank thought back to the time Violet had tried to get her university degree. It had been his idea for her to return to school and get a teaching degree so when the kids were all in school, she could get a job teaching to help the family income. Violet took several courses, about two years' worth, but finally quit, telling Frank she couldn't keep up, and in fact, it wasn't what she really wanted. He faintly remembered her having said something about pursuing writing, but dismissed it at the time.

The pictures began to tell more and more about the woman he loved. Soon, there were few pictures of her with the family, and the ones there were, she was always standing in the background and not smiling at all anymore. As each of the kids left home, there were fewer pictures, just the odd one of when they would take a few days off, and it was mostly him in the forefront of scenery photos. The minimal amount where she would pose, despite them being on holiday, Frank noticed how forced her smiles were.

Frank closed the final album and returned it to the shelf. "How could I have missed all this?" he asked himself. Tears began to form in his heart, running down his cheeks as Frank felt the pain of what he prayed was the temporary loss of the woman he knew now he couldn't live without. He made his way to the kitchen and fixed himself a cup of coffee, then returned to the living room and turned on the news. What he watched did not do anything to appease his uneasy feeling that Violet might be in trouble.

The headline news story was about the escaped convict, Syd Lance, who escaped from the Kingston Penitentiary. He was considered extremely dangerous, and roadblocks had been secured throughout the area. It was mentioned that a team of bloodhounds was getting ready to head out with the hope that the trail would not be too cold for them to follow, the authorities having had to wait for the dogs to finish a previous commitment.

There was a brief back-story as to what Syd Lance had done, and authorities felt he wasn't finished what he started before incarceration. Several individuals had been warned to be on the watch for him.

Frank shut the television off and paced the room. "Where can she be … I wonder if she left me any clues … why didn't I think of this before?" he murmured as he strode in the direction of her office.

~

George placed a call to Joe Simmons at six in the morning to confirm their meeting time and place. Joe confirmed all was on schedule and his dogs were ready to go. He'd meet George at the gas station at seven.

"How many officers will be meeting us there?" Joe asked.

"I have a team of five men, plus myself," George replied. "I know it isn't many, but most of our extra manpower is manning the roadblocks."

"No sign of the guy yet?"

"Obviously not," George replied sarcastically. "We wouldn't be calling out the dogs if we had a locate on him."

Joe laughed, realizing he'd asked a stupid question, and hung up the phone.

George clicked off his phone and threw it on the table. He was tired of dealing with ignorant people. He figured with what he'd saved so far, he'd have enough to leave his job in five years. Maybe sooner if he put more pressure on some of the more affluent inmates.

He showered, after which he had a hearty breakfast and packed some water bottles and a couple sandwiches for his lunch. It could be a long day.

~

The warden placed an early call to Larry and told him he should join George at the meeting place where they'd lost Syd. The warden knew George needed to be watched. He was aware of some of the underhanded activities his guard was involved in, and it was only a matter of time before he would be forced to make a move to take George down. He had never been lax when it came to controlling everyone within his prison—that is what he considered it to be: his prison.

"Morning, Larry," the warden greeted. "I trust since you answered your home phone, you managed to reach everyone on the list last night?"

"Yes, sir. It took a while but by eleven o'clock, I spoke to the last one on my list."

"Good, good." A brief halt. "Larry, I want you to go along with the search team … keep your eyes and ears open while you're out there. I need this to be a clean recovery, if you know what I mean. Sometimes, others can be … how should I say it … too anxious to take matters into their own hands. Get my meaning?"

"Yes, sir … I think so, sir." Larry wasn't exactly sure where the warden was going with this but figured it best to wait to hear more.

"Stick close to George," the warden proceeded. "You can learn a lot from a veteran guard like him."

Larry shuddered. He knew then the warden didn't trust George but trusted him. But Larry was afraid of what George could and would do to him if he ever found out he'd squealed to the warden about any of his activities, or how he handled many of the inmate circumstances—especially ones beyond prison protocol.

"Larry?"

"Yes, sir," Larry finally returned. "Stick close to George."

"Good man. And Larry, one more thing: I want you to pay close attention to everything so *you* can write up the report; tell George I gave you this job, you know, so he could focus more on the task at hand. All this clear to you, Larry?"

"Yes, sir." Larry swallowed hard, hoping the warden couldn't detect the nervousness in his voice.

"Good man. Good luck today. Hopefully, we'll have Syd Lance back behind bars before nightfall." The warden hung up the phone.

Chapter Seventeen

Syd gazed into the mirror. Violet stood behind him, realizing how vulnerable the young man looked now: he could pass for a woman. She had offered to put his hair in two braids for an added feminine touch.

"Not bad," Syd grinned. "Maybe all the times I was used by men as a female has turned me into one," he uttered with disdain. He turned and left the bathroom, Violet on his heels.

Standing in the middle of the room, Syd ran his hand over his head, taking care not to undo the braids. Violet had assumed he'd decided his plan, but this nervous gesture suggested maybe he still wasn't sure about what to do with her.

Proving her thoughts were correct, Syd turned to her and told her the way it was going to go down. "I've changed my mind about leaving you behind," he began. "I think I'd stand a better chance of getting through any road checks if you were with me. I think you should do the driving; you could say I'm your daughter, and we're heading back to … where is it you live?"

"Brantford."

"We're heading back to Brantford after spending a few days away for some mother/daughter time. How does that sound to you?"

Violet's nerves were rattled. She'd thought she was home-free, that Syd was going to go and leave her. She'd promised not to contact anyone for a few days, and after hearing his entire story, planned on keeping her word. Violet resolved she had no choice but to follow his lead and hope, at some point, she could motion to someone for help.

"Gather your clothes and your computer, and let's get on our way," Syd ordered. "I can't waste any more time. Knowing the warden as I do, he's probably already got the dogs out looking for me. Actually, just grab your computer and your suitcase, don't worry about any clothes. Maybe we can throw a bit of food in your cooler … we want to make sure if one of the officers looks in the van, they see enough evidence of us having been away to believe our story."

Violet realized she had no more say in the matter. She walked to her computer and packed it up. Syd went into the bedroom and returned with the empty suitcase. He proceeded to fill the cooler with food, closed it, and took it out the door toward the van.

Taking her time packing the computer, Violet saw Syd's scowl when he returned from outside. "Sorry, it took some time to shut down the computer," she mumbled apologetically.

Syd was no fool. "Don't start messing with me, Violet," he approached and yanked the computer from her hands and shoved it into the case that was on the floor by the table. "It won't end well for you if you start playing games."

Violet drew in a shuddering breath. "I'm sorry, Syd. I wasn't messing with you, really." She reached for her purse but hesitated. "Do you mind if I go to the bathroom before we leave?"

"Go ahead. Make it quick." Syd shuffled his feet nervously. He was overly anxious to get on his way and thinking maybe it was a mistake to bring the woman along.

Violet took as much time as she dared in the outhouse, but not wanting to upset Syd and have him do something drastic, she went faster than she'd initially intended. Coming out of the outhouse, she saw Syd standing on the porch, her purse in his hand. He handed it to her and motioned for her to go to the van. Syd followed her, carrying the empty suitcase and the computer.

~

Toby and Jack finally met up. Jack reached down to scoop the old cat into his arms, happy Toby was safe, however, Toby skirted away, meowed, and started back in the direction from which he'd come.

Jack realized Toby had something important to show him. "Okay, old man."

Toby paused, looked back at him, and meowed loudly. Jack followed as quickly as he could. Toby, realizing Jack was coming, picked up his pace.

Hang in there, Violet—I'm coming—and I have reinforcements!

~

George stood outside his car, leaning on the trunk, a coffee in one hand and a cigarette hanging from his mouth. The smoke wafted into the low-hanging mist. He'd arrived early to the meeting site, wanting time to think about what he intended to do once they caught up with Syd. And catch up with him, they would; George had no doubt about that.

Strolling to the back of the building where the bathroom Syd escaped from was, George looked up at the small window and shook his head. "Hadn't realized you were that skinny," he grumbled, knowing it technically was his fault for not having monitored behind the station. Larry had wanted to. He was a good kid, Larry, knew how to keep his mouth shut.

George heard a couple vehicles approach and returned to the front of the station. A van filled with his team and Larry in his car. No sign yet of Joe and the dogs. "What the hell is Larry doing here? He wasn't on my team list for this operation…" George approached Larry's car.

"Morning, George," Larry greeted as he exited his vehicle. He didn't like the look on his fellow officer's face; he seemed upset. Probably wasn't expecting him to be there. "Everything okay?" he inquired.

George took a drag off his cigarette: "Yeah, everything's fine, just wondering what you're doing here. I didn't call you for this operation."

Larry straightened his shoulders. He knew George was a bully and didn't want him to suspect anything untoward about his presence. "Warden asked me to tag along and make a full report of how this goes down. Said he wanted you to be able to concentrate on getting the job done and didn't want you to have to worry about all the finer details that would have to go in a police report." Larry hoped that would satisfy his co-worker.

From the scowl on George's face, it hadn't. "How nice of the warden to send me a babysitter," he spit, sarcasm saturating his words. "Since when haven't I been able to do my job?" He smiled tightly and threw his cigarette to the ground, grinding the butt into the pavement. "Oh well, not your fault, right, Larry?" George slapped Larry on the back. "Just stay out of my way; observe and learn."

As the rest of the team gathered around George, another van pulled up, and from the sounds coming from within, the dogs had arrived. Joe exited the van. He was short and stocky and wore his hair in a mohawk. His clothes were well-worn buckskin and his feet were clad in a pair of knee-high moccasins. Between him and his dogs, there were no better trackers in the province, that George knew of, anyway.

Introductions were made all around, and then Joe went to his van and brought out the dogs—three large, male bloodhounds, pulling anxiously on their leads. This was their life's work, tracking, and they were ready to start.

George went to his car and returned with a shirt he'd procured from Syd's cell. He handed it to Joe, who in turn held it to the nose of each of his dogs. Their bodies twitched with the eager anticipation of the hunt they were about to begin.

"Okay, boys," George shouted above the din of the dogs' excitement, "follow me around back here, where the little bastard escaped."

Larry took up the rear of the group. He felt it was a better position to be able to observe everything going on.

It didn't take long for the three dogs to pick up Syd's scent. Their baying filled the early morning air and they pulled impatiently on their leashes. They kept looking back at their owner, wondering when he was going to give them the word.

Joe turned to George. "You guys ready? My boys picked up the scent pretty quick."

"We're ready," George replied as his crew nodded. "How about you, Larry? You ready with your pencil?" George guffawed mockingly.

Larry swallowed his anger, not wanting to let George see he was getting under his skin. *Arrogant prick. Keep treating me like this and you better not make a wrong move, or I'll nail you to the fence!* Larry smiled and tersely replied, "Yes sir, George, pencil and I are ready for duty." His finger pushed the button on the small recorder he had tucked in his coat pocket.

There were a couple chuckles from the other officers, but they were silenced by a scowl from George. It appeared everyone knew his reputation. George waved his hand to Joe and the search party started off, the hounds setting a fast pace.

The morning crept by slower than George had expected or wanted it to. There were several times the dogs seemed confused and they circled until they managed to pick up the scent again.

"The scent is likely compromised by the moisture on the ground from the mist that rolled in last night," Max, one of the officers in the group, mentioned.

"Yep ... makes things a tad more difficult. But my boys are good. If there's but a trace of the bugger, they'll pick it up. Won't be long before he's back behind bars where he belongs!" Joe replied.

Larry watched everyone with open curiosity. They were a strange crew, and all seemed quite familiar with George. Larry wondered how far George's influence went. There was a lot of laughing and joking about different episodes that had happened within the prison walls— stories George told with great relish—stories the other officers lapped up with an almost overzealous glee for the unfortunate plight of the prisoners involved. Larry began to have a sinking feeling for Syd's fate, who was supposed to be returned to the prison in one piece—alive.

He kept himself as close to George as possible without raising suspicion, hoping the recorder was picking up the stories. Stories Larry was sure the warden would want to hear.

Chapter Eighteen

Violet's mind raced a thousand miles a second as she and Syd walked to the van. She hadn't anticipated going along on this road trip and she sorely missed Frank and her kids, and her life back in Brantford, as lacklustre as she had thought it had become. This was way too much excitement for her.

Syd gave her a little shove from behind. "Got lead in your feet, Violet?"

She stumbled but managed to stay on her feet. As she did so, though, she got an idea; noticing a small dip in the ground, Violet took a few more steps, picking up her pace, and then suddenly twisted her ankle and went down hard on the earth, letting out a horrific scream. She grabbed hold of her foot and began moaning.

"Oh, God … Syd … oh, God … I'm so sorry, I didn't see that dip in the ground." Violet moaned again.

Syd looked at her, anger and frustration etched on his face. What else could go wrong? He set the suitcase and computer case down and hurried to Violet, who was still on the ground, rubbing her ankle. "Do you think you can walk?" he asked, his voice overwrought with frustration. He made a feeble attempt to help her up.

Violet pretended to try and stand, groaning with pain. "I think I should get some ice on this right away," she said.

Syd let go of her arm. *I should just go and leave her here, maybe help her into the cottage and just leave and take my chances. She won't be going anywhere with a sprained ankle.*

Syd crouched beside Violet and reached out to check the swelling in her ankle. She flinched as he touched her. Thank goodness she was wearing long pants and thick socks, which helped hide that her ankle was not hurt at all—temporarily, at least. Violet wondered how long she could keep up the façade.

Deciding the best thing to do would be to let Syd help her back into the cottage, Violet attempted to stand. She reached out and put a hand on Syd's shoulder for leverage. With his assistance, she got to her feet, and together they hobbled to the cottage. Violet winced every time she put weight on her left foot, pausing after each effort, leaning heavily on Syd. She could tell from the tenseness of his muscles he was irritated.

As they approached the steps, the sound of footsteps entering the yard reached their ears. Syd whirled around, relinquishing his support of Violet. She thought quickly, and let herself fall to the ground.

Toby, taking in the scene, raced to his friend. Jack followed close behind. Kneeling beside Violet, Jack looked up at Syd: "What happened here?" Then, back to Violet, "Are you okay, ma'am?"

"Twisted my ankle," she replied. "We were just getting ready to go for a little drive," she added, glancing up at Syd.

Jack noticed the nervousness in Violet's eyes. He reached out. "Here let me help you," he suggested as he assisted Violet to her feet.

Toby raced ahead, up the steps to the door. *What's going on here? Going for a little drive ... he was taking her with him! Thank goodness Jack and I got here when we did!*

Violet continued her cover-up as Jack assisted her up the three steps. He turned and gave Syd a look. "Mind opening the door for us?" he ordered more than asked.

Syd shook his head; he had to think fast and not give away he was a man. He glanced at Toby, figuring there was nothing the old cat could do to blow his cover, despite having shown up yet again and at a most inopportune time. He bound up the steps and, giving Toby a boot out of the way, opened the door.

Toby arched his back and hissed at Syd. Jack looked from one to the other, wondering why Toby was so upset. He scrutinized Syd closer. He was dressed like a woman but had a shadow of whiskers. There was a lot more to the story, he figured, and was sure he was not here by accident. Toby led him here for a reason; he just needed to figure out what it was.

"I'll get some ice for my mother," Syd offered. moving toward the refrigerator.

Mother! Well, if that isn't a crock of sour cream! Toby walked protectively beside Violet as Jack led her to the couch.

Jack gazed around the room, looking for something Violet could rest her foot on. Seeing no footstool, he pulled a kitchen chair over to the couch. "Have a pillow anywhere?"

Violet nodded toward the bedroom door. "In there," she said, groaning for effect.

Syd pulled out an ice cube tray and, noticing a plastic grocery bag on the counter, dumped the ice in it. He and Jack arrived to Violet's side at the same time. Jack propped her ankle up on the chair and then turned to Syd to take the ice off his hands.

"Shouldn't you take her sock off?" Syd asked. He wanted to see the ankle—that it was swelling—and the thick sock was not allowing him to do so. He reached to remove the sock.

Toby jumped up on Violet's lap, and hissed at Syd, swatting out with his paw. A bloody scratch appeared on Syd's hand; he jumped back and swore.

Violet, thanking God for the salvation that had walked into her yard—the big orange cat—reached out a hand to stroke Toby. "I'd rather keep the sock on," she began, "so the ice won't be so cold on my skin," she added with a grimace.

"Settle down, Toby," Jack said. "That wasn't very nice." He placed the ice pack on Violet's ankle, then turned to Syd and extended his hand. "I'm Jack Nelson," he pointed to Toby, "and this is my cat, Toby. He must have got lost exploring the area."

Syd didn't take the proffered hand, nor did he give his name. How could he? He was supposed to be a young woman and he and Violet hadn't even thought of a name for him.

Jack shrugged, thinking again there was more than a mother/daughter adventure here and not believing Syd was a daughter, Jack turned to Violet. "You and Toby seem to know each other; has he already been here? From the direction he was coming when I met up with him this morning, and from how he's taken to you, I am led to think he has."

Violet nodded and continued to stroke Toby along his back. "As a matter of fact, yes, he was here yesterday.

When we let him out last night, I just assumed he would head home and I wouldn't see him again."

Syd was skulking in the background, confused as to what to do. He was thinking of a way to leave, maybe with the façade he was going to pick up some supplies for the cottage. There was enough evidence in the cottage to suggest he and Violet hadn't been leaving for good.

"You know, Mother," he began, "maybe I should head out and pick up the stuff we need. It looks like you're in good hands."

Toby hissed again, glaring at Syd. Jack knew that look, which confirmed everything was not quite right here. "I don't think Toby and I are able to stay too long. I need to get back to my cottage; I'm actually expecting company later this morning and I'm not near ready for my guests, having had to come out in search of this old man here." Jack reached out and scratched behind Toby's ears. "Gave me quite a scare, old man," he added for additional impact.

Syd fidgeted with the hat he was wearing, not able to run his hands through his hair. "I won't be long," he mumbled. "I'll make my mother a cup of tea, she should be okay 'til I get back, you can go if you like. Thanks for helping me get her into the cabin, but I think we've got it from here."

Jack noticed Violet tense when her *daughter* suggested he leave. He saw the desperation in her eyes. However, if he and Toby were to make it look like they were leaving, they could watch from the woods if anything untoward were to happen. He decided to make that call.

"Well, if you think everything will be okay, we'll get on our way," Jack stated, keeping his eyes fixed on Toby and Violet. He winked, hoping they would get the message that he knew something was up and wouldn't be far away.

Violet saw Jack wink and smiled in return. "Yes, I think we'll be fine … Jack, wasn't it?"

"Yes."

"You go along to your company. Thanks for helping out; my daughter and I are most grateful, especially me. She has a bad back, you know, and was having a difficult time getting me back to the cottage."

"Yes, I noticed *she* was having a struggle." Jack reached for Toby but he backed into Violet's chest. "It's okay, old man. We can come back and visit Violet later if you like. You have a thing for the ladies, don't you, you rascal? How long will you be staying up here?" Jack asked, looking intensely into Violet's eyes.

Violet glanced furtively to where Syd was staring at them, waiting for her answer, an unpleasant look in his eyes.

"Just another couple days," she answered, a little too nervously in Jack's opinion.

"Maybe even tomorrow," Syd added. "I think we should actually get Mother checked out by a doctor if her foot isn't better by morning."

Jack wisely continued—his intention to leave and keep watch from close by. "Well, if you need anything, we aren't far away—just down the shore. You can reach us from our laneway if you prefer to drive over. The mailbox has the name 'Henderson' on it. Be careful though, there are so many ruts in the lane, it looks like a war zone, and we are in about one mile from the main road; you must be, too, eh?"

"Yeah, about the same," Syd returned. "Maybe we'll drop over on our way out; Mother seems to have taken a liking to your cat, despite him not liking me very much." Syd laughed nervously. He was struggling to keep his voice soft and feminine.

Jack snapped his fingers at Toby. "Okay, let's get on our way; Tessa will be up by noon and she'll be wondering where we are. We can take the shortcut through the woods instead of going along the winding shoreline." Jack hinted to Toby where they would go and hide until they were sure Violet was going to be okay.

Okay, Jack, I got it—you got it! I knew I could count on you. Toby rubbed his nose on Violet's hand, looked at her lovingly and purred before jumping down and following Jack to the door. As he passed by Syd, Toby hissed.

"Enough, Toby, let's get going," Jack reached down and scooped up his companion before Toby could cause any more trouble.

Syd stood in the doorway, watching Jack and Toby until they disappeared into the woods. He turned back into the cottage and took his hat off, pulled the elastics off the braids, and ran his hands through his hair. What to do now?

Violet watched him cautiously. What would his next move be? She had a good feeling Jack and Toby weren't far away; Jack seemed aware all was not right but would they be able to save her if Syd decided to end her life and then leave? They wouldn't suspect anything because they already knew her *daughter* was going to go out for supplies. Violet sighed, resolved she would just have to wait and keep her ankle up.

How she missed Frank.

~

In the woods, Jack found a secluded spot that could not be seen from the front of the cottage. He noticed a log and settled on it. "We'll be able to hear the van leave, Toby, and then can sneak back and find out from Violet what is truly going on in there and get her back to our place. I could tell her ankle isn't hurt, so she should have no problem walking with us."

Toby rubbed around Jack's legs and purred. *You got it, Jack! I'm a genius, and I guess I must admit, you are too!* Toby sat beside Jack and stared through the trees to the cottage. He knew he stood a better chance of not being seen lurking than Jack. *Don't worry one little bit, Violet; Detective Toby and his sidekick, Jack Nelson, are on the job!*

Chapter Nineteen

The sun finally broke through the mist, clearing it out of the area by noon. George looked up and, seeing the sun at its peak, called for everyone to take a break and grab a bite and some water.

"Looks like a clearing just up ahead," George pointed out. "We'll take a half-hour rest, then head out again." Turning to Joe, "Is that enough of a break for your hounds?"

Joe snorted. "These hounds will still be going strong when you guys are snoring in your sleeping bags!"

As they neared the clearing, the dogs howled louder and raced to a large fallen log, sniffing and digging. Joe looked back at George. "Looks like your man spent a night here … see how the leaves are pressed into the ground."

George and Max walked over and knelt for a closer look.

"Yep, looks that way," Max stated matter-of-factly. "But it isn't fresh, so I bet the bugger is long gone from here."

George stood and looked around, studying the ground carefully for a sign of which direction Syd might have taken. Seeing nothing concrete that could confirm a specific course, George turned and walked away, muttering under his breath. "Damn guy is so small and light, he didn't even leave enough of a track in these woods for us to see. Damn!"

121

"Everything okay?" Larry asked as George approached. The team had settled down and were eating.

"Yep." George glared at Larry and kept walking. He was in no mood to sit with anyone, he was trying to figure out the real reason the warden had sent Larry to record everything that happened in the chase. George wondered if the warden was on to some of his less desirable activities within the prison walls. Maybe it was time to get out and just enjoy the rest of his life. He didn't have quite the amount of money he wanted, but it would be better than losing it all because of greed.

George had lost his appetite but he knew he needed some nourishment to sustain his strength for their trek through the woods. The dogs might set a quicker pace if they picked up on Syd's scent beyond the log where he'd slept. George found a rock, sat down, and pulled a protein bar from his backpack.

Thinking enough time had passed for the men to eat and rest, George returned to where they were gathered. They had been talking but when he approached, everyone went quiet.

"Something you guys want to fill me in on?" George looked around the group, a scowl on his face.

Larry was quick to reply: "Nope, just guy talk ... nothing important. Saw you coming and figured it was time to get moving again."

Larry smiled at George, a smile George didn't particularly like. It seemed like a *none of your business* smile. But he couldn't be bothered to pry further, knowing they'd already lost too much time. He made his way to Joe, who had calmed his hounds enough they had stopped baying at the sleep site and were lying in wait for their next command. As Joe stood, the dogs' tails started thumping the ground with anticipation of the continuation of the hunt. The dogs, on Joe's command, rose to their feet and the baying began again.

Within seconds, the dogs were on the trail, noses to the ground, tails in the air. The men hurried along behind the canines, knowing Joe was maintaining their pace to one the officers could keep up to. As they broke from the wooded area, they came upon a narrow trail that curved around a creek. The dogs circled in frustration and George's anger grew.

"Crap!" he shouted, driving his fist into the air in frustration. "This bloody area has too many creeks and rivers and lakes. Makes it easy for creeps like Syd Lance to hide their scent."

Joe looked at George and grinned. "The dogs will pick up the trail, don't you go worryin'. Just a matter of time before you have your boy back behind bars." He tarried a moment, looking around, debating his next move. Then, "You boys wait here 'til my boys pick up the trail."

A man used to getting what he wanted when he wanted it, George hated the waiting game.

~

Syd decided to leave the cabin, feeling he had no other choice. Toby watched as he came out the door and picked up the computer case and suitcase, which had been left on the ground when they'd had to get Violet back to the cabin. To Toby's surprise, Syd returned both items to the cottage before exiting again, this time with Violet's purse.

Running to the van, Syd cursed himself for having hung around for so long. He shouldn't have allowed Violet to get in his head, thinking she sympathized with him and genuinely wanted to tell his story. She'd probably been conning him like everyone else in his life had.

He climbed into the van, shoved the key into the ignition, and turned it. He glanced nervously at the gas gage, and prayed for a miracle, although at this point in his life, Syd reckoned God had utterly forsaken him. If there was a loving God, his dad wouldn't have beaten him or his mom, and his mom wouldn't have died giving birth to his baby sister. He wouldn't have been forced into a system that didn't want him, and would never have been used and abused by the evil men who had crept into his life like a flesh-eating virus.

Syd laid his head on the steering wheel for a moment. Finally, he put the van into reverse, backed up and then, going forward, turned onto the laneway that would hopefully lead him to further freedom. Syd tapped his fingers nervously on the steering wheel.

The way was slow due to the many potholes. Occasionally the overhanging branches of the trees scraped across the van's roof. Syd cursed the long drawn-out time it was taking to get to the main road. Once he got there, he hoped a gas station was close by.

Suddenly, out of the woods, a deer jumped onto the lane. Syd slammed on the brakes and the van veered into the trees, slamming hard against a large maple. Syd, who had forgotten to put his seatbelt on, smashed his head on the steering wheel, opening a large gash on his forehead.

"Damn! Damn! Damn!" he moaned. "What else can go wrong?" He pushed back on the seat and looked around for something he could mop the blood up with. Finally, he noticed a box of Kleenex on the floor on the passenger side.

Holding one hand to his head, he leaned down and reached for the box. A sharp pain shot through his ribs and he winced. Finally, his fingers grasped the box; he seized hold of it and straightened back up. He leaned back again, trying to catch his breath. He had to get out of here. Syd feared—had a suspicion—that maybe Jack and the old cat had not gone far and they might decide to return to the cottage. It was possible Jack hadn't believed a word he'd said and realized Syd was not a woman. The old cat knew it and Syd had a hunch there was more to Toby than met the eye.

The blood was already dripping onto his clothes as he tried to stop the flow. Within seconds, the Kleenex's were saturated, and, not thinking, Syd tossed them out the window into the ditch. He cursed as he pulled the last Kleenex from the box and the blood still hadn't stopped. He decided he no other choice but to tear a piece of cloth off his shirt and wrap it tightly around his head. Then he would have to figure out how he was going to continue if he couldn't get the van out of the ditch.

After Syd finished wrapping the cloth around his head, he sat for a few more minutes, thinking. Slowly, he opened the door and stepped out to inspect the situation.

"Not quite as bad as I thought," he babbled, seeing the back wheels were still on the driveway. He walked around to the front of the vehicle and, although dented, the van was still driveable.

Climbing back into the vehicle, Syd turned the ignition, which had shut off when he'd hit the tree. He put the van into reverse, and after a few unsuccessful attempts, it finally creaked out of the ditch. Moving forward once again, Syd drew a deep breath, wincing as the effort shot another sharp pain through his ribs.

Within a couple minutes, Syd reached the highway. He sat for a moment before turning left, in the direction he knew the men he was after were. Once again, he prayed there was a gas station not far down the route. After a couple miles, Syd's prayers were answered. Turning off the highway, he whispered a thank you for the good fortune.

Syd was happy to see it was a modern station with pay-at-pump availability. He knew in remote areas, the option was scarce. Violet had told him her password for the credit cards, and he hoped she hadn't lied. After punching in the numbers, Syd was relieved to see the transaction accepted.

Another car pulled up behind him and a young woman got out and started filling up. She glanced at Syd and he saw her frown. Syd looked at the amount he'd already pumped and thought to just end it now and leave before she could start asking questions.

Too late.

"Hey, there! Are you okay?" the girl called over. "That rag on your head is pretty bloody … you need some help?"

Syd shook his head, pulled the nozzle from his tank, and returned it quickly to the pump. He didn't care to wait for his receipt and, putting his head down, he hurriedly got into the van and took off. Glancing in the rear-view mirror, he saw the girl shrug and continue filling her gas.

"Guess she didn't care that much," Syd muttered, pushing his foot on the gas.

Black clouds were beginning to form in the sky, the promise of a storm to come. That could be good luck for Syd, because it might mean the cops at any roadblocks would be less careful, not wanting to be out in such inclement weather. Something he could hope for, anyway.

On the other hand, how he appeared now, with a bloody rag around his head, it wasn't likely he would slip through without questions being asked. Syd was sure he would be pulled over, despite the stormy weather.

After driving for about fifteen minutes, Syd noticed flashing lights not far down the highway, blocking both lanes. He slowed, thinking hard about how he might be able to make it through the blockade. He shook his head.

"Maybe I should find another way, even if I have to dump the van and take off on foot again," Syd said, trying to work through the obstacle ahead. He slowed again, and decided to make a U-turn, hoping the cops wouldn't notice.

Heading back in the direction from which he'd just come, Syd thought of his options. He could return to the cottage and make Violet come with him. She could get him through the roadblock as he hid in the back under one of the seats. The more he thought about it, the more feasible it became. He didn't think her ankle was that badly sprained she wouldn't be able to drive.

Chapter Twenty

After waiting long enough to ensure Syd had indeed left, Toby made his way back to where Jack was sitting. He rubbed around his friend's legs, meowed, and then took off in the direction of Violet's cabin. Jack, knowing Toby as well as he did, got up and followed.

"Second thoughts about leaving Violet on her own?" Jack called after the disappearing tail.

Toby looked back and meowed, then hurried his pace. When he reached the cottage, he ran up the steps and sat by the closed door, waiting for Jack to open it.

Jack, being the retired cop he was, needed to double-check there was either no one in the cottage, or just Violet. He crept quietly onto the porch, crouched down and duck-walked to one of the windows. Raising his body enough to get a look inside, Jack scanned the open room.

"Looks like Syd flew the coop, Toby. You must have seen him go, eh, old boy?" Jack stood and looked where the van had been parked. "Her vehicle is gone," he added as he approached the door and opened it.

Toby rushed through the door and ran straight to Violet, happy to see she was still there, and alive. He rubbed around her legs, purring. Jack walked swiftly to her chair and hurriedly undid her restraints.

She looked up at him. "Thank you." Violet's eyes were filled with tears, some escaping down her cheeks.

Jack pointed to Toby. "It was all Toby. He's the one that kept a close look at what was going on here, and he brought me to you in the first place." Jack scanned the room before pulling another chair over to where Violet was sitting. He sat, leaning toward her. "Now, tell me: what *is* going on here?"

Toby jumped onto Violet's lap. He arched his back, waiting for her to give him another one of her first-rate massages. He looked into her eyes, and she could have sworn the cat was telling her she could trust Jack. He was rewarded with a scratch behind his ears.

After a few seconds, Toby curled up on her lap. *Okay, Violet, spill the beans!*

Slowly, Violet's story unravelled. She told Jack how she'd left home to try and have some peace and quiet to write the novel she'd wanted to write for years. She said she loved her husband, Frank, and was sorry she'd done it, especially with the way things were turning out.

Jack nodded as Violet filled him in, trying not to get frustrated with the amount of time she was taking, especially since she hadn't even touched on who her captor was. Jack had no idea a prisoner had escaped the prison because he'd not listened to the radio, not even the one in his camper on the way up to his cottage. One thing he was sure of, though, was they were definitely not mother and daughter!

"On the way here, I heard on the radio a prisoner escaped his guards when they were taking him to the hospital," Violet said; her statement caught Jack's and Toby's attention immediately. Toby, who had been about to close his eyes, perked up. Jack raised his eyebrows questioningly, and thought how stupid it had been not to listen to the radio on the way up to his cottage getaway.

"Did that not make you apprehensive about continuing alone and staying here without anyone knowing where you were?" Jack asked.

Violet shrugged. "I was a bit scared, but decided I was so far out of the way no one would bother me here. I thought to use the situation in my novel—I could embellish on a real-life event. When Syd showed up, it crossed my mind he could possibly be the escaped convict, so I was careful with what I said and did. I learned a great deal about how to personalize situations from the detective shows I watch."

Toby nodded in agreement. He and Jack also watched a lot of detective shows. *That's how I learned a lot about being a detective … must have paid more attention than Jack, too, because, despite all his book learning, I always seem to be the one figuring everything out!*

"I thought it was working," Violet proceeded, "Syd appeared to relax somewhat. I sympathized when I heard his story, and it is truly a horrible one, Jack. I don't know if you or I could have endured what he did and not cracked."

"Are you sure what he told you is the truth?" Jack knew criminals try to maintain their innocence and often blame their crimes on what other people did to them.

Violet sighed. "It was the truth. No one could make up that kind of story, showing the emotion he showed. He is definitely a victim of the cards life dealt him."

"Bad enough to murder a man?"

"From the time he was a little boy, his father was always beating on someone in the house, especially his mother. If he dared to say a word or try and protect her, his father beat him, too. Sometimes, he got beat just because. His father was a monster. When his mother died giving birth to his sister, the baby died, and his father was sent to jail for manslaughter; there was enough evidence of abuse on both his wife and unborn child, which left no doubt it was the reason they died.

"There were no family members to take Syd in and he was thrown into the foster care system. He didn't have much good to say about those years … granted, he did acknowledge a couple good families, but the rest…

"His father was finally released from jail and came for Syd. Jail hadn't tempered the man, and it wasn't long before he began beating his son again. Blamed him for the years he'd spent in prison. One night, Syd had enough and fought back, leaving his father severely beaten on the floor.

"Syd was sixteen. He hit the streets, and no one bothered to look for him, because, well, who cared—who was in his life to care? His abusive father? Syd said he made out okay, but winter hit, and it was a bitterly cold winter. He described scavenging for food in dumpsters and curling up in corners of back alleys to sleep. That is where Arthur met him and took him in, promising money and security."

"Arthur was his victim?" Jack questioned, putting some pieces together.

"Yes, and he won't be the last if Syd manages to get through the roadblocks." Violet sighed.

"What did Arthur do to the boy?" Jack inquired, even though he suspected.

"He pimped him out. And not to women—to men." Violet stopped there for impact.

Jack nodded in understanding, but he still believed that what happened to Syd was no reason to kill someone. Many were the criminals who spent time behind bars having committed crimes of passion, but as a cop, Jack accepted the letter of the law, which said murder was not acceptable. There were other ways of dealing with the scum that preyed on those weaker than them.

Violet leaned forward, looking Jack straight in the eyes, her own eyes filling with tears again. "And they were not nice men that Arthur pimped Syd out to. They were abusive beyond words. I have it all written down, Jack. Syd's story needs to be told; hopefully, he doesn't do any more damage to his case."

"What kind of damage?" Jack asked.

"He has a list of names in his head, and he doesn't think anyone on that list deserves to live for what they did to him; he's sure they are doing the same thing to other young boys or men, like he was at the time. He wasn't the only teenager working for Arthur."

Violet stood and walked to the window. Jack noticed she wasn't limping now and smiled that she had orchestrated her injury to buy time.

Leaning on the sill, Violet stared out into the yard. Turning back to Jack, "I have their names, and I think some of these men should be charged with child molestation and rape."

Toby, who had jumped down to the floor when Violet stood, couldn't help but to think about what had happened to his friend, Emma, and how that had affected her life, and that of her brother, Camden. Camden took it upon himself to protect his sister and seek revenge for what had been done to her. He, too, had murdered because of the deviant behaviour of others.

"I hear what you are saying," Jack made his way to where Violet stood. "However, we just can't have everyone going around playing vigilante, killing people. That is what we have the law for, police officers…"

"But the law failed this young man!" Violet's voice broke off Jack's statement. Her words rose in a passionate crescendo: "The system failed him, all his life. He didn't have a chance. You can't deny that. Where were the police when Syd's father was beating his mother—when he was beating his son?"

It was Jack's turn to butt in now. "We can only do so much, Violet. And there are more times than not that we don't know what's going on behind closed doors. I agree, the system fails a lot of people, but that still does not give anyone the privilege to take the law into their own hands."

Toby circled Violet's legs and meowed. He gazed up at Jack and scowled. Jack couldn't figure out the old cat sometimes. One minute he was after the criminal, the next it appeared he agreed with them.

Suddenly, Toby stopped and growled. He ran to the door and scratched at it. *Sounds like a vehicle coming down the lane—good thing I have extra-sharp hearing!* He looked at Jack and meowed loudly. *Come on, Jack, can't you hear it? We gotta get out of here … and take Violet with us; I think Syd might be coming back, he probably discovered he couldn't get through the roadblocks!*

Jack recognizing Toby's signals, realized something was amiss. He put his fingers to his lips, cautioning Violet to be quiet.

"What's wrong?" Violet whispered.

"Toby senses something," Jack murmured quietly. "He's a smart old cat, has solved numerous crimes … had them all figured out before the cops did!" Jack knelt beside Toby. "What is it, old man?"

Toby pawed the door. Jack opened it for him and Toby ran out, stopping at the top of the steps and looking back at Jack and Violet. He meowed loudly. *Come on, guys! Let's get out of here—to the woods—at least until we see who's coming up the lane!*

Finally, Jack heard the vehicle engine approaching. "Violet, let's get out of here until we know who's coming up the lane."

Unexpectedly, Violet shook her head. "I'm not going anywhere. If it is Syd, he might need my help."

"Really, woman?!" Jack shouted in frustration. "After he tied you up..."

"He could have killed me, but he didn't," Violet yelled back. "If he needs my help, I'm going to give it to him. I have a bad feeling in my gut that the cops, or whoever it is chasing him down, won't go easy on him if they do catch him. He might not make it back to the prison alive."

The sound of the engine was getting closer.

"You go, Jack; I'll be fine."

Jack, infuriated, punched the porch post. "You aren't being reasonable—a desperate man will do desperate things. You won't be safe with him."

"I will. Now go, Jack. I trust that you are a good man, and you must know some honest cops who will make sure Syd's story gets told. Get hold of them, and get them up here as fast as you can. If this is Syd returning for me, I'll do my best to keep him here ... that's all I can guarantee you."

"I..."

"Go. Leave Toby with me, and if things go bad, I'll make sure he gets out and can get to you."

Toby looked at Violet and meowed. He moved protectively to her side before meowing at Jack. *Go ahead, Jack—listen to Violet—I got this. If things go south, I'll get out and get you here.* Toby went into the cabin.

The vehicle was almost upon them. Frustrated, Jack sighed dispiritedly and retreated to the wooded area. He lingered just inside the trees, waiting and watching. Within a few seconds, Violet's van appeared in the yard and Syd stepped out. The van looked as though it had been in an accident, as did Syd, whose head was bandaged. Syd made his way to the cabin. Jack headed back to his cottage, intent on calling in the people he knew could be trusted to get a job done right.

Chapter Twenty-one

Frank heard the phone ring just as he was about to take the garbage out. He turned on a dime and rushed back into the house, answering the phone on its fifth ring.

"Hello."

"Hello, is this Frank Saunders?"

"Yes."

"This is Francine Conklin from TD Visa; your visa card was just used at a gas station near Kingston, Ontario."

Frank started to shake. He needed to know precisely where. "Do you have an address?" he asked, barely able to breathe. He thought he might be having a heart attack.

"Of course." Francine gave Frank the address and then hung up.

As soon as the line closed, Frank reopened it and dialled 911. He was worried more than ever now. Kingston was the area where the criminal had escaped from prison. Hopefully, Violet was on her way home and just stopped for gas, but she'd said in her note she'd be gone for about a month. It had been less than a week.

When Frank explained his situation to the dispatch, they told him to phone the Brantford police station directly; someone there could direct him as to what to do.

Frank hung up, agitated at getting, what he thought, was a run-around. He called the Brantford police and asked to speak to someone in charge.

"What's the problem, sir?" the dispatcher asked.

"My wife is missing … well, not really missing, but not here … she left but said she'd be back. I don't know exactly where she went but our credit card was just used at a gas station up in the Kingston area, and there is an escaped prisoner and…"

The dispatcher tried to be patient with the man on the other end of her line. "Slow down … Mr. …?"

"Name is Frank Saunders, and…"

"Yes, I got it, Frank. Your wife is missing, but not really missing because she just went away. What do you want us to do?"

"You aren't hearing me—I think she's in danger. There's a criminal running around up there, and she filled gas at a station in the area close by the Kingston penitentiary."

The dispatcher drew in a deep breath. *This guy's an idiot. His wife runs off and now he's worried some escaped con kidnapped her. Maybe she's better off without him … sounds like a nutcase…*

"Are you listening to me, lady?" Frank shouted into the receiver. "Give me someone in charge that I can talk to!"

"I'm afraid, sir—Frank—you do not have an emergency…"

Frank pushed the OFF button on the phone and slammed the receiver back in its base. He grabbed hold of his car keys. If he couldn't get someone on the phone, he'd go down to the station and demand to speak to the man in charge.

~

George was getting more pissed off by the minute. Joe had been gone far too long with the dogs and time was flying by. The longer it took to pick the scent back up, the further away Syd was getting. George looked at his team, lounging around without a care in the world, all except Larry. He'd caught the young guard staring at him more than once, studying him, and George didn't like it.

Finally, the baying of the hounds echoed through the woods. George leaped to his feet and snapped his fingers to his team. "Sounds like we have a scent—let's get ready to move out, boys."

A few minutes later, Joe appeared with the dogs. He walked straight to George. "Picked up your boy's scent not far from here, on the other side of the stream. Not sure how far we'll get before getting hung up again with more water but my boys are good. Let's get moving." Joe turned and let the dogs pull him across the creek and down to the location they'd picked up Syd's trail.

Larry brought up in the rear. He'd been watching George while they'd waited and noticed the nervousness on his face. Larry wondered exactly what George was up to, and what it was the warden knew about his fellow guard that made him mistrust him. Larry almost lost his footing on the creek bed but quickly recovered and caught up with the rest of the team.

The dogs were already running into the woods, their tails in the air, baying loudly. They were hot on Syd's trail.

~

Jack hated to leave Violet but he knew she would be in good hands—paws—with Toby on the job. He needed to return to his cottage and get hold of Tessa. She was an excellent profiler and had really helped when he was working on the Camden Gale case. She might be able to reach his other friend, Captain Bryce Wagner, from the

Brantford police force. They would know the best people to contact in this area.

Toby hid under the bed when he saw Syd moving toward the cottage. Violet watched him slink there and figured it was best for the old fellow to keep out of the way, so if there were a need for him to slip out, it would be easier to do so if Syd didn't know Toby was there.

Syd lurched into the cabin and looked wildly around for Violet. She had gone into the bathroom when she knew Syd was approaching so she could make an entrance for him.

"Violet!" Syd called out, a tremor in his voice. "I need you; where are you?"

"Just a minute … I'm in the washroom," she called back. She ran water in the sink for a moment. Grabbing a towel off the rack, she exited, drying her face. She remembered at the last minute to limp. Trying to keep her voice calm, "I didn't expect you to be back."

"Neither did I, but the main road is blocked. I'm going to need you to drive the van and hide me in the back. I'm small enough to squeeze under the rear seat, and you can make sure that stuff is piled around and on top of me." Syd's voice shook with nerves. "You're walking," he noticed. "Is your ankle better?" Then, realizing she was walking and remembering that before he'd left, he'd tied her up, "How'd you get lose?" he inquired sharply.

Violet had to think quickly of a good answer: "You didn't really tie me very tight; I managed to wiggle free," she informed. Then, recalling his initial question, "As to my ankle, must have just been a minor twist, not as bad as I thought."

Violet, noticing his bandaged head, walked over to the door and looked out into the yard at her van. "What happened?" she asked, turning back to Syd.

"Deer ran across the laneway when I was on my way out. Swerved to avoid hitting it and crashed into a tree."

"I see. That looks like a nasty bump on your head, seems to still be bleeding. Mind if I take a look and maybe clean it up a bit?" Violet needed to waste some time, enough for Toby to get out and retrieve Jack back to the cottage. She moved for the door.

"Where do you think you're going?" Syd yelled, rushing to her and grabbing her by the arm.

Violet wrenched her arm from his grasp. "Calm down, Syd. I have a first aid kit in the van. I'll be right back."

Syd blushed, embarrassed. He stepped back and let Violet pass. "I'll be watching you," he stated. "No funny stuff."

Violet hesitated in the doorway. "Really, Syd? I have no keys, and if you remember correctly, I also have a sore ankle, even though it's not as bad as I first thought. I am sure, even if I did try and make a run for it, you would have no problem catching up with me. Now, I am going to get the kit and come back here and dress your wound properly."

Despite the nervous troops doing drills in her stomach, Violet walked to the van, limping slightly for effect. She planned to leave the door slightly ajar when she returned to the cottage, take Syd into the bathroom to clean the wound, and hope Toby would get the message and sneak out while Syd was distracted.

As Violet returned, Toby watched her from under the bed. *I have a feeling you have a plan, here, Violet ... what is it? I need to get out of here and reach Jack. I don't like the sound of Syd's plan ... way too much can go wrong.*

"Ready, Syd. Let's go to the bathroom where I can wash that wound before re-bandaging it."

Toby noticed the door hadn't closed all the way. *Good woman, Violet; won't be a problem getting out of here now, just need to wait for you guys to get into the…*

"No need to close the door, is there?" Toby heard Syd tell Violet. "We're alone, aren't we?"

Violet didn't miss a beat, and speaking a little louder than she really had to, "I just want to grab this towel from the back of the door."

That was Toby's cue. He scuttled out from under the bed and raced across the floor and out the door. As he sprinted down the steps, he heard the door bang and Syd holler. But there wasn't time to turn around and see what was happening. He had to get to Jack and get him back to Violet's cabin before she and Syd left—or he did something awful to her.

~

"What was that?" Syd pushed Violet aside and ran out into the main room.

Violet swallowed hard as she followed Syd. "I have no idea… Maybe a 'coon or squirrel knocked something over on the porch; there are a lot around here."

As though someone from above was looking out for Violet, when Syd opened the door, a couple squirrels scurried off the porch toward the nearest tree. Returning inside, Syd still looked puzzled. He didn't think two squirrels could make as much noise as what he'd heard. Something wasn't right.

Violet went to the bathroom: "Come on, let's finish up in here."

The cloth Syd used as a bandage was stuck to his skin and Violet had difficulty removing it. She took her time, careful not to reopen the wound.

"Can't you hurry it up?" Syd asked impatiently.

"I could, but the wound would open again; I'm trying to prevent that from happening."

Syd finally relaxed and Violet continued tediously chipping away at the cloth. Finally, it was free. She stood back and whistled.

"Wow! You definitely made a mess of your head!" she exclaimed as she turned the tap on, filling the sink with warm water. "Can you sit down here?" she motioned to the stool sitting by the shower stall. When he didn't move, "It will be easier for me to clean you up."

Violet stretched the cleaning and dressing of the wound for a good half-hour. During that time, she thought about how to delay leaving, giving Toby enough time to reach Jack and get him back to save her from having to go with Syd. Violet knew, despite feeling sorry for him, Syd was still a killer, and he was desperate, which in turn might make him unpredictable. In the end, she decided she could only do so much—the rest was up to the man upstairs!

~

Toby raced through the woods, following the half-beaten path. It was at times like this when he wished he didn't eat so much and that he exercised more. It took what he felt was forever to finally reach the cottage Jack had rented. He raced up the steps and meowed at the door.

Footsteps and a familiar voice approached the door. Jack had his cell phone to his ear, talking with someone. "Thanks, Tessa." The phone snapped shut, and the door opened. "Toby!"

Toby circled around and around, then ran back down the steps and took off into the woods. Jack, knowing this was the signal for him to follow, charged after Toby.

Pausing at the edge of the trees, Toby turned to make sure Jack was following him. Assured of that fact, he continued on his way. *We're coming, Violet! Keep him busy—you were doing great when I left!*

Chapter Twenty-two

Frank rushed into the police station, straight for the reception desk. "I need to speak to whoever is in charge here," he demanded.

"What's the problem, sir?" the young woman behind the desk asked.

"I need to talk to someone in charge; I don't have time to keep repeating myself."

Something about the look on Frank's face told the receptionist he was a desperate man, one she didn't want to mess with. "Just a moment, sir. I'll get Captain Wagner."

Frank nodded, and seeing a nameplate on the desk, "Thank you, Cynthia."

Cynthia approached Captain Wagner's office and knocked on his door. He was just hanging up the phone. He had a worried look on his face.

"Captain…"

"What is it, Cynthia?" he asked, shuffling some papers on his desk.

"There's a gentleman in the lobby insisting on talking to someone in charge. He's very agitated. Wouldn't tell me anything; said he was tired of repeating himself. Would you like me to show him in here or do you want to meet him out there?"

Captain Wagner considered the situation. He'd just had a call from Tessa Bannister, who was dating his old friend, Jack Nelson. She'd informed him she'd just received a call from Jack asking for the name of someone near Kingston whom he could trust. A prisoner had escaped from the penitentiary and was holding a woman hostage in a cabin near where Jack was staying. Toby, of course, the old detective cat, had come upon the situation. Jack told Tessa the circumstances were dire, and he feared not only for the woman, but the convict; said there was a possibility the young man wouldn't make it back to the prison alive. He had a back-story that needed to be told and he was a desperate man. Even though the woman had managed to get him to trust her, one never knew when the bubble of contentment would burst.

"I'll come out first to see what this guy is all about," he finally replied. "Give me a sec; I'll be right there."

Cynthia returned to the front lobby: "The captain will be with you in a moment, sir."

Frank stopped pacing and rushed to Cynthia, taking her by the hand. She froze, worried what this seemingly desperate man was going to do, but all he did was say, "Thank you so much." Frank shook her hand.

Cynthia relaxed and breathed a sigh of relief. She gave him a gentle smile. "No problem, sir." The phone on her desk started ringing. "Excuse me," she said.

Frank dropped Cynthia's hand and looked toward the door through which she'd just come, waiting impatiently for the captain to appear. Finally, Captain Wagner entered the lobby, extending his hand to Frank.

"Captain Bryce Wagner, and you are?"

"Frank Saunders. Thank you so much for agreeing to listen to me. Might we go somewhere private?"

Bryce, studying the man in front of him, felt he was not dangerous. "Follow me," he directed.

Once inside his office, Bryce motioned to a chair: "Have a seat."

"I'd rather stand," Frank wrung his hands nervously, praying that this man, once he heard his story, would take some action.

"Whatever you like, Frank. Now, what's the problem?"

Frank drew a big breath and began: "My wife might be in danger. She went up to the Kingston area for a bit of 'R and R'..." Frank figured he was safe saying that now that he knew where their credit card had been used. "But I heard there was an escaped prisoner up there and I am worried. I haven't heard from her for days." Frank decided to leave out how Violet had left, reckoning that would probably delay any action the police might take.

To Frank's surprise, the captain looked up sharply. "You say your wife is in the Kingston area? Do you know exactly where?"

"I'm not exactly sure ... but it is near Kingston—just west of the city, actually; she filled some gas there yesterday. She was going to call me to join her but I haven't heard from her. I'm beginning to worry."

"How long since you've heard from your wife, Frank?" Bryce inquired.

Frank, not used to lying, swallowed hard, his Adam's apple bobbing nervously. Bryce noticed but said nothing, waiting for the man to answer. He had an eerie feeling Frank's wife might be the woman Jack was talking about.

"Frank—how long since you heard from your wife?" the captain repeated.

"A few days ago," he lied, although technically, it had been—it had only been a few days ago his beloved Violet left.

Bryce made a decision based on his gut feeling. "Sit down, Frank, I have something to tell you. Nothing concrete at this point in regards to your wife, but there is a possibility…" he drew in a breath, then, "A good friend of mine, a retired officer, rented a place up on a lake in that area…went with his cat, an exceptional cat with a set of whiskers for solving crimes. From what I understand they came upon a woman in a nearby cabin being held captive by the fellow who'd escaped the penitentiary. My friend placed a call to a colleague of ours, not having been able to get through to me, asking her for the name of someone trustworthy in that area…"

Frank jumped from the chair he'd finally sat in a couple minutes earlier: "Is it my wife? Did your friend give you a name?"

"No, he didn't, but, if what you are saying is true, and I have no reason not to believe you, right, sir?" The captain raised his eyebrows, indicating he needed an answer to his question before he would continue.

Frank nodded, not able to speak at the moment.

Bryce continued. "The woman may possibly be your wife. My colleague, Tessa, is already on her way to Jack, and I've given her the name of a trustworthy officer in the area. I've already placed a call to him, just waiting to hear back, he was out of his office."

"I need to get up there," Frank moaned. "I need to find my wife."

Bryce studied the broken man in front of him, feeling there was much more to Frank's story than he was letting on. *You poor bugger! Wife left you for whatever reasons and you can't let her go. Maybe, if this is your wife being held hostage, this situation of almost losing her will bring you two back together…*

147

"What you need to do is leave me your phone number and as soon as I hear anything…"

"I'll leave you my cell, but I'm heading up to Kingston as soon as I leave here. I have the address of the gas station and am guessing my Violet won't be far from there. I just hope we're not too late—that I'm not too late!"

"There are hundreds of cottages up there," the captain stated. "It will be like trying to find a flea on a husky dog. Why don't you let the police do their job, and we'll get hold of you as soon as we have something concrete." Bryce removed his glasses and looked straight into Frank's eyes. "It may not even be your wife, Frank. You don't want to go off on a wild goose chase."

Frank's lips set in a firm line. When he spoke, his voice was filled with controlled emotion. "I'm heading to Kingston, Captain Wagner. If anything transpires, call my cell." With that, Frank turned and left.

Chapter Twenty-three

Toby stopped at the edge of the wood and surveyed the area.

"Looks clear," Jack commented, kneeling down beside Toby.

Toby meowed and started across the yard. Jack followed cautiously, trying to stay out of sight of the front windows. Sneaking up to the end of the porch, Jack crawled over the railing, then inched to the window. Luckily, it was open, so he could hear what was going on inside.

"There, Syd … how does that feel? That's the best I can do; I think, though, you should get yourself to a hospital. The wound looks pretty ugly and it might need stitches."

Jack looked at Toby. "He's wounded?"

Toby blinked and meowed.

"You already knew that, didn't you, old man?" Jack whispered.

You bet I did.

Jack gazed around and saw the van. He had a thought. He scratched Toby behind the ears and leaned closer. "I think it would be a good idea if I disable the van; what do you think, old man?"

Brilliant idea! Why didn't I think of that? Must be getting slow in my old age!

"Here goes, Toby. You wait here." Jack backed up and climbed over the railing again. He moved stealthily across the yard toward the van, keeping as low to the ground as possible. He prayed the door was unlocked.

Upon reaching the van, Jack decided to try the sliding side door, thinking it would be less likely to be noticed once it was opened. Luck was with him. He crawled inside and made his way to the steering wheel. He fiddled around beneath it, looking for wires. It was an older van; there should be something he could disconnect to disable the vehicle. Finally, his fingers touched some cables and he gave them a good pull.

Jack was satisfied that if Syd tried to get away again, the van wasn't going to go anywhere. He hoped Tessa had managed to contact someone and that they would be on their way sooner rather than later. For now, he needed to think of a reason he'd returned to Violet's cottage. Approaching the cottage, he noticed Toby sitting at the door, meowing. Taking a leap of faith Toby had a plan, Jack walked nonchalantly to the steps.

As he reached the porch, Syd opened the door. Toby rushed through and headed straight for Violet. Syd looked at Jack. "What the hell are you doing back here?" he hissed, before realizing that the last time Jack saw him, he was dressed like a woman.

Not missing a beat, Jack replied: "I got back to my cottage and my friend called, said she was delayed and wouldn't be up until tomorrow. I thought to come over and check on Violet to see how she was, in case you got delayed with the shopping. Never can tell with the crowded malls how long it will take."

Syd hesitated.

Jack pushed his way into the cottage. "But you weren't going shopping, were you? Why don't you tell me what's really going on here? I was under the impression when I was here before that you were a young woman. Now, here you are, actually a young man, and, you're wounded." Jack joined Violet and Toby where they stood in the middle of the room, placing himself between Syd and them.

But the next thing that happened surprised the trio. Syd collapsed on the floor and folded up, crushing his knees to his chest, resting his head on his knees. He began rocking and moaning, and his shoulders were soon shaking as the tears flowed from his eyes.

Violet moved to go to him but Jack laid a hand on her arm, trying to stop her. She smiled at him and patted his hand. "It's okay … he's not going to hurt me. Can't you see how defeated he is?"

Toby put a paw on Jack's leg and meowed, then moved to Violet, pushing between her and Jack. Jack, baffled, dropped his hand. He couldn't fight them both.

Violet went to Syd, stooped beside him and pulled him into her arms. Toby had no idea how long they sat on the floor like that, she rocking Syd in her arms, stroking his head and telling him everything would be okay. She would make sure the authorities heard his story. Toby joined her, sitting close enough he could lean on his new friend. Jack wandered into the kitchen area and put a pot of water on the stove to boil for tea.

Setting the drinks on the table, he called out: "Come on now, let's have a bit of tea and then we can talk about how to get Syd out of this mess he's put himself into."

Syd finally looked up at Jack. "You have no idea … I can't go back there … I'll never make it back alive, and if I do, I won't last a day."

Jack scratched his head. "Why is that?"

"All I'm going to say is there are people in the prison that want to see me dead because of what I know, and I ain't talkin' about fellow prisoners!"

Toby walked around to Jack and sat at his feet. He looked at his friend, then to Syd, and back again. *I have a feeling that despite this kid having killed someone—a dirtbag in my estimation if we can believe what Syd told us—there is a bigger fish than him to fry.* Toby fixed his eyes on Jack. *I think we better help this kid, Jack ... best we be the ones to get him back to his prison cell and not whoever is coming after him!*

As though picking up on Toby's thoughts, "I think you need to trust me enough to tell me everything," Jack asserted. "I was a cop for a lot of years, and even though I'm retired now, I still do freelance work..."

You and I work together, bud! Toby glared at Jack, emitting a small growl.

"Okay, old man. *We* freelance for the police department." Jack returned his focus to Syd. "I still have good connections—good cops who can be trusted—and I've already contacted one of them to get me someone up in this area whom we can trust. But, I need to know exactly what is going on. What is it you know that could put your life in danger? Is that what made you run, as much or more so than revenge on those you have on your list?"

Jack pointed to the couch. "Let's sit over there where it's more comfortable."

Once settled on the couch, Syd still hesitated. There was so much to tell. Where should he begin? Finally, "There's a guard at the prison who rules the roost ... his name is George, and if anyone—prisoners or fellow guards—dares to cross him or not do what he orders, well, they pay the consequences."

Syd went on to tell some of the things George had done to prisoners and guards and mentioned there had been a couple prisoners who died under mysterious circumstances. They'd been in George's cell block at the time. Syd had been on the wrong side of George for a time and learned pretty quick to do what he was told and to keep his mouth shut.

"But I know and saw a lot, and George isn't happy about that. So, I faked being sick with the hope of getting a trip to the hospital. That part worked fine, but my heart went to my mouth when I saw George was one of the guards transporting me. The only thing that saved me was that George didn't dare do me in front of the young guard. Larry is new at the prison and hasn't fallen under George's charm or felt his full wrath when not obeyed. I knew if he got the chance to get me out of Larry's sight, George might have caused me to have an unfortunate accident. I don't think I was ever meant to make it to the hospital—not on George's watch."

Jack looked at his watch. It had been two hours since he'd talked to Tessa, and there was still no sign of the promised backup. It would be another two hours before she made it up to his cottage, maybe an hour and a half if she pushed the speed limit.

"I think we need to get Syd out of here," Violet said. "Is there any way we can get him to your cabin without leaving a scent for the dogs to follow? We can wait for your people there and let them know what's going on."

Despite feeling sorry for Syd and everything he'd been through, Toby wasn't sure it was a good idea to take him to Jack's cabin. Syd could use the opportunity to escape again, maybe even hurt Jack. There had to be a better way. *Come on, Jack, can't you think of something?*

"I agree it might be wiser to remove Syd from here and get him someplace where he'll be safe from this George guy, but then again, we've no proof George is even part of the search party. Plus, it'll be tricky to get Syd to my cabin without leaving his scent for the dogs to follow, if they've called in the hounds. Also, if we move Syd from here, I have to make sure he can't escape; he'd have to be tied.

"Once we get to my cabin, I'll call Tessa, and we can arrange a different meeting place. I don't want to get caught out here with an escaped prisoner, and have a trigger-happy prison guard bust in on us."

"What if we were to wrap his shoes with something so there would be no scent? But we'd have to worry about tracks... I guess my idea won't work." Violet realized she'd not been thinking straight. She shook her head in frustration.

"I don't think there's anything you guys can do to save me at this point. It was foolish of me to even try and escape, especially from George. He'll be out for revenge, and the prison warden won't be too happy either."

Jack scratched his head. He remembered something he'd noticed in the woods, just off the trail between the two cabins. It appeared to be a pit in a clearing—most likely an animal trap of some sort. Jack thought if they could somehow get Syd to that spot and hide him there until Tessa and her people arrived, the young man would be safer.

Looking at Syd, Jack figured he could carry him that far. He explained his plan, and when he was finished, he added: "I will still have to tie you up down there."

Syd nodded. "Can't be any worse than being in solitary at the prison." Syd stood and walked into the

154

kitchen area and opened the fridge. "Do you mind if I grab a little something to eat before we go?"

Toby thought it a fabulous idea, and he followed Syd to the fridge. He meowed to let them all know he was hungry, too. *I hope Violet brought some cans of tuna or salmon with her.*

After everyone had a quick bite to eat, Jack put together a small bag of food and water for Syd. He wasn't sure how long he'd have to leave him in the hole, or when he'd be able to return to him if the search party passed by their way.

"Ready to go, Syd?" Jack asked. "I need to get you there and then get back here and try and erase as much of you having been here as possible."

"Is there anything I can do while you're gone?" Violet queried.

Jack thought for a moment. "Yeah, I noticed a hose at the side of the house; water the yard and around the van … make it look like you washed your vehicle, and then water down the porch. I'll help you when I get back. We'll need to scour the inside of the cabin as well; do you have any strong cleaners?"

"I'll see what I can find around here; most of what I brought with me is already used up," Violet replied as she made her way to the bathroom where she'd previously noticed a supply cupboard. "See you soon, Jack." A pause. "Do you mind leaving Toby with me? He brings me comfort, and if by chance a search party shows up while you are gone, I'd like to have something—someone—to hold on to."

"No problem. Okay, Syd, climb on my back."

Toby stood at the door watching his friend leave with Syd. *I really hope you know what you're doing, Jack.*

Having that guy on your back could be a pretty dangerous move. If Syd decides to change his mind about hiding out, you could be toast. I know Violet needs me here, but I am genuinely concerned about you!

Chapter Twenty-four

George was pissed because of all the delays they faced due to the streams and ponds. They were stopped, yet again, while the hounds attempted to pick back up Syd's scent. Nevertheless, he felt they were closing in on Syd; the lake was nearby, and there were a lot of cottages there, many in ill-repair and seldom rented out. He knew the owner of a few of the more derelict ones.

Larry was taking countless notes, many of them observations of his superior's behaviours. He also recorded how most of the team George had assembled left him alone to do whatever he wanted; this scared Larry. He couldn't help but wonder what they would do once they caught up with Syd. Abandon the prisoner to George? Turn blind eyes?

The sound of the hounds baying reached the clearing where the men had stopped to wait for the signal from Joe. George ordered everyone to their feet and they moved out in single file, Larry bringing up the rear.

The dogs were straining hard on their leashes and Joe struggled keeping control of them. "Must be close to something!" Joe shouted back to the team.

After about ten minutes of following the fast pace the dogs set, they burst onto the lakeshore. The dogs continued along the shoreline, the trail remaining close to the tree line. Soon, a cottage came into sight, with a van parked out front and a woman watering the grass. From the looks of the earth around the vehicle, and the water drops still on its surface, it appeared to have just been washed.

The woman looked up as the dogs approached from a distance.

Suddenly, though, they became confused and started circling. Violet knew enough that the dogs had lost the scent. She prayed Jack returned soon. From the looks and sounds of things, a new game was about to begin.

A large, burly man strode across the yard. He'd motioned to the man with the dogs and the men who were with him to stay behind. As he approached Violet, she noticed the surly look in his eyes. Her best guess was this was George.

"You alone here, lady?" George got right to the point.

Violet blinked as she watched the intruder to her domain. "Yes and no," she answered evasively. She grinned as she pointed to Toby, who was sitting on the porch bathing his bright orange fur.

Toby, having a cat-sense that something big was going down, bound down the steps and raced across the yard to Violet. *Darn this water all over the place! I'll have to rewash my feet with this mud getting between my toes ... disgusting ... I sure hope Syd is telling us the truth and he's worth the trouble trying to protect him!* When he reached Violet, he brushed around her legs, then sat and glared up at George. He hissed.

George snorted in disgust as he observed Toby, he hated cats. He looked around the yard at all the puddles Violet created when she'd saturated the area with the hose. "Why so much water, lady?"

Violet scooped Toby up in her arms, holding him close against her thumping heart. "I think, sir, you are here on business, and before I talk further with you, I would ask who you are and what your business is." She squeezed Toby tighter. Toby scowled at George and hissed again.

At this point, Larry, who noticed Violet's discomfort, came forward and joined George. "Hey, there, George, what's happening here?" Not waiting for George to reply, Larry turned to Violet. "We're from the prison, ma'am, tracking an escaped convict. You haven't had any unexpected visitors within the last day or so, have you?" He thrust his hand toward Violet: "I'm Larry, and this big guy beside me is George," Larry introduced. "Who might you be?"

Violet didn't reach for Larry's hand. "As you can see, Larry, my hands are quite full, so you will have to forgive me for not shaking yours."

You squeeze me any tighter, Violet, you are going to have me poop on you! Toby groaned. Catching a glimpse of Jack coming out of the woods, a load of logs in his arms, Toby wiggled to get free, and to get Violet's attention.

Picking up on his cue, Violet glanced in the direction Toby was wiggling. Seeing Jack, she decided she had no choice but to add something to this dangerous game she and Jack were playing. "Finally," she called out, "I thought you were cutting down the forest just to bring a few logs for tonight's campfire."

George whirled on Violet. His voice was ripe with anger: "I thought you said it was just you and this cat!"

"Well, it was at that moment," Violet replied, trying to remain calm. She put Toby down and attempted to walk across the yard toward Jack.

George grabbed her arm roughly. Violet wrenched out of his grip. "Who do you think you are? I'm not one of your inmates," she shouted. "I'm just going to help my husband."

Having heard what Violet called him, Jack hollered over, "Honey, can you help me here? This load is heavier than I thought." And to make an impression on the group of viewers, Jack allowed a couple of logs to drop to the ground. "Damn!" he cursed.

"Let the lady go, George," Larry said with a soft firmness to his words. "We are not here to interrogate her."

George, realizing he was in the wrong and had no right to treat a civilian as he had, backed away with an angry scowl. He didn't like the looks of the area around the cottage, and he had a gut feeling the woman and the guy were hiding something. If it was Syd, they'd be sorry!

Jack piled the logs beside a used fire pit, and Violet retrieved the two pieces he had dropped. Standing up, Jack put his arm around Violet's shoulder and looked over at the men in the yard. He addressed George first.

"I don't know exactly what you want, sir, and I can see that whatever business you are about is important; however, if you lay a hand on my wife again in such a manner, you will answer to authorities far above you." Jack's voice was harsh and imparted the message he was not a man to be messed with.

Toby swished his tail and hissed at George. *That a boy, Jack. You tell him!*

George's fists clenched at his side. He was thinking about what else could go wrong. It was Larry who stepped forward, though, to speak on behalf of the group.

"If you don't mind, sir, we'd just like to take a look around. The fellow who escaped is a pretty dangerous criminal, and as of yet, there has been no indication he's tried to get through our roadblocks. This leads us to believe he may still be in this area. We'll just check the perimeters and then be on our way. The dogs picked up his scent and it led us here, which means he possibly passed by your cottage and seeing it was occupied, he just moved on."

"We'd also like to check inside the cottage," George added, still with the gut feeling that Violet and Jack were hiding something.

As Jack opened his mouth to reply, Larry spoke up: "That won't be necessary, George. I think we've bothered these good people long enough."

George turned on Larry, his mouth set in a thin line, eyes filled with venom. "I am in charge of this operation, officer, and you will stand down now. You've interfered enough already. When I say we check out the inside of the cottage, we check out the inside of the cottage. Is that clear?"

Larry blushed and his Adam's apple quivered. He swallowed hard. He was glad for the tape running in his pocket and prayed it was picking up enough of the conversation to be credible.

"Quite clear." Larry gathered as much courage as he could and faced George: "However, remember, anything you do will be going in my report to the warden, so I suggest you tread carefully, even if you are in charge." With those words, Larry turned and walked away.

George spat on the ground and headed toward the porch but Toby raced ahead of him and backed up against the door. The closer George got, the louder Toby hissed. As the prison guard bent his leg back, ready to kick Toby, Violet lurched forward and to everyone's surprise, knocked George over.

As he regained his feet, George clenched his fists and was ready to strike Violet when a hand grabbed hold of his wrist, stopping the blow in midair.

"I wouldn't do that if I were you. I've already warned you about touching my wife—you will answer to a higher order. You have no idea, sir, who you are dealing with here."

George opened his mouth to speak, but Jack cut him off.

"I happen to know the law as well as you do, probably even more so, having spent most of my life as a police officer, and the final fifteen years as a detective. I still freelance for the department in my city—I bet I've forgotten more laws than you know.

"I know the other fellow may not be as high up the totem pole as you are, but I'd suggest you listen to him and just check around the parameters and then move on. You will not be stepping one foot inside my cottage unless you have a search warrant." Jack held an arm out to Violet. "Shall we, my dear?"

With that, he and Violet went inside and shut the door. Toby slipped in with them, not wanting to be left in the line of fire of George's boot.

George fumed at what Jack had just done to him; however, he was not going to test the already tepid situation. He had his ways of getting even, and Jack hadn't heard the last of him. He turned and headed toward his team and Joe and his dogs.

"Take the dogs and walk around the entire area," George ordered Joe, and then turning to the rest of his team, "Spread out and check every inch of this yard and the woods close by. There's something not right here, and if those two in there are hiding something, they'll be the ones answering to a higher level of the law!"

~

Inside the cottage, Violet collapsed onto the floor and began to weep. Jack, uncomfortable with the situation, laid a hand on her shoulder. "Don't worry, Violet. That guy isn't going to do anything right now. We have time, and hopefully they aren't going to find any traces of Syd."

Violet looked up, worried about something she had just thought of. "What if they check the inside of the van? Syd's scent will be all over the inside … remember … he took the van."

Jack grinned sheepishly. "Don't worry; when I disabled the van before leaving it, I locked the doors. With the good washing down you gave it, they won't pick up anything."

Violet breathed a sigh of relief. Gathering herself together, she stood and walked to the bathroom. Jack could hear her throwing up. He turned and looked out the window, watching the goings on in the yard. Taking out his phone, he dialled Tessa's number.

Tessa picked up after the third ring. "Jack, what's up?"

"How close are you to getting here?" Jack asked. "Things are heating up around this place."

"I'm less than an hour from where you are … still want me to come to your cottage, or is there somewhere else we should meet?"

"Well, it's become complicated. I'm not at my cottage, but at one just down the lake, where all the action seems to be taking place at the moment." Jack took a breath, then filled Tessa in on what had just taken place.

"Violet is a wreck," he ended with, "yet, at the same time, one hell of a woman. Quick thinker, too."

Jack hadn't told Tessa yet what he'd done with Syd and wasn't sure how much he should say. "The search party is still here at Violet's cottage, combing the perimeters, looking for any clues of the escaped convict..."

"And he wasn't there ... or, he was?"

"He was, and then he wasn't. We hid him."

Tessa was having a difficult time with what she was hearing. "You did what?"

"I need to see you and talk to you in person, Tessa. This young man, despite being a killer, is in danger. If we let the search party take him back to prison, he wouldn't see the inside of a cell—he would end up a box! And, after meeting the lead man on the search team, I have no doubt."

"Really?"

"No doubt in my mind." Jack switched the phone to his other ear. "For now, just get yourself to my cottage and have whatever backup you have put together meet you there. When you are all in place, call me, and I will get this young fellow to you as soon as I can."

"He's in your custody then?"

"Sort of."

"Okay. I hope you're right about this guy and this doesn't backfire on you and blow up in your face," Tessa said worriedly.

Jack laughed. "Even if it does blow up and go south, not much damage can be done to this ugly old mug."

"Funny man, Jack." Tessa giggled, despite the urgency of the situation they were finding themselves in. "Talk to you soon."

Jack was worried. He didn't like George; the man was a loose cannon, and there was no telling what he was capable of. Jack also worried about the young officer, Larry, having seen the way George looked when Larry overstepped what George thought was his line of authority. Jack was well aware of how quickly *accidents* could happen.

Toby jumped up on the windowsill and rubbed his head against Jack's hand. He purred. He was happy they had managed to hide Syd, especially after having met George. The guy was scum. He turned his head and looked out the window to watch George's men as they scoured the area. He specifically watched George, who was trying to get into the van. *Good man, Jack, for thinking to lock it. We'd be toast if they managed to get inside there.*

George looked at the cottage, as though he knew he and his team were being watched, another reason he mistrusted what was really going on here. In frustration, he kicked a tire, then turned and walked over to one of his men.

Jack watched as George talked to his colleague. The man nodded and walked away. Jack turned back into the cottage and met Violet as she was coming out of the bathroom, her face pale.

"It'll all work out," Jack assured her. "I just talked to Tessa, and she and whomever she's contacted up here will be going straight to my cottage. She'll call me when they are all in place and then we'll get Syd over there—I'll get Syd there. I think it's time you took a step back, just in case things don't go well. I'd prefer the professionals handle the situation from here on."

Violet shook her head. "I'd prefer to be there. Syd trusts me more than he will trust any of you. He trusted me enough with his whole story, and even though, at first, I was just doing it to try and save my skin … well, he got under my skin. Even into my heart, if I have to say so. I've always had a soft spot for the underdog, I guess."

Jack wasn't ready to make a firm commitment to Violet being involved. He looked down at her. "We'll see," he said, then turned and walked to the door and out onto the porch. He wanted to see George and his team finish and be on their way.

Once on the porch, Jack leaned against one of the posts. He watched as George's team gathered together, as George gave instructions, pointing down the laneway. Jack watched as they left, the dogs leading the way. But he had counted the men and knew there was one missing; George had left one behind to keep an eye on the cottage. Jack knew he was going to have to be careful. Maybe he'd send Toby out to snoop around and find out where the officer was hiding. The man wouldn't suspect an old cat wandering around; probably assume he was just out hunting for mice.

Jack went back inside. Violet was sitting at the table with her computer open. She was studying a document, and Jack noticed the tears brimming in her eyes. She looked up at him and pointed to the screen.

"Read this, Jack. Then you might understand why we must help Syd, why his story has to be told."

Jack leaned over and started scanning the document. It was the telling of the last man who had used and abused Syd. The details were sadistic, and Jack couldn't imagine anyone having to go through such torture and pain, willingly or otherwise.

He stood back when he finished reading: "Syd cut the root of the snake off, but the branches are still out there. Those are the men that must be taken down, regardless of who they are. God knows how many other young boys these men have abused." Jack put a hand on Violet's shoulder.

"You came up here to write a story, Violet … you just didn't expect one so real, did you?"

Violet was so choked with emotion, she couldn't reply. Instead, she shook her head and returned her attention to the computer, her hand hovering over the mouse.

"I need to have a talk with Toby," Jack said. He wasn't sure he should tell Violet about the man George left behind, but on the other hand, it was better she knew. "Our friend out there left someone behind to keep an eye on us. I'm going to send Toby to find out where he's holed up. There are advantages to being a feline, and when one knows a feline that is also a great detective, all the better!"

Toby, having heard his name and the praise that went with it, made his way to Jack. *I'm on it, Jack; don't need to ask me twice.* He ran to the door and scratched to be let out.

"He already knows what you want, doesn't he?" Violet pointed out.

"That he does," Jack returned as he opened the door and let Toby out to get busy with the next part of the mission.

Chapter Twenty-five

Tessa, before leaving Brantford, had called Captain Wagner at the station and informed him of what Jack had told her. She'd asked him for the name of someone she could trust in the Kingston area and he'd passed on the name of an old friend, Sam Cranks, he'd gone to the academy with, and was the captain at the Kingston police station. He'd said he would call him and fill him in on what was happening and ask if he'd be willing to step in and assist in making sure the young convict was transported safely back to the prison.

Bryce phoned Tessa while she was on her way to Kingston and told her Sam would meet her at Jack's cabin, along with some of his officers. She could fill him in on anything else she might have learned from Jack when they met.

~

After leaving the Brantford police station, Frank filled his car with gas, then hit the highway. If the traffic didn't hold him back, he would get to Kingston within three and a half hours. What he was going to do when he got there, he really hadn't thought about yet.

~

Violet had been thinking about asking Jack if she could use his cell to call Frank and let him know she was safe. She was afraid he might have heard the news about the escaped convict near Kingston, and he knew how much she loved that area; they had spent part of their honeymoon there.

Knowing her husband the way she did, Violet knew he would worry and think the worst. He would think she'd been kidnapped or killed, and he would have a heart attack—or worse—if there was something graver than that. She decided to ask Jack to borrow his phone.

"Do you mind?" Violet asked, pointing to his cell. "I think it's time I called my husband."

Jack handed it to her. "Would you like some privacy?" he asked.

Violet nodded. "Please."

Jack stepped out the door onto the porch. "May as well take a little stroll," he muttered and took off down toward the lake. Had he known how closely he was being watched, he might have stayed nearer to the cottage.

~

Violet dialled Frank's cell, and after five rings, his voicemail picked up. "Hello, this is Frank. Can't talk right now … Leave a message."

"Frank, this is Violet … I need to talk to you … it's important." She quickly rattled off the number Frank could reach her on and shut Jack's phone off, then sat down at the table where her computer was. She tapped her fingers impatiently on the table, hoping Frank had his phone on him and would be picking up the phone messages sooner rather than later.

~

Frank saw an unfamiliar number come up on his Bluetooth and ignored it. "Damn solicitors," he cursed and kept driving.

~

Toby had covered a lot of ground but hadn't been able to pick up on where the guy who had stayed behind was hiding. *Must be losing my touch ... where could he be ... he has to be close by so he can see what we're doing.* Toby looked up into the trees. *That's it! He has to be up in the limbs. Getting too old for this.* Toby started up a tree with sturdy-looking branches. *I'll have a cats-eye view from up here.*

Scanning the area, below and beyond where he was, Toby still saw nothing of any interest. He noticed Jack down by the lake, though. *What are you doing down there, Jack! You shouldn't be leaving Violet alone!* Toby turned on the branch, just about losing his footing. Had he not turned, he would have seen George hold a gun to Jack's head and lead him back toward the cottage.

~

Jack didn't hear the footsteps behind him until it was too late. He felt the cold muzzle of a gun press against the back of his head.

"Not a good idea to leave the little woman alone so much, especially with an escaped convict in the area," George's voice grated in Jack's ear. "Turn around, slowly, and let's go back to the cottage and see how she's doing."

Jack felt a chill run up and down his spine. This was not good. If George was here with him, where was the other guy? With Violet? *Toby, old man, I hope you are seeing this, and have the foresight to go back to our cottage and wait for Tessa. You'll know what to do then.*

~

Violet heard the footsteps coming across the porch, despite whoever it was trying to tiptoe. Some of the boards were old and creaky. She hoped it was Jack returning but had a bad feeling it wasn't. Before she had time to hide, the door swung open and one of the men who had been with the search party entered.

"What are you doing, sir, and who are you to think you can just walk into my cottage without an invitation?" Violet's words did not relay how she was feeling inside. *Where are you, Jack?*

The man cast a sardonic look Violet's way. "George got to thinking that you and your man were trying to hide something. George is no one's fool, you know, and if I were you, I wouldn't be trying to lie to him about anything."

Walking over to the table where the computer sat open, the man leaned over and looked at the screen. Luckily, Violet had exited out of the document detailing Syd's life story.

"You were working on something here?" the man probed, a cynical curl on his lips.

"Not really. If I was, I don't see that it would be any of your business." Violet was trying hard to keep the butterflies in her stomach at bay.

The man laughed, an unpleasant sound. "You know," he began, "I think I'm going to tell you a story; maybe you will want to write it down. What do you think?"

Violet swallowed. "What kind of story?"

"Oh, maybe the story of a man and a woman trying to conceal something—someone—but they got caught in their lies. Does that sound like it would make a good story?"

"Sounds like a story that's already been told. I write fiction, sir, but not mysteries; more romance and children's books," Violet lied.

The man laughed again. "Oh, look," he said, pointing out the window. "Look who George found—your beloved husband. He is your husband, isn't he?"

Violet couldn't think how the situation could get any worse. What if Frank called back now and this guy or George answered the phone? She had to think quickly of a solution in case that happened.

"Actually, he isn't my husband," she blushed. "I left my husband home. Jack and I are having an affair." Violet's revelation was spoken as George shoved Jack through the door.

Violet continued, to ensure Jack heard what she said. "I've told this fellow here the truth, Jack—we're lovers, not husband and wife."

"Well, isn't this something," George guffawed. "The little lady is telling us another lie! Why should I believe you now? First, you're husband and wife, now you're lovers; what next? Tell me," George waved his gun around before pointing it at Violet's head. "What would you say if I said you were lying about having seen my escaped prisoner?"

Violet looked at Jack, trying to deduce an answer from his body language. He just stared at her hard for a moment. "We have no reason to lie," Jack commented through clenched teeth, taking the onus off Violet. "Like the lady said, the only thing we lied about was our relationship."

"Well, I think you're lying, and I am going to tell you why and how I know." George swung back to Jack and traced the barrel of the gun down his neck and across his back, ending in his belly. "Guess what I found halfway down the laneway leading out of here?"

"What?" Jack glared at George, despite the sinking feeling in his gut.

"I found a section of laneway where a vehicle must have gone off into the ditch and hit a tree. Made quite a dent in the tree—almost a match to the dent in the fender of that van out in your yard."

"So, how do you know one of us didn't do that," Jack spit out. "Not something we would have thought necessary to tell you," he added.

"There's more," George looked over at Violet. "Let me ask you, lady … you really love this guy? If so, how about telling me the truth. I don't want to have to hurt this old man."

Violet blushed. "Aren't you an officer of the law?" she asked. "What would your superiors say if they knew you were harassing two innocent civilians?"

"I don't think I am harassing two *innocent* civilians." George paused for effect. "We found something interesting at the accident scene; want to know what we found?"

When neither Jack or Violet commented, George finished his thoughts. "We found some bloody tissues in the ditch."

Another pause.

"I sent them with Larry to have them tested for DNA."

Another pause.

"Do you want to tell me whose blood it is, or should I just tell you who I think it is?"

"Enlighten us," Jack grumbled.

"Are you a betting man, Jack?" George asked.

"Not really."

"Well, I'll tell you, then—I think its Syd Lance's blood. I think he was here, and he took the van in an attempt to escape, but something happened that caused him to have an accident. I think he returned here, and for whatever reason, you either let him go or are hiding him somewhere. How am I doing so far?"

Before either Jack or Violet could answer, Jack's cell phone rang. "You want to answer that for me, Mike?" George motioned for his colleague to grab the phone.

Mike snatched the phone from the table before Violet could reach it. He pressed the button for the speaker but didn't say anything.

"Violet?" Frank's voice came over the line. "Violet? Are you there? You left this number for me to call." Frank's voice began to sound desperate.

Finally, Mike spoke: "You must be the husband of the little lady here; do I have that right?"

"Who the hell are you?" Frank shouted into the phone. "Where's my wife?"

Mike snickered. "You mean the lady shacked up with Jack—oops—have I said too much?"

"Frank!" Violet called out, but before she could say anything more, George shoved the gun in her face.

"Violet! Love, what's going on?" Frank's desperation was unmistakable to everyone in the cottage.

George took over the conversation: "Violet ain't liking you too much, Frankie boy; told us she found a real man up here, although I don't think he's too much of a man, hasn't protected his woman—I guess your woman—but he says he's been bangin' her pretty well." George couldn't help himself; he was on a roll.

Frank wasn't to be so easily fooled. He knew his wife; she wouldn't do anything like this. He'd picked up her

174

message when he'd pulled into a gas station to use the washroom. He'd heard the desperation in her voice, and when she'd called out his name on the phone, he'd heard it again. No, his wife was in trouble, and whoever else was there with her.

He deduced two men were holding his wife and another man prisoner, but why? Frank made a decision. He clicked end on his phone, then dialled 911.

George threw the cell phone back on the table and laughed hysterically.

~

Toby had finally come down from his tree and headed back to the cottage. However, as he'd come close, he'd heard a man inside with Violet, and it hadn't sounded like a friendly man. Toby hid in the long grass at the side of the cottage and listened. Just as he'd thought he'd heard enough, he saw Jack and George coming across the yard: Jack had a gun trained on him. Toby crouched down lower in the grass.

Finally, having heard enough, Toby turned and headed back to Jack's cottage. Tessa would be there soon with her reinforcements, he hoped. All he needed to do was convince her to follow him back to save Jack and Violet— and Syd Lance.

Chapter Twenty-six

L arry wasn't happy when George ordered him to take the evidence to the penitentiary and have forensics analyze the tissues. He'd asked George what he was going to do, but George told Larry it was none of his business.

George had taken out his cell phone and called someone to come and pick Larry up. As Larry waited for his ride, George had dispersed everyone else into the wooded area, telling them to turn over every needle, leaf, log, and twig.

After dropping the evidence off at the prison lab, Larry went straight to the warden's office. He knocked on the door but didn't wait for an answer. Bursting through the door: "Warden, we need to talk."

John Harley looked up from his paperwork, startled at the intrusion. "Larry! What are you doing here? Shouldn't you be with the search party tracking down our convict?"

"There's been a development, sir ... actually, more than one. And I don't think you are going to like some of what I am going to tell you."

The warden frowned, exasperated. "Well, get on with it; what's going on?"

Larry relayed his fears about George to the warden. "The man is completely out of control, warden. He resented the hell out of having me there in the capacity you sent me in on. It also seemed to me the crew he picked are in his pocket—if you know what I mean. They do his bidding without questioning any of his motives.

"We came across this couple in one of the cabins and George got right nasty with them—a husband and wife just taking a few days off away from the hub-bub of city life. When I tried to interfere, pointing out we had no right to be interrogating the couple, he got pissed and ordered me to back off."

"You mentioned he dispersed the team into the woods to continue his search; did he go with them?" the warden questioned, thinking he already knew the answer.

"I don't know for sure, but I know he left one of the men behind to keep a watch on the couple's cabin. I also overheard him say to another guy that he had something that needed to be taken care of and he'd catch up with them later."

The warden's eyebrows rose in surprise. He knew George was getting out of hand but, if he was picking on civilians now, for no reason, he was going too far. "I'm going to make a phone call and gather a couple men I know I can trust. Grab yourself a sandwich from the cafeteria if you want and meet them down front in half an hour. I want you to guide them back to this cottage and make sure nothing untoward is going on." The warden picked up his phone, dismissing Larry with a wave of his hand.

~

Syd was shivering from cold, or possibly fear. He hated that Jack had felt it necessary to tie him up, but he also understood why he'd had to do it. If the shoe were on the other foot, he would have done the same.

He had a lot of time to think about his life, what had been done to him, and what he had done to others. He thought about his years behind bars and the things he'd done to survive, things like he'd had to do when he wasn't in prison. Neither had been his choice. Syd thought about George and the number of times he'd used him, and for more than just sex. George used sex as a weapon to control Syd, promising if he didn't cooperate, there were others who might enjoy a sweet piece of ass. Syd cursed the fact that he was small, blond and blue-eyed. That alone was a green light for the perverts out there.

Syd thought about his father and how cruel he'd been. He thought of his mother, a gentle soul, who always tried to protect him and had the bruises to prove it. He thought of the little sister he never got to hold because his father had viciously struck his mother, thus beating his little sister before she could breathe in the world. Maybe she was the lucky one.

Thinking about it all caused Syd to tear up. He prayed he'd put his trust in the right people. Violet, he felt was sincere, but Jack … he wasn't too sure about him. But he was better than George.

~

Toby struggled through the woods. He was tired, but time was of the essence. *I can't afford to be old—no excuses, Toby—Jack and Violet are in danger! Must get to Tessa.* Toby pulled an extra shot of adrenaline from deep down and picked up his pace.

Soon he was rewarded with the sight of Jack's cottage, but the only vehicle in the yard was Jack's. Toby ran up the steps and curled up on the doormat. *May as well take a catnap to rejuvenate a bit before Tessa arrives.* He was sound asleep within seconds.

~

Tessa turned onto the laneway leading to Jack's cottage. She smiled at the thought of seeing him again but wasn't happy about the circumstances of the situation. She'd have preferred to be coming for a couple days of relaxation, not another case that demanded their attention. If only Toby had just stayed curled up in the cottage while Jack had been out fishing.

"Don't be selfish, Tessa," she grumbled to herself. "If Toby hadn't come upon the situation, this Violet woman could be in worse danger, or sadder yet, dead."

Tessa had to drive slowly because of the potholes in the lane. "I hope the cabin is in better condition than this laneway," she said as she tried to avoid another deep pothole.

Finally, she reached the cabin and saw a giant ball of orange lying in front of the door. Tessa smiled, recognizing Toby. "What are you doing here, Toby? Jack said you guys were at Violet's cabin, and I was to call him when I arrived..." Tessa automatically thought there was something terribly wrong.

She got out of her vehicle and headed up to the cottage. Toby heard the footsteps approaching and cracked open one of his eyes. Seeing it was Tessa, he shook himself awake, stood up, and stretched.

Tessa leaned down and gave him a scratch behind the ears. "What's going on, Toby? Where's Jack?" she asked, checking the door. It opened effortlessly into a quiet, empty space. Toby ran in after her and rubbed around her legs, meowing, before returning to the door and looking back at her.

"Do you want me to follow you somewhere?"

Toby meowed even louder.

Tessa glanced at her watch. The officer Captain Wagner called should be arriving any time now. She needed to wait for him. If Jack and Violet were in trouble, Tessa couldn't take the chance of helping them alone; she was a profiler, not an actual police officer. Not that she didn't know how to use a gun when necessary.

"We have to wait for my backup, Toby. He should be here anytime."

Toby meowed then growled, hoping that would stress the importance of the situation. *We need to go, Tessa! We can't wait!*

The sound of a motor approaching alerted Toby to the vehicle that a few seconds later crept into the yard. An elderly police officer exited, followed by another officer who appeared much younger. They approached the cottage and Tessa came down the porch steps to greet them.

"You Tessa?" the older officer asked, his voice quivering with age.

"Yes, you must be Sam Cranks," Tessa greeted him.

Sam nodded. "Want to fill me in on what's going on here?" He drove right to the point.

Tessa told Sam and his partner what little she knew. Then, "But I think there's something terribly wrong; Toby wants me to follow him."

"Toby? Who's Toby?" Sam asked, looking around.

Tessa pointed to Toby.

"A cat?"

She nodded. The young officer snickered.

"You're telling me the cat wants us to follow him?" Sam shook his head in disbelief.

"Yep." Tessa grinned. "And he wants us to get moving. Whatever is happening where he's taking us must be serious. Toby has an honorary detective certificate from the Brantford police for having helped solve more than one crime."

Not honorary, Tessa, but I won't argue the point now; we need to get going! Toby meowed and headed toward the woods. Tessa shrugged her shoulders and followed, looking back at Sam and the young officer: "You coming? We better get moving or we'll lose him."

Sam, still shaking his head in disbelief, decided he had no other recourse but to follow the cat and Tessa. "Never heard anything so ridiculous in all my life; a cat detective, my ass!" He noted his rookie officer hadn't moved yet: "You coming, Greg? Don't want to get too far behind the pussycat!"

Chapter Twenty-seven

Frank burst into the police station: "I need someone, a technical person who can track a location on a cell phone from the last call. My wife is in danger; she's being held by what sounds like some very dangerous men!" Frank's face was red from the physical exertion of running into the station and from his blood pressure, which had skyrocketed after the phone call to Violet.

The officer behind the reception desk stood and came around to Frank. "Please, sir, settle down and tell me what the problem is so I can point you in the right direction."

"I just told you! My wife is being held hostage—it might be that guy who escaped from prison here—I don't know, but I do know she's being held against her will. I … I have the number of the cell I called. Is there any way to trace its location?"

"Just a moment, sir. I'll get someone for you to talk with."

The young woman disappeared around the corner. Frank paced back and forth across the lobby, his blood pressure going up by the second. He kept looking at his watch, wondering where the girl had gone, what she was doing. Finally, she returned, followed by another officer.

"This is Officer Lawrence; he has certain information that might be of some help to you."

"Follow me, sir," the officer directed as he led the way into a small office down the hall from reception. "Have a seat," he pointed to a chair.

"I don't have time to sit down. The girl said you might have some information for me."

Officer Lawrence proceeded to tell Frank that his boss had had a call from a friend—fellow officer—from Brantford, and that one of his former officers was up here and in some kind of difficulty. There was a civilian woman in trouble, plus suspicion the escaped prisoner was in the mix.

"I think it best, though, that you wait here until we hear from my captain."

Frank's fist came down on the desk. "I can't wait— that's my wife out there! Can't you trace this number?" He held out his cell phone, showing the phone number Violet had called from.

"I'm afraid we can't trace a number unless the call is being made. We don't have the technology here to do that."

Frank started to crumble. His face went from dark pink to beat red. He clutched at his chest. His breathing came in gasps.

Lawrence rushed over to him: "Are you okay, sir?" He reached over and laid a hand on his shoulder. Then, seeing how pale Frank suddenly went, he stood and raced to the door. "Melanie," he called to the receptionist, "call 911. I think this guy is having a heart attack!"

~

The dogs weren't picking anything beyond where the van had crashed. Joe turned to the officer George had left in charge. "I don't think your guy went anywhere from here on foot. We're barking up the wrong tree, so to speak."

The officer scratched his head. "I think you might be right, but the boss thinks the guy is still in the vicinity. He thinks he doubled back to that cottage where the couple was, so why don't we head back in that direction and comb the woods around there? If he isn't in the cottage, he must be in the woods somewhere. George thinks the couple is hiding him; maybe even in another cabin close by."

"Okay, then. Let's head back, but stay in the woods," Joe suggested, "so the dogs will pick up any scent if there's one to pick up."

The men turned back in the direction of Violet's cabin but kept deep in the woods. The dogs kept their noses to the ground, but there was no baying for the longest time. Suddenly, one of the dogs started growling and picked up his pace.

~

Not far away, in a deep hole, lay Syd Lance wondering why it was taking Jack so long to return.

From the other direction, Toby was leading Tessa and the two officers who had come to assist her, and they were getting closer to where Syd was hidden.

Syd awoke to a lot of commotion above him: dogs baying, people shouting. He scuttled as best he could into a corner of the hole, his body shaking with fear. Jack had deserted him. Violet had abandoned him. They'd both betrayed what little trust he'd put in them, and now George was going to get his hands on him.

"Maybe that will be better in the long run," Syd whispered to the elements around him. "It will end my nightmare of a life."

Above him, the search team met face to face with Tessa, and Officers Sam and Greg, and Toby. Both groups gazed at the area Sam was holding the dogs back from. The baying was deafening, evidence that they'd found what they were looking for.

Sam stepped forward, taking the lead over Tessa, and approached one of the men who appeared to be the leader of the search party. He extended his hand: "I'm Captain Sam Cranks from the Kingston precinct. You, sir, would be…?"

Refusing the proffered hand, the officer smirked: "I'm Officer Duncan, and I'm with the search party looking for what I believe we've just found, from the actions of these dogs—a dangerous criminal who needs to be locked up behind bars again. I think it will be in your best interests if you and your companions step aside and let us retrieve whoever is down there under all that brush."

Tessa was about to say something when Sam spoke up again. "Don't think I can let you do that, son."

Duncan pushed his face right up to Sam's and leered: "Try and stop us."

Sam rested his hand on his gun holster. "Come on now, officer, I think we're both on the same side of the law and want the same thing for the poor bugger who's in that hole. How say, since you seem to be without benefit of a vehicle, I take him into custody and transport him to my jail until the warden can send someone out from the prison to get the kid back behind the penitentiary bars?"

Greg stepped up beside his boss, hand on his gun holster, despite the locusts that had taken root in the pit of his stomach. He didn't like the looks of the group of men in front of him. Tessa joined her colleagues.

Toby sat off at a distance, fearing the three big dogs that were only being controlled by their owner. *And I thought Emma's dog was a bruiser! These three will eat me alive! Of course, I'd be up that tree behind me quicker than I could catch a mouse in front of my nose. I sure hope Sam can defuse this situation but it's five against two and a half. Tessa doesn't have a gun and they have the dogs—not good, not good!* Toby hissed and growled toward the group, the best he could do.

Duncan heard the hiss and growl. He sneered. "You brought the pussycat along to protect you!" He turned to Joe. "Your dogs hungry, Joe?" he sniggered.

Joe was sizing up the situation and didn't like it. He was contracted by the prison to retrieve prisoners, and he had no stomach for what he was thinking might be going on here at the moment. He'd spent enough time with George to realize the man was up to no good most of the time, and this was one of those times. Joe pulled his dogs back and turned to Duncan.

"I think you should let this good officer take the prisoner back to his jail and go and find George and tell him the prisoner is now *safely* in custody, which was the mission we were sent to do. I'm sure Captain Cranks is a man of his word."

Tessa, thinking ahead as she always tried to do, pulled her cell phone from her pocket. "I can call your warden right now and have him meet us at the station with transport for the prisoner."

Duncan attempted to step forward, intent on grabbing Tessa's phone, but Joe, anticipating Duncan's move, placed himself and the dogs between the two groups. He looked over his shoulder to Tessa. "Make your phone call, lady."

"You bastard," Duncan shouted at Joe. "You've no right to interfere! Step aside before I arrest you for interfering with a criminal recovery."

A clicking sound came out of Joe's mouth and all three dogs stood at attention and bared their teeth at Duncan as he attempted to approach Joe. "You won't be arresting me or these good people, and you won't be taking the prisoner into your custody either."

Duncan and his team backed away from the snarling dogs. "Okay, have it your way—for now. But George isn't going to be happy, and he's one dude you don't want to cross." Duncan made a last weak attempt at scaring Joe.

"I know all about your boss, George," Joe snorted. "A real piece of work. But every kingdom eventually falls—a warning to you boys if you are too firmly planted in George's kingdom!"

Sam motioned for Greg to begin removing the branches from the top of the hole. Peering down, he saw the young prisoner curled in the fetal position, his face streaked with tears. Sam noticed his hands and feet were tied securely, disabling him from being able to climb out of the pit on his own.

"Go down and fetch him, Greg," Sam instructed.

Greg jumped into the hole and made his way over to Syd, who cowered against the earthen wall. "It's okay, buddy. You're safe. Captain Cranks is in control now." Greg stooped over to undo the rope around Syd's ankles.

Syd looked up into a pair of kindly eyes and relaxed as the rope fell away.

"Can you stand?" Greg asked as he assisted Syd to his feet.

Syd nodded.

Greg was hesitant as to how he was actually going to get Syd out of the pit, especially with what was going on above. He wasn't sure his boss could handle the search team, despite the old fellow, Joe, having stepped up to be on their side. He called up to Tessa: "Hey, Tessa—I'm going to boost Syd up to you—help him, please. His hands are still tied."

Tessa had finally reached the warden at the prison and she motioned for Greg to wait a second. "Is this the warden?" she asked, wanting to confirm she was talking to the right person.

"Yes, how can I help you?"

"My name is Tessa Bannister, and I am a criminal profiler. I was called up here because a colleague of mine found someone you lost, but there is a great deal more to the story, and no time now to tell it. The good news is, we have your prisoner, Syd Lance, in our possession—"

"Have you spoken to the retrieval team, to George, who is leading the search?" the warden interrupted.

"No." Tessa glanced at the group of men who were standing back from the bloodhounds. "However, some of your men are here and they aren't too happy about me and the people I am with bringing the prisoner back to you. In fact, if you were to ask my opinion, as a profiler, I would say these men would not deliver your prisoner to you alive." Tessa turned her back on George's team, not wanting them to hear what she was saying to the warden.

"I have a gut feeling they are under authority from your man, George, to make sure Syd doesn't make it back. I'm here with Captain Sam Cranks and another officer from the Kingston precinct. Joe, who owns the bloodhounds, is holding George's team back from taking Syd into their custody. I have the feeling Joe has seen enough not to trust them either."

"What is it I can do to make this easier for you, Tessa Bannister?"

"One of two things—your choice. We can take Syd to a cabin, which is not far from where we presently are, and I'll give you the address, or we can take him into Sam's police station, and you can pick him up there."

"What's the address where you're at?"

Tessa gave him the location and then added, "We also have some new evidence that needs to be revealed regarding your prisoner, and I have been instructed to pass on the following information, as brief as it is. All the details will be filled in later. Make sure Syd is put in solitary confinement and George is not allowed anywhere near him—or any of George's patsies."

"Okay, Tessa. I'm willing to look at any new evidence, not that it is going to exonerate our prisoner, but I'm a reasonable man. We'll get there as soon as possible; keep my prisoner safe until then." John Harley hung up the phone and cursed. He didn't need this kind of crap! What the hell was George trying to prove?

Tessa pushed the off button on her cell, then turned and reached for Syd's hands. Greg held his hands like a stirrup, and gave him a lift up, far enough so Tessa could grip his wrists and wrest Syd the rest of the way. She was surprised at how light he was. Once Syd was safely out of the hole, Tessa reached down and assisted Greg.

With a nod, Joe motioned for Tessa, Sam, and Greg to move along with Syd. "I'll keep these fellows here 'til you are well clear," he affirmed.

Toby, still fearing for his life with the three big dogs around, took the opportunity when everyone was busy to climb up one of the trees. *Oh no! Trouble coming! Oh, Jack, what have you gotten yourself into now?!* Toby saw George and Jack approaching; Jack's hands were tied behind his back, a gun pointed at his head. *Where's Violet?*

Oh damn! I bet he left the other guy with her, using her as leverage to get Jack to show him where he'd hidden Syd. Toby scuttled behind some leaves on the branch to ensure he wouldn't be seen.

Within seconds from Toby catching sight of George and Jack, George shoved Jack into the clearing near the hole. "Well, well, what do we have here?" George's voice grated harshly as he witnessed the standoff. "What's going on, Joe? You forget your place, turning your dogs on my men?"

In the second it took for Joe to turn and make sure Tessa and her people were on their way, George turned his gun on the dogs.

"Call them off, Joe, or I'll start picking them off—one by one!" George threatened.

Joe's mouth dropped in shock. He was speechless. He knew George was capable of a lot of things, but Joe hadn't dreamed the man would go so far as to threaten to kill the dogs. George must have toppled over the precipice of insanity.

George, realizing Syd was being whisked off, hollered: "Hey you, up there, running like scared little rabbits—turn yourselves around or there's going to be a bloodbath back here!"

Tessa stopped in her tracks. Sam and Greg, one on each side of Syd, hesitated. Syd began to shake, tears of terror flowing from his eyes.

"There's no escaping him!" Syd muttered between gasps of tear-filled breaths. "I don't want to be responsible for innocent deaths; just take me back to him."

Sam had been a police officer for a lot of years and he wasn't used to buckling to men like George. However, without being face to face with what was going on, he had no idea what was happening, and if Joe and his dogs were still safe.

Once again, George's voice reached them: "I don't see any bodies returning here, doggy number one is going to go to dog heaven!"

Tessa was trying to think of a way out of this situation. She looked at Sam and Greg, then made her decision. After all, she was a profiler; she should be able to buy time until the warden sent in support.

"Greg—you get Syd to safety, Sam and I will go back. I'll try and buy us some time. Move as fast as you can. Don't question me—I've negotiated before."

Greg took Syd and shoved him in front of him: "Okay, let's get going, as fast as your legs can take you."

Syd stumbled forward, not believing these people would go to this extent to save his life. As he and Greg disappeared in the trees, Tessa called out to George.

"Okay—hold your fire—we're coming back." Tessa nodded to Sam, who unlocked his gun holster. Tessa motioned to him to take it slow, giving Greg time to get away.

Toby was watching from his tree branch, trying to figure out his next move. *What's your plan, Tessa? Hope you have a good one. George is out of control. Oh, Jack, I wish I could jump down and knock that gun out of George's hand but the other guys all have theirs out now and those dogs … they're big bruisers, and they might not know if I'm one of the good guys or not! Better just wait and see what Tessa has planned.*

Joe had pulled his dogs back to him and they were sitting by his feet, low growls emitting from their throats. He was thinking about what he would do to George if the man shot his dogs—there wouldn't be a place on earth the prison guard would be safe. George had no idea what Joe was capable of when necessary. He scanned the area, looking for a possible out. The only place that would offer temporary shelter was the hole, but that would be short-lived, for sure. Joe realized there was nothing he could do and hoped the lady profiler had a plan.

George paced back and forth in front of his men, ordering one of them to keep a gun held to Jack's head. The rest of the crew had their weapons trained in the direction Tessa and Sam would be returning.

Finally, Tessa appeared, followed by Sam. She motioned for him to stand back, and proceeded to approach the group in the clearing. "Hello, Jack. You okay, my friend?"

Jack nodded.

"Where's your friend, the lady that was with you at her cabin?" Tessa continued, trying to get a lay of what was going on and how much leverage she was going to have with George.

George, wasting no time, answered for Jack: "The little lady is back at the cabin with one of my men. She's safe—well, will be safe—as long as I get what I want, and you know what I want, right?" George's lips curled upward in what should have been a smile; however, on him, it looked more like an evil grin. "Where's my prisoner?"

Tessa smiled. Jack noticed the look in her eyes and knew she had a plan. He hoped it worked.

"Your prisoner is safe and will soon be in the custody of the prison warden, which is what you wanted, isn't it?" Tessa tilted her head to the side.

"What do you mean?" George shouted angrily. "He's my prisoner and I was instructed to bring him in!"

"Well, we have a situation then, don't we?" Tessa looked around at the pointed guns. "I think you gentleman should lower your guns. If you were here in the clearing earlier, you know I made a phone call. I spoke with your warden and he is on his way to get Syd. Is following a rogue guard's direction going to benefit your jobs—your future in the prison—and in life?"

George whirled and faced his men. "Don't let the bitch get in your heads, boys. You know I have your best interests at heart—and you also know that if I go down, so do all of you! I know all your secrets, what you have done on the side, in and out of the prison, to line your own pockets."

Tessa observed each man, looking for one that might be willing to cave onto the side of good. For now, she needed to keep talking. "You've lost, George. I think you should call your man back at the cottage and tell him it's over and he's to let the woman go. Syd Lance is in custody. I think you also need to let Jack go. He's a police officer, and killing one will never sit well with any police force or jury."

"You know, you got a lot of guts, but I make a phone call to my buddy, and the lady is dead—unless I get the prisoner. Now I'm sure you can call whoever has him at the moment and get his ass here pronto. You aren't scaring me one bit." There was bravado in George's voice that denoted he meant business. He pulled out his cell phone and held it up in the air.

"Well, there's a problem, George," Tessa began. "I don't know the officer's number."

"Do you think I'm a fool?" George pointed to Sam, still standing in the background. "He's got the number."

Toby was taking all this in and finally made a decision. Violet was alone with another madman, and he needed to get to her before George could call him to kill her. Toby had no doubt George was whacky enough to carry through with his threat. Toby leaped from the tree, landing just a few feet from George.

"What the—!" George exclaimed. "That cat again!" He swung his foot at Toby, barely missing him, as Toby high-tailed it in the direction of Violet's cabin.

Turning to Tessa, George picked up where he'd left off: "Now, since you seem to be the one in charge, tell that guy back there to call his partner and get Syd back here."

Tessa stared at George, her eyes hard and unflinching. "Maybe we should hear from your friends there; I don't think some of them are up for what you are planning. Do they know exactly what you're thinking of doing to that young man? That he's not going to make it back alive?

"What was your plan, George? Were you going to do it in front of everyone? Probably not; you're too much of a coward to do that. You were going to make up some excuse and get Syd alone, weren't you? Accidents happen is what you would tell everyone when Syd showed up dead. Or maybe a shot in the back because he was trying to escape again? Who would believe he hadn't tried since he is already an escaped convict?"

Tessa looked at George's men. "Like I said before, are you willing to forfeit all your years of service and your families for this man? Isn't there one amongst you who can stand up to him? He's just a man—a bully."

Finally, one of the men spoke up. "We have no choice, lady. He's got too much on us. If I were you, I'd just do as he says, then we can all go our separate ways."

Tessa laughed, low and sarcastically. "You think so? We all know too much now. George can't take a chance on letting us go when we know he intends to kill that boy, can he?" She paused. "So, is he going to pull the trigger or is he going to tell one or more of you to? Which one of you is willing to kill a police officer?"

George noticed the hesitation on a couple of his team members. He had to think quickly of something that would make this woman realize he meant business. "I see you think you have me over a barrel, but you don't. I have the advantage here, and I'm going to take that right now." He chuckled as he began to dial a number on his cell phone.

Pushing the speaker button, George held the phone up so everyone could hear what he was saying, and the other side of the conversation.

"Hey," a voice came over the speaker. "What's the score, boss?"

George laughed. "At the moment, I'd say it's one nothing for me! How's the little lady doing?"

"Not bad, other than she pissed her pants; didn't tell me in time how bad she had to go and it took me a while to untie her." The laugh that came through the phone was pure evil.

Tessa and Jack cringed.

"Well, Nabil, I have a situation here that I need a little help with. I told these good people, who have scooped our prey away from us, I wanted him back, and they don't want to listen. So, I guess I have no other alternative than to convince them the hard way that I mean business." George tarried a moment before resuming the conversation.

"But, just to show I'm a reasonable man, Nabil, I'm going to give these people five minutes—you hear that lady in the cottage? Your life is in the hands of some hotshot police profiler who thinks she can manipulate me! If she doesn't give me what I want within five minutes, Nabil, you are to shoot your hostage. If they give me what I want, I'll call you and they can be happy they've saved an innocent woman's life."

"Got it, boss." Nabil disconnected the conversation.

George turned back to Tessa: "So, lady, what's it to be? You going to make the phone call to have a no good lowlife like Syd brought back to me, or should we just continue and have the responsibility of the death of an innocent woman on your head? Your choice."

~

Toby ran as fast as his legs could carry him. *I have to get to Violet! Please let me get to her in time! I'll figure out what I'm going to do once I get there, but I can't allow anything happen to such a sweet lady!*

Soon, Toby saw the cabin. He raced across the yard, hoping a window or the door would be open. Luck was with him: whoever left the cabin last had not closed the door. Toby shoved his nose through the opening and entered the cabin.

Violet was sitting on a chair in the middle of the room. Her hands were tied behind her back and her feet were bound to the chair legs. Toby noticed her clothes were wet. *Bastard! How could they do this to a harmless woman? Prison guards, who were supposed to be on the law's side!*

The man in the room was glancing at his watch but when Toby burst into the room, he looked over to the door in alarm, then laughed. "Well looky here, Violet, a pussycat has come to rescue you." Nabil looked at his watch again. "Too bad, though, your time is up!" He took a gun out of the waistband of his pants and pointed it at Violet's head. "Say goodbye, sweetheart … any last words?"

Violet's eyes were wide with terror. She couldn't believe her life was going to end this way, all because she'd wanted to get away from her lonely life and have some time to do what she wanted to do—write a novel. Now, she'd never be able to do that—not the one she'd started or Syd's story. She knew if George went through her computer and saw what was written there, he'd destroy it.

As Nabil pulled back the hammer on the gun, the sound of a car coming to a screeching halt in the yard filled the air. Toby took a jump of faith, hoping whoever was in that car was friendly. Nabil hesitated a moment, just long enough for Toby to leap at his arm and knock the gun out of his hand. A second later, Larry and two other guards burst through the door.

Seeing the gun on the floor and Violet tied up and terrified, Larry directed his companions to restrain Nabil as he went straight to Violet and undid her restraints. She fell into his arms, but after a few seconds, pushed back from him and reached for Toby.

Looking at Larry, she explained, "He saved my life. If he hadn't knocked the gun out of that guy's hand, I'd be dead right now." She pulled Toby close to her and buried her face in his fur.

All in a day's work for a detective cat like me…all in a day's work! Toby purred loudly and rubbed his head on Violet's chin.

Chapter Twenty-eight

George looked at his watch and grinned, confident that Violet was dead. "Proud of yourself, lady? You just killed a woman."

Tessa sucked in her breath. She prayed that wasn't so. One thing she'd learned over the years when negotiating with madmen like George was that most of them were bluffers. She hoped it was right in this case, as well.

"I'll just call Nabil and confirm the job is done." George dialled the number and waited for Nabil to answer. After six rings, he was about to hang up when the line opened and a familiar voice answered, but it wasn't Nabil.

"Hello, George," Larry said casually. "You looking for Nabil? Just a second, I'll get him for you … oh, wait—I can't. He's handcuffed in the back of my car. Seems he was going to shoot this nice lady here, but a big orange cat knocked the gun out of his hand just before I burst into the cabin. You wouldn't know anything about that would you, George?"

George had again placed the phone on speaker, and Tessa, Joe, Sam, and Jack listened to the conversation. George's face paled. Tessa and the others smiled. Even some of George's own men grinned.

Recovering from his initial shock, George returned to his arrogant self. "So what if you have my guy in your custody, Larry? I have a few people here just waiting for me to drill a bullet into them—"

Larry laughed. "I don't think so, George; it's over for you. The warden is on his way and he has plenty of backup. He knows all about your activities, and he's none too pleased with you at the moment. I'd reconsider your next action, George."

George wasn't going down without a fight. He fired a shot into the air, hoping to frighten everyone. However, his men, realizing George's game was over, stepped forward, guns drawn on George.

"It's over, boss, lower your weapon," one of them ordered. "We ain't willing to kill any cops, not even for you. We might be going down for some of the things we've done but at least it won't be on death row!"

George hesitated as a whirring sound filled the woods. He looked up and saw a helicopter; recognizing it as the one used by the prison. Slowly, he lowered his weapon. It was as though a soft wind blew through the woods as everyone let out a sigh of relief.

Sam was the first to step forward. He took the gun from George's hand, then drew out his handcuffs and secured George's arms behind his back. "Looks as if the helicopter is going to land on the beach by the cabin where Greg was taking the prisoner." He turned to Tessa and Jack. "I'll take this fellow back that way; I'm sure the warden will want to take him into custody. I assume you guys want to get back to the lady's cabin and make sure she's okay."

Joe stepped forward with his dogs. "I'll accompany you, Sam, make sure this bastard gets to where you're taking him." Joe approached George and shoved his face up to his. "You're a lucky man that I don't end you right here for what you threatened to do to my dogs! But for now, I, and my boys, will make sure the system does their job and puts you behind bars, where I'm sure you'll be well looked after!" Joe chuckled.

George paled for the second time, knowing what awaited him behind bars. He kicked himself for having not gotten out of the racket he'd started sooner. He could be basking on a beach somewhere now, not heading to a ten by ten cell with bars and no window, and a lot of prisoners who might make it their mission to pay him back for what he'd done to them.

The other members of George's team seemed confused as to what they should do. They didn't trust that George wouldn't turn them in, having been privy to and part of many of his schemes. Sam solved their problem for them.

"I think you boys better come along with Joe and me. So far, to my knowledge anyway, you had no idea what George's real intentions were toward the escaped prisoner. Might bode well for you boys if you were to testify about what you witnessed here."

After the group left for Jack's cabin, Tessa untied Jack's hands. She moved immediately into his arms, and after about a minute of just holding each other, Jack took Tessa by the hand.

"Let's get to Violet's cabin and check on her and Toby. Sounds like the old fur ball had a lot to do with saving her life."

Tessa smiled and fell into step with the man she'd begun to think might be a big, important part of her future.

Chapter Twenty-nine

When Tessa and Jack arrived at Violet's cottage, she was curled up on the couch with Toby sitting on her lap. She was stroking his back absentmindedly. Larry was in the kitchen making tea.

Jack noticed a cruiser with an officer leaning against it and someone in the backseat. He assumed it was the man who had been ready to kill Violet and Larry had asked the officer to wait until someone came to be with Violet; Larry hadn't wanted her to be alone after such an ordeal.

Hooking a thumb in the direction of the car, "Thanks a lot, Larry. I got the impression earlier, when we first met, you were an upright guy—nothing like George."

Larry walked over and handed Violet her cup of tea. "I'm just glad no one got hurt. Now that you're here with Violet, I need to go and get Nabil to the police station and get him processed."

Violet looked up, a startled look on her face. "I need to find Frank. I know he was up here somewhere, and he's probably worried sick, going crazy trying to find me." She looked up at Larry. "Can you do me one more favour? See if you can locate my husband?"

Larry tipped his hat to Violet. "I'll do what I can, I'm sure he's still in the area. Give me a number I can call; I'll phone, either way."

Jack retrieved a piece of paper and wrote his cell phone number on it and handed it to Larry. "Best you call my cell. Tessa and I will stay with Violet until we hear from you."

With Larry gone, Jack introduced Tessa to Violet. "This is Tessa Bannister, my friend, and a criminal profiler. She's the one I called to get in contact with someone we could trust in this area. Tessa, as you've probably already guessed by now, this is Violet," Jack grinned and then added, "Toby's friend."

Everyone laughed.

An hour passed, during which Jack and Tessa filled Violet in on what had gone on in the woods. Finally, Jack's cell phone rang. He grabbed it quickly, knowing how anxious Violet was to hear any news of her husband.

"Hello."

"Hey, Jack—Larry, here. I've got good news and bad news. I know where Violet's husband is, the bad news is, he's in the hospital—had a heart attack here at the police station trying to find his wife." Larry proceeded to give Jack the address of the hospital and the room number. "I called the hospital just before calling you, and they said he's stable and keeps asking for his wife."

"Thanks, Larry. We'll get Violet to the hospital right away." Jack turned the phone off and filled Violet in on where her husband was.

"This is all my fault!" she cried. "I should never have come here." Pulling herself together, she grabbed her purse and the keys that were sitting by the computer and took off out the door. "You guys coming?" she called back.

"You bet," Jack replied. "I'll drive."

Toby raced out the door as well, beating all the humans to the van. *You aren't leaving me behind!*

"Okay, old man, get in," Jack chuckled as he opened the door.

~

The warden met Sam and Joe and the remainder of the search party at Jack's cabin. He strolled toward the approaching group, straight for George.

George knew what was coming to him. The warden was a hard man and took no nonsense from anyone, even to the point of resorting to physical punishment in some cases. George anticipated this might be one of those cases.

"Hello, George," the warden began. "I've heard some very unscrupulous rumours about you lately … didn't want to believe them, especially about one of my best guards. Been around a long time, eh, George—maybe a little too long." There was a pause in which the warden took out a cigarette and lit it. Handing it to George, he continued: "I've looked away from some of your activities … hell, a man has to make a bit on the side occasionally, doesn't he? However, lately you seemed to be taking more liberties than you should. Then—can you believe this—I get a call from a lady who says she's a criminal profiler, and tells me a story about what is going on in these here woods." The warden jut his chin toward the trees. "She tells me one of my guards—George, she said his name was— one of my guards was out of control and threatening to kill people, demanding the return of an escaped prisoner to him. She went on to say how the prisoner was safe and in the custody of a police officer but that this George fellow was still demanding he be released into *his* custody. Now, why would that be, George? Why weren't you just happy with Syd being recaptured, even if it wasn't you who made the collar? Can you answer me that, George?" The warden took out another cigarette, for himself this time.

George stood there, waiting for the final blow he knew was coming his way any moment. He flexed his stomach muscles. When it came, it was not to his stomach as anticipated—not at first.

The warden took his foot and swept George's feet out from under him. Without warning, he kicked him hard in the stomach, knocking the wind from him. The warden turned and walked away.

Everyone in the yard stood in shocked silence at the justice the warden had delivered. He stopped in front of Joe and his dogs and extended his hand: "I want to thank you personally for all your help, Joe. I also want to apologize for George's behaviour. I give you my guarantee he will be dealt with accordingly. Your usual compensation will be sent out to you, plus a bonus for this extra inconvenience you've had to endure." The warden shook Joe's hand, holding it a bit longer after the initial shake. "I trust this episode will not jeopardize our relationship."

Joe was not one to bear a grudge against a man who'd never done him a wrong, and the warden had always been a fair man. "We're all good," he responded. "Now, if you don't mind, I'd like to get my dogs home; it's been a long couple days."

"I've ordered the vehicles you guys left at the gas station to be brought here; they should be arriving any time now," the warden informed.

~

Syd watched the entire scene from inside the cabin where Greg was standing guard over him. What he saw the warden do to George gave him hope for his case. He prayed the nightmare of his past few days was over, and Violet would be faithful to her word and get his story to the warden. Maybe, just maybe, if she did, his case would get reopened and others who had done him wrong would find themselves behind bars, as well. Syd knew he was still going to have to serve out his sentence, and because he'd tried to escape, there was also the possibility he would have some time added on.

The warden spoke to some of the people he'd brought with him and Sam. "We'll take Syd from here, Sam," he began. "Thanks for all your assistance. I'll be in touch to get statements from you and your man, and the others who were involved." He motioned to one of his men to go into the cottage and bring out the prisoner. "As for George, I think he should go with you."

With Syd loaded into the helicopter, along with the men the warden brought with him, the warden motioned to George's team and his vehicle. "I drove here, so you boys may as well ride back with me."

Chapter Thirty

As soon as Jack pulled up to the hospital door, Violet and Tessa jumped out and rushed through the front doors. It had already been agreed Jack would follow them after parking the vehicle.

The lot was full of cars, being visitors' hours at the hospital, and it took Jack almost five minutes to finally land a spot.

"Been a rough couple days, eh, old man?" he said to Toby.

You got that right. Toby was curled up on the back bench of the vehicle, content to get a good nap in before his next adventure.

"You okay here, Toby, while I go in to meet Violet's husband?"

Toby opened his eyes and then closed them quickly. *Of course I'm okay.*

Jack chuckled and got out of the van and headed to the hospital. Walking into Frank's room, he noticed Tessa sitting in a chair in the corner: Violet was standing beside the bed, holding her husband's hand. The reunited couple had tears streaming down their cheeks.

As Jack entered, Violet turned to face him and smiled through her tears. "Jack, I want you to meet my husband, Frank. Frank, this is Jack." She looked behind Jack at the empty doorway. "Where's Toby? I want Frank to meet the cat that saved my life."

Jack cleared his throat and grinned: "Toby's catching up on his sleep. There'll be plenty of time once Frank gets out of here for him to meet the old cat."

Tessa stood and made her way to Jack, hooking her arm into his. "Why don't we give these two some privacy?" Turning to Violet, "We'll be in the cafeteria. Nice to meet you, Frank. Get better soon."

After Tessa and Jack left, Frank reached for Violet's hand again. He was unable to speak because he was still hooked up to oxygen, but his eyes said it all.

Violet bowed her head: "I'm so sorry, Frank; I'll never do anything so foolish again. I've made such a mess … how will you ever forgive me?"

In response, Frank squeezed her hand.

A half-hour later, a nurse entered the room and told Violet she'd have to leave, visiting hours were over. She invited Violet to the nurses' station to get updated on Frank's condition.

"Your husband will be out of here in a couple days," she began. "It was a minor heart attack, caused by elevated blood pressure. He will need to recuperate somewhere quiet for a bit, though."

Violet thanked the nurse for all they'd done for Frank, and as she walked to the cafeteria to meet Tessa and Jack, she sent a prayer to God, thanking Him for saving not only her life, but her husband's.

As she entered the cafeteria, Violet saw Tessa and Jack in earnest conversation. She thought how lucky she was to have met such decent people. If it hadn't been for Toby, she wouldn't have met them. What a blessed day that was when the old cat wandered into her cottage. Violet approached their table; they looked up and smiled at her.

"How's your husband doing?" Tessa inquired, motioning to the empty chair beside her.

Violet sat. "The nurse said it was a minor attack, but that he should take some time to relax somewhere quiet. I was thinking of staying at the cottage with him for a couple weeks since it's already paid for. He'll enjoy the peacefulness of the lake."

"Sounds like a great idea," Jack put in. "Tessa and I were just talking about staying up here for another week, as well. The police will want to talk to all of us and get our statements about what went down. It will be easier than driving back and forth from here to Brantford."

"Maybe we could get together for a barbeque," Violet suggested. "And I'd like to take a trip up to the prison and see Syd. I want him to know I am serious about getting his story out there. At first, I was just writing his story as a ruse to buy some time, but after hearing what he went through, and then meeting George and seeing what he was capable of, I changed my mind. Men like George, and like the ones who abused Syd, need to be brought to justice."

"Would you like me to accompany you to the prison?" Tessa asked. "Jack can stay with Frank," she added.

"That would be nice of you," Violet replied, standing. "I think I would like to get back to the cottage now, though. I'm beginning to feel the exhaustion set in … oh, one thing: do you think you could loan me Toby for a couple days? I'd rather not be alone. Just until Frank gets out of the hospital."

Jack grinned and chuckled. "I'm sure Toby won't mind."

~

Instead of cooking supper after such a long day, Tessa suggested they pick up some chicken dinners from the Swiss Chalet she'd noticed close to the hospital. Everyone agreed it was a good idea.

After the meal, Tessa and Jack headed back to Jack's cottage, leaving Violet and Toby sound asleep in the bedroom. Jack had asked Violet if they could borrow her van since it was late and he and Tessa preferred not to walk through the woods in the dark.

"We'll bring it back first thing in the morning," Jack affirmed.

When Tessa and Jack returned to his cottage, Jack suggested they make a fire. He was tired but knew he wouldn't be able to fall asleep until he'd relaxed a bit. A campfire by a beautiful, calm lake should do the trick.

Sitting by the fire, Tessa opened the conversation. "How does Toby do it, Jack? The old cat seems to have a nose for flushing out trouble."

"Your guess is as good as mine," Jack chuckled. "Guess the old boy has hung around me for too long, listening to all the cases I mulled over when we were alone at night."

Tessa laughed softly. "He's a brave cat. People say cats are selfish and only think of themselves, but Toby is different."

"Don't you go painting him as a saint," Jack tried hard to look stern. "He's still a cat—trust me on that one!"

They sat for a few more moments, listening to the night sounds: the crickets, the frogs, the soft lapping waves on the lake. As though on cue, they both reached out a hand to the other, and sat there, hands clasped, staring into the fire. After a time, Tessa heard soft snoring coming from the chair beside her. Looking over at Jack, she saw his head had fallen to his chest. She leaned back in her chair and stretched her legs out in front of her. It was a warm enough night; why wake a sleeping lion?

Chapter Thirty-one

Syd spent his first night back behind bars in solitary confinement. The warden told him he would be there for a while, saying it was for his own protection. For the most part, Syd agreed, all depending on who his guards ended up being. Hopefully, not one of George's lackeys.

Unable to fall asleep right away, Syd paced his cell, thinking about how the past few days had gone, how the events would carve his future. He wondered over and over if Violet would be sincere to her word now that he was incarcerated again. It was essential to his easily broken faith in humankind that she was.

Finally, Syd lay down on the narrow cot. He stared up at the grey ceiling and visions of the men who had abused him flashed before his eyes. He began to feel the anger build at not having been able to take his revenge. His fists were still clenched as he finally fell asleep.

In the middle of the night, Syd felt someone shaking his shoulder. "Wake up, boy," a voice ordered.

Syd jolted up and scuttled back to the top of his cot, clutching his knees to his chest. *Oh, God! Not again!* His eyes were wide with fright.

"It's okay, boy ... I'm not here to hurt you. Heard you yelling out in your sleep; must have been having a nightmare. Didn't want you waking the others on the block. Some of them can get right mean when they don't get a good night's sleep."

Syd opened his eyes wide enough to study the guard in front of him. He wasn't one of the usual guards, one of George's friends. The guard sat on the edge of the bed.

"Warden asked me to keep an eye on you … told me some of your story. Had a rough go in life, haven't you? Told me some lady is going to tell your story and maybe get your sentence reduced. If you ask me, I think you should do your time for killing that man and maybe a bit extra for causing us all this trouble with your attempted escape, but who am I to say? I might have done the same thing if someone treated me the way you were treated."

Syd sat quietly, listening to the guard droll on, wishing he would leave, fearing what he might do if he stayed—like some of the others had done before. Finally, the guard stood and walked toward the door. Before leaving, he turned and smiled.

"See you around, Syd."

His statement sent a shiver down Syd's spine.

~

Jack awoke just as the sun crept into the morning hours. He glanced over at Tessa, who had fallen asleep on her chair. Reaching out, he gently shook her shoulder. She opened her eyes, and stretched her arms up in the air and yawned.

"Good morning," she whispered sleepily, shuffling up in the chair and then leaning over with her elbows on her knees. "I guess we both fell asleep."

Jack stood and looked at his watch. Five o'clock. "Guess we better take some time to freshen up and then make our way over to Violet's. I'm sure she won't be sleeping in too late with Toby there. You can shower first if you like; I'm going to take a walk down to the lake."

Tessa had a bright idea. "Why don't we change into our bathing suits and both go down to the lake for an early morning swim?" she suggested seductively. "Used to be one of my favourite times of the day when I was at camp," she added.

"Hmmm ... sounds like a plan."

Fifteen minutes later, Tessa and Jack were floating in the lake, enjoying the warm water and the tranquility of early morning, broken only by the chorus of birds awakening in the trees.

~

Toby woke early, as well. He gazed at Violet, who was still peacefully sleeping, then jumped down off the bed and padded out into the living area. Fortunately, Violet had the foresight the night before to leave the window open for Toby in case he needed to go out and attend to business.

Jumping up onto the windowsill, then down to the porch, Toby headed for the lake. Even though he wasn't fond of getting his feet wet, the water breaking onto the shore was a comfort to him. Upon reaching the beach, Toby sat down on a scrubby piece of grass and gazed out over the lake.

Well, Jack, our peaceful two-week vacation sure turned into a doozer, eh! Good thing you know people in law enforcement or we might be toast by now—you probably at the bottom of the lake with cement around your ankles and me ... well, perhaps left to the elements in the forest. George likely would have crippled me so I couldn't climb a tree.

Poor Violet ... I wonder what he would have done to her? Once he realized we were all lying to him, he got even nastier. I guess things will be okay now that she's going to be reunited with her husband. Poor guy must have been worried sick when his wife just up and left him like that ... I know she didn't mean any harm to him, she told me so last night, but boy, was she sorry for what she did.

And that poor kid, Syd. I wonder how he spent the night? Hope that warden is as good as his word and he'll protect him. He sure has a hard-luck story, a bit unbelievable but after meeting George ... how do they let guys like that work in a prison system?! I know inmates all have a story to tell about why they ended up behind bars, but really, a lot of them were victims of the life they were born into.

Toby's thoughts were very un-catlike. He couldn't think of another one of his feline acquaintances who would be thinking of crimes and how to solve them. They'd be thinking about their next meal and how many catnaps they could get throughout the day. Toby's thoughts wandered to a cute Siamese he'd become acquainted with while he was in the hospital recuperating from saving Jack's friend, Andrew.

Time to head back, I guess ... Violet will be getting up soon, and Tessa and Jack should be here any time. I wonder how they spent their night... Toby wandered back to the cottage just in time to see Tessa and Jack drive up and park.

"Hey there, Toby, old man," Jack called out as he exited the van, "you're up early."

Toby sauntered over to Jack and rubbed around his legs. *Missed you too, older man!*

Jack bent over and tousled the fur behind Toby's ears.

As the three entered the cottage, Violet was filling a pan with water to make a pot of tea. "Just in time," she said, turning the stove on. "I was about to start breakfast. Bacon and eggs?"

"Sounds perfect," Tessa replied, joining Violet in the kitchen area. "Let me help."

Within a half-hour, they were sitting down to a hearty breakfast and Toby was rewarded with a few pieces of cut-up bacon mixed in with the kibble Jack had thought to bring over.

"I'd like to go to the prison today, after seeing Frank," Violet mentioned as she and Tessa cleared the table.

"Sounds like a plan," Tessa replied.

~

After visiting Frank, and being assured he was doing fine, Tessa and Violet left for the prison. Jack and Toby had opted to stay back at the cottages to do some tidying up. Jack was hesitant at first because he felt he should be with the women when they went to the prison, but Tessa assured him she was a big girl and had been in several before—part of her job, she laughed.

"I've never been inside a prison before," Violet commented, making small talk.

"It can be scary but we'll be well-protected," Tessa noted. "I think we should stop by the warden's office first, though, before seeing Syd."

Violet nodded in agreement.

As the two women approached the main gate, Tessa flashed her I.D. and the door was opened for them. "Could you direct us to the warden's office, please?" she asked.

"One moment. I'll page someone to take you there."

A few minutes later, a young guard appeared. "Follow me," he said.

After five minutes walking down several hallways, the guard stopped in front of a door and knocked. "Here we are," he informed.

"Come in."

The guard opened the door for Tessa and Violet and motioned them in.

"Thank you, Michael," the warden said. "You may wait outside the door; I'll need you to guide the ladies back out shortly."

Tessa tilted her head to the side, wondering what the warden meant. Maybe he didn't realize they were here to see Syd.

"Have a seat, ladies, and tell me what I can do for you today? I am not quite prepared to take your statements as to what happened, so I am afraid you've probably made this trip for nothing." The warden smiled, showing a set of perfect false teeth.

"Actually," Violet spoke up, "we came to see Syd."

"Oh." The warden scratched his head, leaned back in his chair, and clasped his hands on his stomach. His eyes narrowed as he studied the women in front of him. "I'm afraid you've wasted a trip. Syd had a rough night and is unable to see anyone today. In fact, I just sent the doctor down to solitary to check on him."

Alarm bells went off in Tessa's head, but she knew from experience it was better not to make waves with a man like the warden. She stood and nodded. "Well,

216

hopefully, he will be feeling better by tomorrow when we return. Let's go, Violet."

Violet looked bewildered but she followed Tessa's lead. "Yes, hopefully, Syd will be able to see us tomorrow."

"I'll call if he's able to have visitors," the warden said through clenched teeth. The women, especially the profiler, were proving difficult.

"No need," Tessa returned as she and Violet walked to the door. "We'll be back tomorrow."

Once the women left the office, the warden brought his fist down on the desk. "Damn! The last thing I need is a nosey profiler with major connections poking around in my prison." He picked up his phone and dialled a number. "Send Henry up to my office when he's finished his shift."

Ten minutes later, a young guard stood in the doorway. "Come in, Henry. Have a seat." The warden pointed to a chair in front of his desk. He paused for what seemed like forever to Henry before speaking. "What happened last night? You were supposed to watch out for Syd Lance and keep him safe."

Henry lowered his head and cleared his throat. He'd had no part in what took place and he'd not dared to interfere. One didn't mess with the kind of hierarchy there was in the prison guard system. George, despite being behind bars, still had a long reach and more than enough faithful followers.

"I'm waiting," the warden tapped his fingers impatiently on his desk.

"I heard the patient crying out in his sleep, and I went to see what was wrong," Henry began. "He was having a nightmare, so I sat with him for a bit. He was acting weird, though, as if I was going to do something to him … pushed himself back into a corner on his bed. I finally left and told him to get some sleep. As I was leaving solitary to make my report, a couple guards walked past me."

"Do you know their names?"

"No sir, I haven't been here long enough to get to know many of the guards by name," Henry replied.

"Describe them for me."

Henry proceeded to describe the two guards he'd seen and the warden shook his head in disgust. He knew exactly who they were.

"Did you happen to see where they went once they were in the solitary cell block?"

"I did."

"You know, Henry, I'm going to need a more specific answer."

Henry's face blanched with fear. "They went to Syd's cell," he finally answered.

"And you didn't think to call for backup under the circumstances?" The warden's eyes narrowed menacingly.

Looking at the warden, Henry cleared his throat again. "One learns quickly that there are some things you just let be. They gave me a look before they entered his cell and it wasn't friendly!"

"I see." The warden frowned, eyes narrowed as he continued: "Had you called for backup, that prisoner would not be in the infirmary right now." The warden paused and turned his back on Henry before asking the next question. "Do you have any idea how many times Syd Lance has been sent to sickbay since he's been here?"

"No, sir."

"Too many." The warden informed as he turned back. He approached Henry, leaning on his desk as he looked into the guard's eyes. "You know, Henry, I know there's a lot of underhanded things going on in my prison. Some of the stuff I can turn a blind eye to, but when it comes to one of my prisoners being beaten and God knows what else, I try and draw a line. I'd hope some of my guards could help me with this. Wouldn't you agree that would be a good thing?"

Henry nodded.

The warden stood. "Okay, then. Now that we have that out of the way, here's what I'd like you to do: you are to go to the infirmary and stand guard over Syd. Make sure no one other than the doctor has access to him. Do I make myself clear?"

"Yes, sir."

"I will send a replacement for you in a few hours, another guard I know I can trust. His name is Larry, badge number 23678. No one but him is to replace you. You are dismissed. Don't let me down, Henry."

"I won't, sir," Henry replied as he stood and scuttled out of the room toward the infirmary.

Once Henry was gone, the warden hit his fist on the wall. He was upset about what transpired the night before in Syd's cell. John Harley didn't really care what happened to the kid—he knew Syd had been a victim of George's games before. But there were outsiders interested in protecting Syd and it seemed they weren't going away anytime soon; the warden couldn't have too many prying eyes inside his prison walls.

"The sooner I get their statements about what went on out there, the sooner I can send them on their way," he muttered as he returned to his desk and picked up his phone.

Chapter Thirty-two

"There's something wrong," Tessa informed Jack when she and Violet returned to the cottage.

Toby's ears perked up. *Now what? I thought we had this case wrapped up tight.* Toby shuffled into a sitting position so he could hear better.

Jack frowned. "What do you mean? Didn't you get to see Syd?"

Tessa shook her head. "The warden said there were some issues in the night and the doctor has apparently been dispatched to Syd's cell in the solitary block."

"And these issues were?" Jack's eyebrows furrowed with intensity.

"He wouldn't say." Tessa pursed her lips. "I'd like you to go with us tomorrow."

Toby looked from Jack to Tessa and back again. *Don't wait until tomorrow, Jack. I got a bad feeling about this—big cover-up!* Toby's tail switched angrily and he flattened his ears. A growl slipped from his throat as he made his way to the door. He sat and meowed.

Violet smiled for the first time since her and Tessa's arrival. "I think Toby is telling us we can't wait until tomorrow to do something," she stated. "Maybe we should go to the police station and talk to Captain Sam. Hopefully, George is still behind bars."

Jack scratched his head. "A man like George has a long reach; even if he isn't somewhere physically, there are enough of his followers that will probably carry out anything he wants. We already saw how he controlled the search team. If there was a court hearing this morning, George could have been released on bail." He paused. "I think Toby and Violet are right—we need to check on his whereabouts. We can stop and see Frank afterward."

"Let's grab a bite to eat before we go," Violet suggested, heading to the kitchen.

~

An hour later, the three companions, plus Toby, were on their way to the police station to talk to Captain Sam. When they arrived, he was busy in his office going through a pile of papers. He didn't look happy. As Tessa, Violet, Jack, and Toby were shown into his office, he looked up and scowled.

Standing and coming around to meet his visitors, Sam's voice had a tinge of sarcasm. "To what do I owe this honour?" He looked down at Toby, who was sitting between Tessa and Violet. "You brought your cat?" Sam's eyes narrowed as he studied the group.

Jack was quick to answer: "Toby was instrumental in the solving of this case, and he actually saved Violet's life by knocking the gun out of the guard's hand just as he was about to shoot her."

"I see." Sam returned to his desk, motioning to the chairs. "Have a seat and tell me what brings you in here. I have a lot to do, and a meeting in about a half-hour."

Tessa drove right to the point. "We'd like to know if George is still in your custody."

"Nope. There was a hearing earlier this morning, he was released on bail."

"Who put up the bail money?" Jack inquired.

"I believe it was the warden," was Sam's curt reply. Jack got the impression Sam wasn't happy about the situation.

"The warden?" Tessa absorbed this information, wondering why the prison warden would do such a thing.

"Not much that happens up at the pen' surprises me anymore," Sam replied. "Sometimes I think a change of the guard every few years would be a good thing." Sam stood and walked to the door. He opened it, indicating their time was up. "I'll be in touch about your statements regarding what went on in the woods. I'd do it now but, like I said, I have a meeting."

Jack, Tessa, Violet, and Toby left the office and walked back to the van. As they drove away, silence hung like a dense fog in a deep valley. There was something rotten going on at the penitentiary, but how to get to the bottom of it, and how to save Syd before it was too late, was going to be a big problem.

Jack was first to break the silence. "I think we should see Frank first," he suggested.

No one answered him, so he took the initiative and headed to the hospital.

When they walked into Frank's room, he was sitting up eating lunch. "Hey, guys," Frank smiled. "I swear, I'll never complain about Violet's cooking again," he grinned, a twinkle in his eyes. "Not that I ever did," he added quickly.

Violet just about choked, but a smile still played on the corner of her lips. "Not much, and I'll be sure to remind you of that if you ever do again!"

Everyone laughed.

"Any idea when you can be released?" Violet asked.

"Tomorrow morning, the doctor said," Frank informed.

"We'll stay at the cottage for a few days," Violet said. "We still have to give our statements to the police about what happened. Jack and Tessa are staying as well, and will help us out if we need anything."

"What about the old cat that saved your life? Where's he at?" Frank inquired.

"Actually, he's waiting in the van for us," Jack answered.

"Bring him up here; I want to thank him for saving my Violet's life."

"Oh, Frank," Violet smiled, "you will have plenty of time to thank him once you are out of here. Besides, we have somewhere else we need to go this afternoon."

Frank made puppy-dog eyes and sniffled in an attempt to look as though he were going to cry. "Can't grant a sick man a wish, eh?"

Tessa and Jack stood back and allowed Violet to deal with her husband. Both were smirking.

"I'll grant you your wish tomorrow when we pick you up and take you to the cottage." Violet turned to Jack. "You wouldn't mind parting with Toby for a couple days so Frank can spoil the cat that saved my life?" Violet's eyes twinkled. "Now, Frank," Violet reached over and adjusted his pillow, "we are leaving and will return to pick you up in the morning."

Frank reached up and gripped hold of Violet's wrist, pulling him to her. "Wouldn't leave your old man without a bit of love, would you?" he questioned, puckering his lips.

Violet giggled as she leaned in closer and pecked her husband on the lips. "That's enough for now, old man— I wouldn't want you getting too excited and having another attack."

On the way to the prison, the group stopped and grabbed some tea, buying an extra one for Syd, plus a half dozen muffins. As they entered the gate carrying their wares, the guard stopped them and searched the box of goodies.

"Just muffins," Tessa informed.

The guard nodded. "Protocol, ma'am; everything coming into the prison has to be checked." Satisfied there were no files in the baked goods, he motioned them through.

Once inside, they met another guard, who had them sign in. "Who're you here to see?" he asked as he pushed a clipboard toward them.

"Syd Lance," Jack replied.

As Tessa went to write her name on the sheet, the guard pulled the clipboard back to him. "Wait here," he said, then turned and left.

A few minutes later, the guard returned with the warden. "Back so soon?" the warden asked. "I thought I made it clear to you ladies this morning that Syd was not up to visitors today and I would call you when he was."

Jack stepped forward. "We just want to see the boy. We've brought him a tea and a muffin. Thought it might cheer him up, that, and some friendly faces."

The warden scowled and blew through tight lips. He opened his mouth but shut it quickly, changing his mind about what he was going to say. He turned to the guard. "Show these people out, please."

Tessa decided it was time to pull a trump card. "I don't think you understand, warden. We came here to see Syd, and despite the distress you say he is in, I don't think there is any reason why we can't see him. I wouldn't want to have to pull any strings, like get a warrant, something I am sure neither of us wants to have to bother with, am I correct?"

An irritated look crossed the warden's face. He leaned into Tessa's space, so close she could smell the coffee on his breath—coffee laced with a hint of whiskey. "This is my domain; don't threaten me with *strings*! I am telling you for the last time—you are not going to see Syd today, or tomorrow, for that matter. You will see him when I say you can, and not a minute before!" Once again, the warden turned to the guard. "Show them out, and if they give you any trouble, call for backup!"

As the warden was leaving, Tessa got in the last word: "We'll see who's in charge, warden. We'll be back with a warrant, and Syd Lance better be in one piece when we get here!"

~

On the drive back to the cottages, Tessa was busy on her cell phone contacting a local judge she knew in the area. He owed her more than one favour and she was going to call one in now.

"Violet, we're going to drop you at the cottage; Jack will stay with you until I get back. I'm going to have to go back into the city to see a friend about a warrant."

Violet sat in the back seat, Toby curled up on her lap. Her face showed lines of worry; she was afraid for Syd. She had a thought: "Will my manuscript help—Syd's story?" she asked Tessa. "Maybe you can show it to whoever it is you're going to see."

"Might not be a bad idea," Tessa replied. "Can you put it on a memory stick for me?"

"Yeah, I think I have one in my computer case."

~

Armed with the memory stick holding an unbelievable story, and a determination more enormous than common sense, Tessa returned to Kingston to the address the judge had provided her with. It was dark by the time she arrived and rang the doorbell. An elderly gentleman answered.

"Judge MacGregor is waiting for you in the study," he motioned for Tessa to follow him.

As Tessa entered the room, Judge MacGregor stood to welcome her. He extended his hand: "Tessa, it's been a while. Have a seat." He motioned to the loveseat beside his chair as he retook his seat. "You sounded stressed on the phone, my dear. What can I do to help?"

Tessa filled the judge in on what had been going on over the past few days, and about her worry that something had happened to Syd Lance since his recapture. The judge shook his head and looked at Tessa, dismay written all over his face. He'd had some dealings with incidents from the prison, but the warden and his boys had always managed to come out of the situations squeaky clean.

"Do you have proof something is going on?" the judge questioned. He needed to be completely sure he finally had something concrete on the prison goings-on.

"I have the young man's story on a memory stick. Would you like to look at it?"

The judge rose from his chair and walked over to his desk. Tessa followed, and handed him the stick. She watched as he read the screen, noting his eyes watered numerous times. After an hour, he pushed back from the computer and reached into his desk drawer, pulling out a form, which he placed on his desk. He took out a pen and filled in the paper.

"Here is your warrant. You will need backup when you go in there; I think it wise you take some police officers with you. I suggest Sam Cranks and some of his men; the warden will respect the numbers and not give you any trouble." He paused. "What time are you going tomorrow? I'll call the police station and have them meet you there."

~

As Tessa left, she hugged Judge MacGregor. "Thank you. I know this young man killed a man in cold blood and escaped prison with more killing on his mind, but he is a victim himself. After reading and hearing his story, and meeting Syd in person, he doesn't deserve to rot in prison for the rest of his life. I think he can be rehabilitated—if it isn't too late."

"Let's hope not," the judge stated dryly. "Good luck, Tessa. Let me know if there is anything else I can do for you."

~

When Tessa arrived back at Violet's cabin, she found Jack asleep on the couch. Violet's bedroom door was closed and Toby was curled up on the rug under the kitchen table. Surveying the scene, Tessa decided to leave things be.

"No sense waking anybody up at this time of night," she murmured to herself, looking at her watch. Tessa looked around the room. Noticing a chair with a footstool, she made her way over and stretched out. Within minutes, she was sound asleep.

Chapter Thirty-three

Toby jumped up on Jack and began to knead on his chest. It had been a long night and he needed to take a trip outside. No one had thought to bring his litter box from Jack's cabin.

Jack moaned and tried to push Toby off. "Not now, old man."

Toby meowed in protest and dug his claws in. *You think I can wait all morning for you to get up?* Toby jumped down and ran to the door. Jack stumbled off the couch, and opening the door, gave Toby a little shove with his foot. Toby looked up at Jack and growled before heading outside. *What's up with that, Jack? Talk about me being a grumpy old cat!*

The commotion woke Tessa. She stretched in the chair, then stood and walked over to the kitchen sink. "I'll put the water on for coffee."

Violet, hearing Tessa and Jack, ventured from her room, rubbing the sleep from her eyes. She'd had a fitful sleep for the first part of the night, dreaming about all the horrid things that might have happened to Syd. She thought of how she tried to run away from the loneliness she'd been feeling at home, and if she hadn't done so, where would Syd be now?

"Good morning, Violet," Tessa greeted as she put the pot of water on the stove.

"Morning." Violet walked to the door and stepped outside, taking in the beauty of the lake and the trees. Jack joined her after a few minutes.

"I guess we'll pick Frank up after we see Syd, if that's okay with you," Jack said.

Without looking at him, Violet nodded. "Sounds good. I don't think Frank will be up to a trip yet, especially to a prison."

"You don't have to come either if it's too much for you," Jack suggested. "Tessa and I can let you know what's going on."

"I need to see Syd," was all Violet said. She turned and headed to the outhouse.

~

The trip to the prison was conducted in silence, no one felt like talking. Toby, once again, sat on the backseat, curled up beside Violet. He'd heard Violet ask Jack if they could sneak Toby into the prison and Jack had said he'd try. It would all depend on the prison rules about animals entering the premises because Toby was too big to hide under a coat.

Toby glowered at Jack through slit eyes, hearing the comment about his weight. *Don't need to rub it in so deeply, Jack—you're getting a little round about the waistline, too! I admit, I am moving slower these days, and it might not hurt to eat a little less … I'll think about it … maybe tomorrow.* Toby closed his eyes and snuggled closer to Violet.

~

The guard wasn't pleased when Tessa handed him her search warrant. He knew the warden would be pissed this out-of-town woman went over his head to see the returned

229

prisoner. He decided it was his duty to give them as hard a time as possible, even if it were only for show.

"I don't think this warrant has any jurisdiction here in the prison," the guard stated with a smug look.

Tessa laughed. "Would you like to tell Judge MacGregor that? I can get him on the phone right now; he's on my speed dial." Tessa looked back at the parking lot, wondering where the police backup was. The judge had said he would arrange it for her but there was no sign of them.

Taken aback, the guard reached for his phone. "I still have to call the warden," he grumbled.

It took almost a full minute for the warden to answer the phone, and when the guard explained to him what was going on, the warden slammed the phone down so hard that the prison guests heard the crash.

Within minutes, the warden was at the gate. He walked straight to Tessa, who was holding out the search warrant, and snatched it from her hand. Glancing straight to the bottom for the signature, the warden snorted disdainfully. "This old bugger has been out to get something on me for years!" Handing the warrant back to Tessa, he gazed over the group. "Can't let you all in, and," pointing to Toby, "especially not the cat!"

Jack stepped forward, drawing himself up to his full height, which, despite having lost an inch or two since his prime years, was quite impressive. "I think you have no choice but to let us in. If you read the search warrant, it says Tessa Bannister and her team." Jack grinned roguishly. "We're her team."

"You're telling me that cat is part of your team?" The warden looked down his nose at Toby.

Bet your bottom dollar I am, buddy! I'm the most essential part of this team, having solved more than one crime in my time, and, by the look of it, I might be about to crack another one!

"I'm telling you this cat is part of the team. In fact," Jack pointed to Violet, "Toby's the team member that saved this woman's life back at the cottage when one of your guards, under orders from George, almost killed her! Toby is well-known for figuring out 'who done it' in several crimes back in our hometown."

The warden wasn't happy about the predicament he found himself in, but he needed to buy some time to prepare Syd Lance for this visit. The last thing he needed was Judge MacGregor stopping by the prison to say hello. As he was about to open his mouth with an excuse to stall, the sound of sirens burst into the parking lot. "Damn!" he cursed under his breath.

Two police cars roared to a stop and four officers exited and made their way hurriedly to the prison gate. "Sorry we're late," the lead officer said. "We were delayed on the highway by a bad accident."

Tessa recognized Sam Cranks. "Nice to see you again, Sam," she grinned. "Better late than never. The warden here seems hesitant to let us in, although, for the life of me, I can't fathom why it would be such a problem to let us see one little prisoner." Tessa showed Sam the warrant.

Sam flicked his finger on the page after reading it, even though he already knew from Judge MacGregor what it said. He looked directly at the warden, his eyes a piercing green. "Is there a problem here, John? Been a while since I've had to come out here; I hope there are some improvements from my last visit."

The warden disliked the tone in Sam's voice, and he detested Sam even more. He was an old-school cop, like a hoary bulldog, who once he sunk his teeth into something, didn't let go until he drew blood. "I think you will find everything in order in *my* prison," the warden replied mockingly.

"Well then, shall we see for ourselves?" Sam pointed to the gate. "I think enough time has been wasted here. Take us to Syd Lance—all of us!"

Atta boy, Sam, put that foot down heavy on this warden fellow! He smells as bad as that crooked guard, George, and I bet it won't be long before he goes down, too! Toby glared at Warden John Harley, eyes slit in disgust.

~

John Harley was beyond annoyed. He wasn't even being allowed a moment to warn the guards to remove Syd from his cell, to get him out of the way. He'd thought of having the guards inform them, upon arrival to Syd's cell, the prisoner had been sent to the hospital, this time his stomach troubles being for real. He glanced over his shoulder, still contemplating how he could pull it off, but the group following him had a look of determination on their faces that told the warden time was up.

Entering the solitary confinement block of the prison, all seemed deserted other than two guards busy on their cell phones at the reception desk. They looked up, embarrassed, when the warden directed them to open the door into the cell area.

"We're here to see the prisoner, Syd Lance," the warden nodded to the guards. "I hope he's feeling better than he was yesterday and up to all this added, although unnecessary, attention."

One of the guards grabbed a set of keys and led the way through the door. "He refused breakfast this morning," he stated. "Said he needed to see a doctor," he added nervously. Even though he hadn't been part of Syd's welcome back committee, he knew what had happened. Everyone in the prison did.

Approaching Syd's door, Violet began shaking. The bad feelings she'd been having increased their hold on her. She shut her eyes as the door clanged open. When she reopened them, she gasped as she saw the young man curled into a fetal position in the corner of the cell. She ran to him, pushing her way past the warden and the guard.

"What have you done to him?" she admonished, turning to the warden.

It was Tessa's turn now to push past the warden. She knelt beside Syd, putting her hand under his chin, forcing him to look up at her. He squeezed his eyes shut, not wanting to look at her, his body shaking uncontrollably.

"Talk to us, Syd; what happened here?" Tessa's eyes followed the trail of bruises and cuts that littered the man's face and arms, the only exposed skin. As she turned to ask Sam to call for an ambulance, Tessa saw the officer already on his phone, barking orders to have an ambulance dispatched immediately to the prison.

Toby struggled out of Jack's arms and raced into the cell, pushing his nose against Syd's arm. *It's okay, man, we're here now. We'll get you out of here!*

Syd finally opened his eyes. The look of hopeless despair greeted his friends. Both Violet and Tessa knelt beside him, each taking one of Syd's hands warmly in their own. Together, they encouraged Syd to his feet.

"Come on, Syd," Tessa encouraged. "We're getting you out of here; we'll make sure you're safe." Syd staggered. "Are you able to walk?" Tessa questioned.

Syd nodded. He couldn't believe his luck at being rescued from what he'd begun to think was his imminent death. He also couldn't help thinking, as he glanced at Violet, that it had been his lucky day when he'd walked into her cabin.

~

An hour later, Syd Lance was settled into a private room at the Kingston General Hospital. Two police officers stood guard, one inside the room, one outside the door. They had been instructed not to let anyone in or out that looked like they didn't belong. The officers were aware of who the medical team looking after Syd was, and a code word was given to any officer who would be coming to relieve the ones currently on duty.

The doctors had gone over Syd and found, besides the visible bruises and scratches, several broken ribs and hairline fractures on his left arm. They bound him up as best as possible and heavily sedated him, eliminating the need to handcuff him to the bed.

Once they were sure all was secure, Jack, Tessa, Violet, and Toby left the room and headed up to the floor where Violet's husband was waiting to be discharged. Frank chuckled when his wife walked into his room, holding a large, orange tabby cat in her arms.

"So this is the famous cat, Toby, you have told me about?"

Violet put Toby down on the end of the bed: Toby sat, staring at Frank, *his* Violet's husband. *He looks of good character ... a sense of humour, too, by the sound of it.*

Frank reached out and scratched behind Toby's ears. "Thanks for saving my Violet, Toby." Turning to his wife, "How much longer before I can get out of here?" he asked.

"The doctor is signing your release papers right now," Violet responded. She looked her husband up and down. "I can see you're ready. However, there is one thing I want you to understand, Frank: you will be going from this bed to one at the cabin; you will take quiet walks along the beach and forest trails. We'll stay there for a couple weeks, and then head home."

Frank sniggered: "It sounds as though you have everything worked out."

Violet gave her husband one of her famous "yes, I have" looks. Nothing more was said as she led the way to the nurse's station. Once the paperwork was signed by Frank, the group made their way out of the hospital to the van. Toby chose to be in Tessa's arms, wanting to give Violet and her husband the opportunity to walk arm in arm.

~

Jack and Tessa dropped Violet and Frank at their cabin, Jack parking Violet's van as close as possible to the door. Violet invited them in. "Won't you come in for a tea?"

Tessa shook her head. "I think I'd like to take a walk over to Jack's place. You two probably have a lot to catch up on."

"We sure do," Frank interrupted. "I'll be drilling my wife as to why she felt it necessary to leave me like she did." Despite the sternness in his words, there was a twinkle in his eyes.

Violet and Frank watched as Tessa, Jack, and Toby headed toward the lakeshore. Once they were out of sight, the two turned and walked, hand in hand, into the cottage.

Chapter Thirty-four

George poured another drink. His entire world was falling apart. He downed the liquor in two gulps and threw the glass across the room, smashing it against the fireplace.

"How could I have been so stupid!" he shouted. "I had enough to live out the rest of my life in comfort on a remote island of my choice, and now it's all going down the sewer because of one lousy little prick with a sob story to tell!" George picked up the bottle and put it to his lips.

"I'll see the bastard in hell for what he's done! And that nosey bitch who wrote his story … I'll make sure she never gets a chance to publish the lies." George emptied the rest of the bottle down his throat, then collapsed in a chair.

~

Violet and Frank spent a quiet evening talking. Frank couldn't apologize enough for what Violet had gone through for the sake of needing time to herself to sort out her life. She apologized for thinking she was running away from loneliness, assuming that going away alone to a cabin in a remote cottage area would solve all her problems.

"I was so frustrated with my life, with all the interferences," Violet started to explain to Frank. "The years I spent longing to write a great novel, something more than a few short stories and poetry. You know how many people read poetry nowadays?"

Frank shook his head. "Not many is my guess." He waited patiently for Violet to continue.

"You always told me when the kids all got out on their own, I could pursue my dream of writing, but you know, Frank ... and this isn't your fault, it's mine ... I still didn't have the time I wanted. I found I was even busier, somehow. There was always someone calling me to do something for them or with them, or one of the kids needed me to babysit, or ... I'm not blaming anyone, really, Frank ... I could always say no, couldn't I? But somehow, I never did, and I felt I was being ripped apart.

"So, I devised a plan, a plan to run away from the loneliness I was feeling had me bottled up. I felt someone had put me in a bottle and put the cork in it."

"Why didn't you talk to me, Violet?" Frank's eyes teared up as he realized how much emotional pain his wife had been in.

"I couldn't," she replied. "I just couldn't. You were busy doing your thing, I was busy doing whatever, and I began to find I was isolating myself from friends and from my dream—mostly from my dream—and I was miserable.

"So many times, I just about told you ... I wanted to tell you. But I didn't, and I'm sorry, Frank, honestly I am. On the other hand, maybe it was providence. If I hadn't run away like I did, what would have happened to that young man, Syd?

"I was in the right place at the right time for him. I was here to hear, and then write down, his story, which I intend to honour for him. I would never have met Toby, an amazing cat, nor Jack and Tessa. All in all, despite the danger I faced, it has been the experience of a lifetime for me!" Violet reached out a hand to Frank.

Frank smiled. "It's okay, my love. We can talk later; we can't solve everything in one evening."

Violet, seeing the fatigue on her husband's face, stood and said it was time for bed. For the first night in a while, they both slept like babies, wrapped tightly in each other's arms.

~

Tessa went into the cottage to make a phone call to Judge MacGregor, filling him in on what had transpired, and to ask what they could do for Syd once he was recovered from the beating he'd taken.

Jack went in search of kindling to build a campfire for later. He pulled up two chairs to the fire pit site, then took a walk down to the lake, giving Tessa her space to deal with the next step in the Syd Lance situation. Jack found a large rock close to the water and sat. A few minutes later, he felt something rub around his legs, and looking down, saw Toby.

"Well, old man, been a hectic holiday so far, hasn't it?" He reached down and rubbed Toby's back. "I think we'll spend a couple more days here and then head home; what do you say about that? I can use the rest; I'm sure you can, too." Jack scooped Toby up in his arms and laid him across his lap.

"Tessa's making arrangements now with the judge to ensure Syd will be okay. Best thing to happen is to get him transferred to a different jail and hope George gets put behind bars again—sooner than later. And anyone who knew what the bastard was up to and turned a blind eye, too!"

Toby looked up at Jack, a worried thought skimming through his brain. *This isn't over yet, my friend. I have a cat feeling that scumbag, George, is going to make a move. How can I delay Jack from returning to Brantford? We shouldn't leave Violet and Frank unprotected. Frank can't protect his wife in his condition, and if he tried to, he'd probably die of a heart attack this time!* Toby jumped down and took off across the sand, heading toward Violet's cabin.

Jack figured where Toby was going. "It's okay, old man, go ahead and say your goodbyes." He raised his face to the sun and closed his eyes.

~

Toby reached Violet's cabin and, seeing all was quiet and in darkness, curled up on the step and went to sleep.

~

George woke from his drunken stupor and began to plan. He didn't need anyone's help for what he was about to do. He opened his computer and logged into the Kingston Airport site. He'd have to get a flight to Toronto, then to the island of his choice. He was thinking Martinique. He searched for a connecting flight.

"Bingo!" he exclaimed. George staggered over to the kitchen table, grabbed his wallet, and pulled out a credit card. It was one with another name on it, an alias he'd cooked up a couple years ago in case he ever needed one. He never knew when he might have to cover his tracks.

After booking his flights, George packed a gym bag with a few clothes and personal items. He reached into the back of the bottom drawer of his dresser and pulled out a bank book, also in another name. There was enough money in the account for him to make a fresh start. Island life would be cheap, especially if one laid low, at least until everyone forgot about what had gone on within the walls of the Kingston penitentiary, and about what he was going to have to do before he left for paradise.

A good night's sleep was what he needed now, to be fresh for the deed, and the getaway. The bank didn't open till nine. He'd be finished what he had to do before supper, with luck, then off to the airport for an eight o'clock flight to Toronto. He smiled as his head hit the pillow. By this time tomorrow night, he'd be on his way to Martinique.

~

Tessa and Jack pushed the lawn chairs by the fire close to each other so they could hold hands. Tessa looked around. "Where's Toby?"

"Probably over at Violet's. I think the old guy is going to miss her when we leave."

"Well, they live in Brantford," Tessa stated matter-of-factly. "You'll have to get their address so you and Toby can pay them a visit."

Jack chuckled. "I guess we can do that." He stretched his legs out toward the fire. "What's going to happen to young Syd now, Tessa?"

"Judge MacGregor is going to see to it that he's moved to a different facility. He's also going to have a team go into the prison and do a full investigation into the goings on in there, not just amongst the guards, but on Warden John Harley, as well."

"What about the guard, George? He's out on bail."

"Not for long. After reading Syd's story and what was revealed in Violet's written account, the judge is going to be issuing a warrant to have George picked up and thrown back in jail. Sam Cranks will receive the notice in the morning."

Jack sighed. "It's all going to work out then—justice all around, especially for Syd."

"Yep. Maybe Syd will finally get the help he needs to get over all the wrongs that have been done to him since the day he was born." Tessa stretched her legs out to join Jack's.

As the fire died down, the retired police officer and the police profiler looked up at the stars, then at each other. Understanding in their eyes, they stood and walked into the cottage, hand in hand.

Chapter Thirty-six

George rose before sunrise, looked around his apartment for the last time, grabbed his bag, and left. Tying his bag to the back of his motorbike, he searched the area for any sign of life. One could never be too careful. The warden was supposed to have called him by now and hadn't—not a good sign. Maybe he shouldn't have gotten his friends to beat on Syd, but he couldn't take that back. Surely there wouldn't be any kickback from the beating— yet.

Thinking it might be a good idea to stop at one of his buddies' places before hitting the bank, George headed out. They would tell him if there was anything amiss. Unfortunately, his chum wasn't home, and neither was the next one he chose to pay a visit to.

George looked at his watch. Almost nine. Time to head to the bank.

~

Violet crawled out of bed quietly, not wanting to disturb Frank. She pulled on a jogging suit and headed out the door. A walk along the beach was just what she needed to clear her head. Syd was safe in the hospital. Frank was safe in bed in the cottage. Her friends Jack, Tessa, and Toby were safe in a cabin down the lakeshore.

Through the night, Toby had found a more comfortable spot to sleep, one that protected him from the night breeze, so he missed Violet tiptoeing across the veranda.

~

George cut the motorbike engine far enough from the cottage that he wouldn't be heard. He'd have no problem getting back to his bike after he did what he had to do. The only problem he might run into was if Jack and Tessa were visiting—he hadn't thought of that scenario. If they were, maybe he'd just hang around in the woods and wait for them to leave.

He approached the cabin cautiously, listening for any sounds of life from inside. All seemed quiet. As he began to move forward, he noticed a figure standing down by the lake—a woman. Looked like Violet.

"Well, good for her that she stays away. This way, I can just grab the computer with the document on it and take off. Eliminate the evidence against me from that low-life murderer."

This time, Toby's keen cat hearing was alert, and the sound of George creeping up the wooden steps to the cottage door awakened him. *Violet must be up.* Toby stood and stretched, and looked toward the door. *That's not Violet—or Frank. That's the son-of-a-dog, George! What's he doing here? Nothing good, I'm sure.*

Toby decided it best to lay low and see what George was up to. He couldn't take a chance on being seen yet, in case he had to run to get Jack. He watched as George looked around before slowly opening the door.

George stepped inside, not bothering to close the door. He looked around the room, and his eyes set upon the table where Violet's computer was sitting. As he made his way across the room, the bedroom door opened.

"Is that you, love?" Frank called out. "Why'd you let me sl— who are you? And what are you doing in our cottage?" Frank's heart beat faster, and he could feel his blood pressure rising. Where was Violet?

The hair on the back of Toby's spine fluffed up, but he still hesitated. He jumped up on the porch railing and padded along until he had a good view inside the cabin. Frank was standing in the middle of the room and George was by the table where the computer was.

Looks like a standoff! But where's Violet? Toby looked back over his shoulder, picking up on footsteps approaching the cottage. *Oh no! There she is!* Toby jumped down from the railing, hoping to head her off before she went through the door, but he was too late.

Violet noticed the door ajar, and feeling something amiss, she bounded up the steps and through the door before Toby could reach her. He stopped in his tracks.

"Fra—" Violet halted at the sight before her.

George had seen Violet coming across the yard, and now he stood in the middle of the room with a gun to Frank's head. "Well, look who it is—the bleeding-heart lady who writes sob stories. Only problem is, none of it was true."

"Then why are you here … George, wasn't it?" Violet was quick to think about what he might be doing in her cabin. "Aren't you out on bail for mishandling the Syd Lance affair?" she taunted courageously.

"I don't like lies being told about me, and I certainly don't like people thinking that the crap Syd told you about me, or anything else for that matter, is true. He's a cold-blooded murderer who escaped a federal prison. He's not a poor, hard-done-by kid who deserves a break. Tell that to the victim's family. He carved Arthur up bad—mutilated him in ways not fit for a lady to see. After everything the guy did for the kid, getting him off the street and giving him a job."

Violet decided to change the subject. "George, could you let my husband go, please? He's not well. He's recovering from a heart attack, and from the looks of him, he's not doing too well right now."

George sneered. "I guess that's going to be up to you, isn't it?" He waved the gun in the air. "All I want is the manuscript to be destroyed. Your being here makes it easy for me, actually; I'll just hold the gun on your hubby here while you fire your computer up and delete the file. Once deleted, you can empty your trash bin so you won't be able to retrieve the document after I'm gone. Saves me from smashing or stealing a perfectly good laptop," George mocked, as he pressed the gun into Frank's temple. "Now, aren't I a nice guy? You do as I say and I'll be out of here, and you two can get back to whatever you were doing.

"And, by the way, I know where you live—where all of your family lives—so don't even think about telling anyone about this. I'd like you to rethink any testimony or statements you might have been going to give." George had researched Violet's family and knew she had five children and some grandchildren. He needed to put the fear of God into her to make sure she reversed anything she might be going to say about the truth of what Syd Lance had told her.

"Probably the wisest thing for you to do is to just go home and forget you ever met Syd Lance, or me, or anyone else up here, don't you agree?"

Toby watched Violet hesitate, a worried look on her face. *Of course, she's scared—the bastard has a gun on her sick husband! There's no time for me to go and get Jack; I'd never get there and back in time…* Toby began to pace along the railing, frustrated. *What to do … what to do … I'm just a cat, and against a man with a gun pointed at my friend's husband, I probably wouldn't stand a chance, he'd see me coming. This situation isn't like when I jumped from the roof and saved Andrew … George will see me coming, maybe even accidentally pull the trigger and shoot Frank … What to do, what to do?*

Toby stopped pacing for a moment and looked back into the cabin. Violet had moved to where her computer was and she was firing it up. *She's going to delete the file, but George doesn't know Tessa made a copy … it doesn't matter if Violet erases this one, he doesn't know a judge has already read Syd's story—Violet knows, though—she can play along and agree to whatever George wants her to agree to, and it won't matter one little bit—he's screwed!* Toby almost smiled, as much as a cat can.

Jumping down from the railing, Toby decided to head into the cabin and cause a stir, if possible. There was no other choice, and he knew it. He pushed his way into the room and meowed.

Violet turned, surprised. "Toby! What are you doing here?" Her fingers hovered over the keyboard as she paused to greet her friend.

Toby ran up to Violet and rubbed against her legs. Protectively, he sat down by her and glared at George. He noticed Frank was sweating more than was usual for anyone just standing in a room. *I hope there's a God out there somewhere, and if so, maybe He'll send a saviour … I don't think Frank's going to last much longer under this pressure.*

~

Jack and Tessa slept in longer than they expected, but once up, they decided to take a walk on the beach.

"Want to drop in on Violet and Frank and make sure they're okay?" Jack inquired casually. He was also worried about Toby, who hadn't come home yet.

Tessa, picking up on the anxious note in Jack's voice, grinned. "Missing the old man, eh?"

"It's not like him to miss breakfast," Jack explained. "Especially after such an exhausting few days."

"Well then, we may as well, since we're walking in that direction anyway." Tessa let go of Jack's hand and pointed to a section of the lake where the water reeds were crowding the shore. "Look! A Blue Heron! Where's a camera when you need one?"

They continued their walk, taking it slow, not a worry in the world—for the moment.

~

Sam Cranks didn't receive the fax on his desk until eleven o'clock. His secretary was at a dentist appointment and had arrived late to work. Sam scanned the paper signed by Judge MacGregor, shoved back his chair, and rushed out of his office.

"Greg! John!" he barked at the two officers. "We have a warrant to serve!"

The two officers followed their boss out the door and into their cruiser. Sam led the way out of the lot. When the vehicles pulled up to George's apartment building, there wasn't a soul in sight. Sam, despite his years, was the first one to the door. He ran his fingers along the list of names until he found the one he wanted. After several attempts, and receiving no answer, Sam pushed the button for the apartment superintendent.

"Good morning," a sleepy voice sounded over the intercom. "How can I help you?"

Sam didn't waste any time getting to the point. "This is officer Sam Cranks from the Kingston police department; I need to get in and up to apartment 601immediately."

A whirring sounded in the top left-hand corner of the lobby. Sam looked up and noticed a camera sweeping the area. Then came a louder buzz, and Greg grabbed the door handle. The officers raced to the elevators and, finding only one in working order, pushed the button impatiently.

It took forever for the elevator to open, and when it did, the officers had to wait for several teenagers to pile out. They were laughing and carrying on, taking their time.

Sam lost his patience: "Move it!" he shouted, flashing his badge.

One of the teens swaggered up to Sam. "Take it easy, old man … we're just havin' some fun."

Greg stepped forward and shoved the teen out of the way before grabbing the elevator door to stop it from closing. The last two young people staggered out and the officers piled in. John pushed the sixth-floor button and the elevator began its slow ascent.

Rushing from the elevator, the three men ran to apartment 601, which was at the end of the hall. Sam banged on the door. No answer. He pounded again, louder. Still no response.

"We should have brought the super with us," Sam grumbled. Turning to Greg, "Go get him. I don't want to break down the door. I don't think George is in there, but we still need to check. Might find a clue as to where he's gone."

Five minutes later, Greg returned with the superintendent and she let them into George's apartment. The emptiness confirmed George wasn't home.

"Look around for anything that might tell us where he is," Sam ordered, heading into the bathroom.

Sam opened and closed drawers by the sink. After a few minutes, he walked out to where Greg and John were searching. "If my guess is right, he's getting ready to flee the country."

"How so, boss?" Greg queried.

"His personal effects are gone," Sam replied. He had a gut feeling George hadn't quite left yet and might be making a stop. Call it an old police dog's intuition. Sam hoped he wouldn't be too late.

"Where to now?" The question came from one of the young officers, but Sam didn't care which one.

"Follow me—and don't put your sirens on. If George is where I think he is, I don't want him warned."

It didn't take Greg long to figure out where they were going as he followed his boss. He was confused, though, as to why.

Chapter Thirty-seven

George waved the gun again at Violet. "Get moving," he ordered. "Forget the dumb cat! I don't have a lot of time."

Violet's hands shook as her fingers hovered over the keyboard. She paused again and looked back at George: "Please, my husband is not well. Please let him sit down."

"The faster your little fingers type, the sooner your old man can sit down. A little incentive, so you work faster." George tightened his grip on Frank's arm and pushed the gun nozzle into his temple.

Frank groaned and swayed, almost losing his balance. George steadied his prisoner. Toby growled and hissed, frustrated he couldn't do anything to help. Violet returned her attention to the computer and began typing as fast as she could.

Finally, Violet pressed one last button. "There, it's gone. Now please, let us go."

No sooner were the words out of her mouth, Frank completely lost control and began to crumble. Toby was watching him closely and got the feeling Frank was faking the fall.

Good man, Frank! Maybe I can do something now! That's it…

Toby watched as Frank went limp and George tried to keep control of the man and his gun. Seeing his chance, Toby sprung for the gun hand, knocking the weapon away.

It flew into the far corner of the room, but not before it sounded off.

"Friggin' cat!" George shouted as he lost his grip on Frank.

Toby gathered himself together after landing hard on the floor. He turned and ran back for another attack. *While I've got you off-guard, may as well finish the job!*

But Toby hadn't taken into consideration the huge boot that met him midair.

~

The gunshot echoed through the late morning air. Jack and Tessa looked at each other and took off running for Violet's cottage. By the time they burst through the door, George had recovered his gun and was holding it against Violet's back. Toby lay on the floor, not moving. Frank lay not far from Toby, also not moving, but acutely aware of what was going on—especially the gun in his wife's back.

George pressed the nozzle into Violet's flesh and Jack noticed how she cringed in pain. He dared not make a move for fear of getting his friend shot.

"I'm leaving now," George stated as he inched toward the door, keeping Violet between him and Jack and Tessa. "I'll be taking a little insurance with me here, so don't try to follow me; I won't hesitate to kill her. Not much more I can lose at this point."

George backed slowly out the door, keeping his eyes glued on Jack and Tessa. He stepped backward down the steps and across the yard until he reached the wooded area by the laneway. At that point, he turned and pushed Violet in front of him.

Jack and Tessa watched, helpless to do anything. When George and Violet disappeared down the lane,

Tessa grabbed her phone and made a call to 911. Jack ran to Toby, who was still unconscious, and picked him up, carrying him to the couch and laying him down gently. The old cat was still breathing; Jack noticed his side moving up and down, but it was weak.

"This is getting a bit much for you, isn't it, old man … might be time to hang up the badge," Jack muttered as he stroked his friend, trying to will Toby awake.

Tessa finished her 911 call and knelt beside Frank, who was sitting now, holding his head in his hands. "You okay?" she asked.

Frank looked at her, his eyes filled with two emotions: sadness and rage. "No, I'm not okay! That animal has my wife, and God knows what he's going to do to her! And I had to stand like a dummy, doing nothing. Back when I was younger, that prick wouldn't have stood a chance against me; I'd have laid him flat in no time!"

"I don't think George is actually going to hurt Violet," Tessa tried comforting the distraught husband. "My guess is, he has a vehicle parked down the lane, and once he reaches it, he'll let Violet go. He's just buying time to get out of here."

Frank shook his head. "I hope you're right … I hope you're right," he repeated.

Jack decided he'd waited long enough. "I'm going after them," he informed Tessa and Frank. "Tessa, please stay here and keep an eye on Frank and Toby for me."

"You don't have a weapon, Jack. George does. And if he sees you coming, he won't hesitate to use his gun on either you or Violet. Think about what you are doing!"

"I am thinking, Tessa; he won't see me coming. Remember, my dear, I'm a retired cop, and even though I worked at a small city police force in my later years, I was an undercover officer on a much larger force for a number of years."

Tessa's eyebrows rose in surprise. "I didn't know that, Jack."

"Never came up in our conversations, I guess; it's not something I advertise."

"The police are on their way. You should wait for them. Sam Crank was already on his way here, according to the dispatcher at the station; said something about Sam figuring things out."

"Well that works out great then," Jack said, moving to the door. "The police can come in from one side, and from this side, I'll make sure George doesn't double back here, or hurt Violet."

Jack left, and when he reached the tree line, he veered off the roadway and advanced into the woods.

~

George hesitated when he reached his motorbike, wondering if he should keep Violet with him a bit longer as insurance against any unforeseen events. His bike was hardly big enough, though, and his gym bag overlapped on the seat extension. He turned Violet around and waved the gun in her face.

"Don't forget what I told you, lady—I know where you live, and I know where all your family lives."

Violet thought she detected a hint of worry in George's voice. "I'm no threat to you, George. Just let me go. All I want to do is to go back to my boring life. I've had enough excitement in the past week to last me a lifetime."

The sound of wheels on gravel reached George and Violet's ears. Jack, who was hiding not far from where the motorbike was parked, also heard the vehicles approaching. He smiled and readied himself for what he might have to do.

~

Back at the cottage, Tessa heard Toby growl softly, a sign the old cat was waking up. Toby sat up slowly, feeling every twitch of the pain in his side where George's boot had made contact.

Damn! Where's Jack? Where's Violet? Tessa's here, and Frank. George is gone, too. Gotta go help my guy … gotta help save Violet … George must have her or Jack would still be here looking after me.

Toby jumped gingerly off the couch and headed for the door, each step getting easier. He heard Tessa call after him but ignored her, picking up his pace as he made his way across the lawn and down the lane.

~

Sam pulled his car to a stop and Greg pulled up right behind him. The three officers exited quickly from their vehicles and Sam drew his gun; Greg and John followed suit. With firearms poised, the three made their way up the lane toward the cottage.

Greg was the first to catch sight of George and Violet. He tapped Sam on the shoulder and raised a finger to his lips. "They're there, just around the bend," he whispered.

Sam nodded, thinking since he was first in line, he should have seen them. He made a mental note to get his eyes checked. He motioned for his officers to take to the woods so George wouldn't see them coming.

~

Toby caught sight of George and Violet. He saw the fearful look on Violet's face. Still feeling off from the blow George had delivered to his side, Toby knew he wouldn't be able to jump up and knock the gun away this time. However, if he could make it up a nearby tree, he could jump down on George and dig his claws in where it would do the most damage: George's eyes.

~

George's nerves communicated he was in trouble. He looked around furtively. *Maybe if I shove her out of the way and fire up the bike, I can still get out of here!* Impulsively, he thrust Violet out of the way. As he ran for his bike, he heard a twig snap. Reeling around, he pointed the gun randomly, searching wildly for whatever—whoever—was in the trees.

Toby panicked when he saw George shove Violet and swing around, pointing his gun in the direction where Toby knew Jack was readying to pounce. As Jack burst out of the woods, Toby jumped, landing on George's head, as planned. George's arm jerked up and the gun went off.

Jack screamed and went down, clutching his shoulder. Violet ran to him. Toby clung on to George's head, digging his claws in, drawing blood.

It was a chaotic scene that greeted Sam Cranks and his fellow officers when they burst from the tree cover. Greg moved ahead of his boss, gun drawn, and pointed it directly at George's head.

"Drop your gun, George; it's over!" Sam shouted.

George, still trying to get Toby off, realized he had nowhere to go. His gun fell to the driveway and both hands reached up, trying to grab hold of Toby. Toby, seeing three armed police officers with their weapons trained on

George, released his grip and jumped to the ground. He ran to where Violet sat holding Jack's head in her lap.

Violet had removed her scarf and was pressing it into Jack's wound. Jack was paler than Toby had ever seen him.

Oh no! Not you, Jack—hang in there, buddy—I'm here for you! Toby pushed his way under Jack's good side and lay down. *Here you go, buddy, I'll keep you warm.*

Toby looked to where Greg was cuffing George. He saw Sam on his cell phone and assumed he was calling 911 to get an ambulance for Jack. John took the gym bag off the bike before he and Greg led George away in the direction of their vehicles.

Sam walked over to Jack and Violet. "Ambulance is on its way," he stated as he knelt beside Jack. He glanced over at Toby. "Quite a brave cat you got there, Jack."

You bet I am!

"Foolish old bugger," Jack grimaced. "But, if it hadn't been for him jumping on George, the bullet would have ended up in my gut. He saved my life." Jack raised his good arm and weakly rubbed Toby behind the ears.

Chapter Thirty-eight

Tessa rushed into the hospital room where Jack was recovering from surgery to remove the bullet. He was just starting to wake up and smiled when he saw her.

"Oh, Jack," was all Tessa could manage as she sat in the chair beside his bed and reached for his hand.

Jack's grip was weak but his smile was genuine as he looked at the woman he was becoming more than fond of. "Some holiday, eh?" he chuckled.

"Yeah."

"How's the other old man? He took quite a beating, between getting kicked by George and then leaping from a tree to attack him. Saved my life by doing that. Like I told Sam, God knows where the bullet might have hit had Toby not attacked the bastard."

Tessa cleared her throat. She didn't want to talk business but felt she needed to catch Jack up on what had transpired over the past few hours while he was in surgery.

"Toby's safe. He's with Violet and Frank. Violet is spoiling him rotten for saving her husband, and, well … you know … for just being Toby. When I left the cottage, he was well fed and curled up on the couch at Frank's feet. Frank is so thankful Violet is okay, he can't stop giving Toby treats. Your old man has probably gained a few pounds over the past couple hours, eating all the goodies, trying to please his friends.

"George won't be getting out on bail this time. The police found a ticket to the Toronto airport, and from there, another ticket to Martinique. He appeared before Judge MacGregor, who has a short fuse when it comes to criminals, especially when they've been in positions of power like what George was at the prison.

"The police have also discharged John Harley, the prison warden, of his duties, while he is being investigated for unorthodox procedures within the prison. A temporary warden has been put in place. Syd has been transferred to another facility, minimum security, where he'll get the help he needs. He's promised he won't try to escape because he really wants to heal—to find peace. He's realized, after telling his story to Violet, how much he wants to be released from his demons."

Jack grinned weakly. "Well, looks like we can go home as soon as I get out of here, eh?"

"Looks that way. We'll still have to give a statement to Sam Cranks at the Kingston precinct, and then we can be on our way."

"Good." Jack closed his eyes and drifted to sleep.

~

By the end of the week, both cottages on the lake were empty, their vacationers on their way home to Brantford. Violet and Frank decided not to stay a second week, anxious to get home to their children, who had placed several distraught calls to their father's cell phone. It wasn't like their parents to just up and leave without reason.

Tessa had stood by, smiling, as Violet gave Jack her home address and Jack returned the gesture. Toby rubbed his face against Violet's chin before she handed the old cat to Tessa. Jack was still hurting too much to lift anything over a few pounds, and Toby was well over that.

Tessa parked her vehicle at the police station until she could send for it, deciding Jack shouldn't be driving yet. Frank did likewise with his, as the doctor had told him he shouldn't drive for six weeks after the heart attack. Violet was more than willing to take the wheel to ensure her husband arrived safely home.

~

Emma was in her yard when Tessa and Jack pulled into Jack's driveway. She walked over to the fence, Duke at her side, and waved. Shock spread across her face when Jack got out of the vehicle with his arm in a sling.

Quickly, Emma opened her gate and rushed down the sidewalk to Jack, forgetting that Duke was free to follow her. Toby hissed and ran to the side door where his cat flap was and pushed his way into the house. He ran to the front window, jumped up on the back of the couch, and stared out at the homecoming.

Emma hugged Jack. Jack reached over and patted Duke on the head. Emma talked excitedly to Jack as he leaned back on the vehicle, tired. Finally, Tessa came around and touched Emma on the arm, saying something. Emma nodded and motioned to Duke to follow her home.

~

Later that evening, after a supper of takeout fish and chips, which all three enjoyed equally, Tessa finally stood and said it was time for her to go.

"I think I'll be on my way, Jack. I'll stop by tomorrow morning to see how you're doing."

"Thanks, that will be nice." Jack tried to stand but fell back in his chair.

"Here, let me get you into bed…"

Jack's laugh cut off the rest of what Tessa intended to say. She gave him a light smack on the uninjured shoulder.

~

Violet and Frank pulled into the driveway of their bungalow on Fairview Drive. Violet put the vehicle in park and leaned against the steering wheel. She and Frank hadn't spoken much on the trip home and hadn't really broached the subject of why she'd left since Frank's first night out of the hospital.

Frank reached over and placed a hand on her arm, understanding her thoughts. "When you are ready to talk more, my love, I'll be ready to listen."

"Thank you, Frank," she whispered huskily, choking back her tears. "Thank you." In her mind, Violet knew she would never be lonely again—leastwise not while Frank was still with her.

If anyone had been running away from loneliness, it had been Syd. Violet had a story to tell—Syd's story—the one she'd promised to write.

Epilogue

Toby decided to let Frank have the bed to himself on their first night back in Branford. Curling up on the back of the couch, he stared out into the night, watching the bugs buzz around the streetlights. Thoughts of what had taken place over the past week raced through his mind, tired as he was.

This is getting a bit much for me. It might be time, as Jack suggested, to hang up my detective badge. Jack and I aren't getting any younger, and both of us could have been killed ... but we weren't. And sweet Violet is okay ... and her husband Frank ... even the kid, Syd; where would he be right now if it hadn't been for Frank and me? Dead, probably.

I hope George gets his just desserts; gets put in the general prison population with a bunch of the guys he did wrong to while he was a guard ... Tessa's connection, the judge, will probably ensure he does. Prison warden, too ... him knowing all along what George was up to and turning a blind eye...

Toby sat up and began to groom his fur. He noticed someone walking along the sidewalk with their dog— Emma and Duke?

What's Emma doing out walking at this time of night? Not safe ... well, I guess she has that oversized mutt with her. She seems to have recuperated well enough from her brother's trial ... better off without Camden in her life, is all I have to say. Note to self: visit Emma tomorrow when I get up…

Toby resumed his grooming. Finally satisfied his fur was clean enough, at least for the time being, he lay back down and closed his eyes. Tomorrow would be another day, and he would face whatever challenges it might bring him and Frank.

For now, Detective Toby had had enough excitement.

Running Away From Loneliness

Acknowledgements

No matter how many times I go over my manuscript, or how many times I might run it through a grammar program, there is still nothing better than a great book editor to "bring my story home!" Thank you to Bethany Jamieson at Cavern of Dreams Publishing for making my dreams come true; and, thank you to Cavern of Dreams Publishing for once again believing in me.

I may be the author of the story; however, many other extraordinary people have helped me through the different stages:

Jennifer Bettio, who worked closely with me to come up with an amazing, unique cover for "Running Away From Loneliness."

Terry Davis from Ball Media, who put the finishing touches on the cover.

Randy Nickman at Brant Service Press, who does a fantastic job of getting the finished copies to print.

I would be remiss if I didn't thank all the individuals who read my books and keep encouraging me to continue on this crazy journey of mine. Your positive comments about my writing are the fuel that keeps me chugging along.

Last, and definitely not least, I thank my family—you all know who you are—from the wonderfully, patient man I am married to, who puts up with my endless hours of writing; to my children, who have been inspirations to me throughout their years, to my grandchildren who excitedly tell everyone that their grandma is a writer!

About the Author

Mary M. Cushnie-Mansour resides in Brantford, ON, Canada. She has a freelance journalism certificate from Waterloo University, and in the past, she wrote a short story column and feature articles for the *Brantford Expositor*. Mary is the award-winning author of the popular "Night's Vampire" series and has also written and published several bilingual children's books, picture books, youth novels, mystery novels, collections of poetry and short stories, and a biography.

Mary has always believed in encouraging people's imaginations and spent several years running the "Just Imagine" program for the local school board. She has also been involved in the local writing community, inspiring adults to follow their dreams. Mary is available for select readings and workshops. To inquire about a possible appearance, contact Mary through her website—

http://www.writerontherun.ca

or via email

mary@writerontherun.ca